Praise for the novels of
New York Times **bestselling author Sharon Sala**

"[T]he Youngblood family is a force to be reckoned with.... [W]atching this family gather around and protect its own is an uplifting tribute to familial love."
—*RT Book Reviews* on *Family Sins*

"[A] soul-wrenching story of love, heartache, and murder that is practically impossible to put down.... If you love emotional tales of love, family, and justice, then look no further... Sharon Sala has yet another winner on her hands."
—*FreshFiction.com* on *Family Sins*

"So many twists and turns, and the ending will shock readers. Another stellar book to add to Sala's collection!"
—*RT Book Reviews* on *Dark Hearts*

"Sala is a master at telling a story that is both romantic and suspenseful.... With this amazing story, Sala proves why she is one of the best writers in the genre."
—*RT Book Reviews* on *Wild Hearts*

"Skillfully balancing suspense and romance, Sala gives readers a nonstop breath-holding adventure."
—*Publishers Weekly* on *Going Once*

"Vivid, gripping... This thriller keeps the pages turning."
—*Library Journal* on *Torn Apart*

"Sala's characters are vivid and engaging."
—*Publishers Weekly* on *Cut Throat*

SHARON SALA

RACE AGAINST TIME

mira

mira

ISBN-13: 978-0-7783-1997-9

Recycling programs
for this product may
not exist in your area.

Race Against Time

ome people never have to face an unexpected fe-or-death situation, so they go their whole lives wondering when tested, how they might have fared.

But there are others who found out the hard way, through no fault of their own, how ugly the dark side of life can be. Some don't make it. But the ones who do are the ultimate survivors. Warriors from another time who, when faced with death, refuse to accept it. They fight with everything in them, raging against the helplessness, to go down fighting rather than roll over and die.

I dedicate this book to my daughter, Kathy, and all the others like her, who fought back and persevered.

RACE
AGAINST
TIME

One

It was a hot Saturday evening in Nashville, Tennessee, when seventeen-year-old Starla Davis came running up the hall carrying an overnight bag in one hand and her car keys in the other.

She stopped by the recliner her dad, John, was sitting in to kiss his forehead.

"'Bye, Daddy, I'm off to Lara's house. We're going to the movies. I'll be home sometime in the morning."

"'Bye, sugar. Drive safely and have a good time."

"I will. Mama! I'm leaving now!" she yelled.

Her mother, Connie, came out of the kitchen, wiping her hands.

"Supper is almost ready. Sure you don't want to eat before you leave? It's meat loaf and mashed potatoes. Your favorite."

"Sounds wonderful, but we'll eat popcorn and junk at the movie," she said and kissed her mother goodbye. "See you in the morning."

"Good. Leaves more for me," her brother, Justin, said as he walked through the living room.

Starla made a face at him.

He was laughing when she opened the door.

"Have fun!" her mother said.

"I will. Love you!"

And then she was gone.

She had a slight twinge of conscience as she drove away because she'd lied to her parents about where she was going, and she'd never lied to them before. But that wasn't the extent of the lie. She'd also lied to get a fake ID last week so she could get in at a club on the outskirts of Nashville to meet the boy she'd met online. They'd been talking for weeks, FaceTiming on a regular basis.

Then he told her he was falling in love with her, and that was his lie, but she didn't know it. She believed him, just as her parents had believed her.

He was already twenty-one, and she didn't want to come across as the high school kid she was when she finally met him in person, so she was going for her idea of sexy when she chose the red leather miniskirt, black knit top and black leather knee-high boots.

She passed the time before their meeting at her friend Lara's house, but they didn't go to a movie, even though Lara knew what was happening and was worried how this might turn out. But they had been friends their whole lives, and Lara wasn't going to snitch.

They were in her bedroom, talking and laughing while Lara was doing Starla's hair. When it was almost time to leave, she got dressed.

"How do I look?" Starla asked, twirling around and around in front of her friend.

Lara smiled.

"You look beautiful, no matter what you're wearing."

"Thanks for everything, Lara. You're the best friend ever."

Lara's parents owned a supermarket and were always late coming home, so there were no other witnesses to Starla's new look as she left the house and drove away.

The closer she got to the club, the more excited she became. The parking lot was filling up fast when she arrived, but she finally found a space toward the back of the lot. She locked the car, put the keys in a little shoulder bag and started walking across the gravel toward the club.

The night air was sultry and still. A bead of sweat rolled out of her hairline and down the back of her neck. The mosquitoes were already out. One landed on her bare arm, but she swatted it before it could bite. The buzz of the neon sign was loud in her ears as she passed beneath it on the way toward the club.

Putting her hair up in the messy-on-purpose look was a good move on Lara's part. It was a sexy style for her long blond hair and made her feel pretty and grown up. Her eyes were alight with the night's possibilities as she neared the club.

And then she saw him leaning against the corner of the building, watching her come toward him. He smiled and waved.

She shivered.

Oh, my God, he is so handsome.

His name was Darren, and when she waved back, he came running.

That first hug was a rush. The first kiss made her ache for so much more. He laughed when she suddenly turned shy, and then they walked into the club arm in arm.

One hour and one spiked drink later, Starla Davis was passed out in his arms. He made a joke about having too much fun, and carried her out of the club, and away from the city of her birth.

When she didn't come home the next morning, John and Connie called Lara. Lara was already worried because Starla hadn't come back after her date and quickly confessed to their ruse.

John and Connie went from concern to panic and called the police. The first thing the police did was confiscate Starla's computer. They found the emails, then the location of a meeting place and found her car in the club parking lot, but no trace of Starla.

The bartender vaguely remembered the guy, and a waitress remembered Starla because of the red leather miniskirt. It wasn't the kind of club that was high on security cameras, because most of the people who went there didn't necessarily want to be found.

After the police found pictures of Darren on her computer, they ran them through facial recognition. Darren Edward Vail popped up in criminal records. He'd been in and out of juvenile detentions since he was twelve, but the files were sealed. He popped up again on police reports after he turned eighteen, but nothing that had put him in prison. Then a year ago last Christmas, he was implicated in the disappearance of four girls from neighboring states, two of whom turned up dead, which connected him to a human-trafficking ring. He had bonded out on the charges and disappeared. After that, he stayed two steps ahead of the law. That's when John and Connie Davis began to realize the possibility they may never see Starla again.

Lara heard the news and collapsed in hysterics. Her worst fear had come true, and she helped make it happen.

Starla woke up in the back of a moving vehicle, hands and feet bound, blindfolded, gagged and certain she was going to die. She tried sending a mental message to her daddy, as if he could read her mind in the miles between them.

Daddy, save me. Help me. Find me.

Then she began praying to God.

God, I'm sorry. Please save me. Please don't let me die.

But neither miracle happened, and the miles rolled on.

She listened to her captors talking, laughing, as if completely oblivious to her presence, which made her reality that much scarier. If they didn't care what she heard, she was probably going to die. And then she heard the words "sell" and "auction," and her heart sank. She hadn't just been kidnapped for ransom. They weren't going to try to get money out of her parents. She was the product they were going to sell.

Her naïveté and rash behavior had put her in the

hands of human traffickers. They weren't going to kill her after all, but she might soon wish they had.

The ride went on forever, and after a time she began moaning and screaming behind the gag, trying to tell them she needed to pee. But they didn't pay any attention, and they didn't stop, and she wet herself, and they kept driving.

The ride ended after dark. Only then did the men in the front seat become real. She heard a door slide back and felt a breeze on her face. One of them stepped up into the van, then began cursing her when he smelled the urine. He grabbed at her breasts and squeezed them hard until she moaned, then dragged her out of the van, still bitching about the smell of urine on her and her clothes.

"Stand up," one of them growled, as he removed the ties around her ankles, then the blindfold and gag.

"I can't feel my feet," she cried, as she went to her knees.

One of them yanked her to her feet and slapped her. She cried out.

"Did you feel that, bitch?"

She nodded. Fear had a whole new meaning.

"Then shut up and do what we say," he growled.

There was nothing on her mind now but survival. She couldn't think about family. There would be no rescue. No one knew where she'd gone. She didn't even know where she was. They were in the middle of nowhere, and all she could see were the stars overhead and what looked like a long metal building in front of them.

Then a light came on inside, and she watched in

growing horror at the opening door. The man who came out was tall and skinny.

"Get her inside!" he yelled.

The two men grabbed her by the arms.

"Walk, or we'll drag you," one said, but her legs were shaking so hard she couldn't make them move.

One of the men punched her in the stomach. With no breath left to scream, she leaned over and threw up until there was nothing left but the faint taste of bile in the back of her throat.

This time when they grabbed her by the arms, she followed.

People in Nashville were holding vigils for Starla. Her last school picture was on flyers posted all over town.

Her brother, Justin, had nightly dreams about her screaming for help. He could hear her voice, but he never found her.

Their family was in mourning. Connie took to her bed. John went to work every day because it's all he knew what to do, then came home and drank himself to sleep. Justin became the boy whose sister was gone. Starla wasn't the only one who had disappeared. Their family unit was gone as well, and verging on implosion.

Starla was thrown into a room with five other girls who appeared to be around her age, and from the looks of their clothes and blank stares, they'd been there awhile. Each of them had a manacle and chain on one wrist and the other end of the chain fastened to a wall.

At first they wouldn't talk to her, and then when they began, she regretted it. They all knew Darren, and they had no idea how they'd gotten here, but they knew where they were going.

The auction block.

Dread shot through Starla like a bullet ripping through flesh. Less than twelve hours later, they moved the girls in the dark, and when they stopped they were taken out blindfolded and led into another building.

An hour later they were forced to strip and, under the watchful eye of three armed men, were sent to a communal shower not unlike the ones in the gym at Starla's school.

The humiliation of undressing in front of strange men was only the first in a long line of horrors to come. The girls scrubbed their bodies and then their hair, then went straight from the shower to another room full of young girls and women in the same state. They didn't look at each other. They didn't speak. They sat on the floor, hunched up to cover their nudity from each other, waiting to be called. Starla's hair slowly dried, as did her skin, then soon beaded with sweat again. When Starla's name was called she stood up. The shame she felt was less about her nudity than the lies that had gotten her here. She had to face a hard truth. Her last hopes were gone.

The room they took her to was air-conditioned, an accommodation to the nearly fifty men there, but it was thick with smoke from their cigarettes and cigars.

The open bar was manned by two young naked men,

who moved among the crowd with shots of whiskey and tequila, and longneck bottles of beer.

Starla walked in with her head held high, past the humiliation of being nude, locked into the fear of what would happen next.

Her hair was dry now and hanging halfway to her waist, and beneath the bright overhead lights, her pale blond hair almost looked white.

A guard marched her up the steps to a small round stage in the middle of the room before he untied her. Then he grabbed a handful of her hair and yanked.

"Look up," he growled.

So she did, and when it was announced that she was a virgin, the crowd, as a whole, moved closer. She began to pray again, but this time not to be rescued. She was asking for something easier—asking God to strike her dead.

The first bid started at a thousand and flew up to ten, and then fifteen thousand, and the bidders were thinning out. She wouldn't look at them and was trying not to cry. Her survival instinct was already guiding her, telling her not to let them see her fear, and so she stared at a spot above their heads.

But then the bidding suddenly came to a stop and the room went quiet. When she realized the crowd was beginning to part, her heart started to pound. Something was happening, and she had to look, because it was going to happen to her.

A fortysomething man was coming toward the stage as if he owned it. Their gazes locked. His eyes narrowed as hers widened.

He was someone important. That much she guessed. He was dressed fit to kill, but she didn't know that he was also willing to do it to get what he wanted.

"The bidding stops now. She is no longer for sale. She is mine," the man said.

The silence in the room was sudden—almost as if men were afraid to breathe, and then the auctioneer slammed the gavel down on the dais.

"The girl known as Star is no longer for sale."

Starla blinked at the name change. She was lost—so lost—and she no longer existed.

"Take the girl down now," the man said.

"Yes, sir, Mr. Baba. Right away."

Baba snapped his fingers. A man came running behind him carrying a long white robe. When Star was led down the steps, Mr. Baba held it out for her to put on and then turned her around to face him and tied the ties himself. The gesture was not lost on her. For all intents and purposes, she was now tied to him.

The first plane ride of her life was in a private jet in the middle of the night. It landed in a city emblazoned with lights. It would be a week before she would know it was Las Vegas.

Her first night in his bed was a learning experience in how much pain she could bear before he would climax. Every time she cried out, he rammed her harder. It was as effective a reminder to shut up as the gag in her mouth had been to keep her silent.

In the daylight he was a consummate gentleman, calling her his shining princess and shining star, saying she was going to bring him good luck. So she set about learning everything she could about how to please him, how to make his climax happen sooner and with more intensity. She made herself indispensable to him in the sex department, but always with an eye on one day making her escape, until the night Anton sat her down and showed her a video. He called it insurance against her urge to run. She called it carnage. Just thinking about her family innocently opening a door to that fate gave her nightmares. In that moment, she gave up plotting for a better future in the hopes that she would be keeping the people she loved safe and alive.

And so one year followed another and then another, when one day, to her horror, after one of their vacation trips to his Mexican villa, she found herself pregnant.

Star missed her period. The shock and the implications were staggering. Women in Anton's houses were not allowed to keep babies. Abortions were SOP—standard operating procedure. While the thought of being tied to him for life by the birth of his child was abhorrent, the idea of aborting her own baby was worse, and she kept silent, still waiting for a way to make a break. And then a week later, the nausea began. She hid it for a while by waiting to get up until after he had left their bed. Then one morning he came back to get his watch and heard her throwing up.

When he rushed into the bathroom, she was on her knees in front of the commode, trembling in every muscle, praying that was the last wave of nausea when he walked in.

"Star! What's happening?"

Startled by the sound of his voice, she rocked back on her heels and started to cry.

He pulled her to her feet, then got a wet cloth and began wiping her face.

"You are sick. I will call a doctor."

If he did, he would know the truth, and someone else would be telling him. If she stood a chance at all, it had to come from her.

"I'm not sick. I'm pregnant. I don't know how it happened. I take my birth control pills as you request. I never miss. I never forget. But…remember the night I got food poisoning when we were in Mexico? I threw up all night and most of the next day. I took my pill as always, but it must have come up before it had time to get into my system."

She dropped to her knees and wrapped her arms around his legs.

"Please forgive me, Anton. I would never mean to displease you. I live to make you happy."

Anton was in shock. The idea of becoming a father had never entered his mind. But this girl he'd taken from an auction block had turned into a woman over the past five years, and in doing so had become entrenched in his life.

He put a hand on the top of her head and then lifted her to her feet.

Star was in desperation mode, and the only thing she could think to do was feed his ego. Make him believe she adored him as much as she pretended to do.

"Please don't make me kill our baby. Please, Anton, don't make me kill a part of you."

Anton believed what she'd said. She worshipped him. She was a beautiful woman who was carrying his child. What if it was a boy? In two years he would be fifty. What would happen to his fortune of flesh when he died? Maybe it was time to think about an heir.

"Don't cry, my shining Star. We will keep this baby. You will give me a son. I will have an heir."

She shuddered.

"What if it's a girl?"

He frowned.

"I do not sire girls. It will be a boy."

He helped her up, had his secretary make an appointment for her at an obstetrician's office and then had the chef bring her something to calm her stomach.

Every day afterward, he did not leave their bedroom until she'd had weak tea and toast in bed, until she was able to get up without nausea.

Eight months later, Samuel Anton Baba was laid in his mother's arms, with Anton standing beside her. But it wasn't love he felt for the child, only pride.

Star went home to a nursery someone else decorated and a nanny who took the baby out of her arms. Anton gave Star a week, and then she was back on the job, satisfying his sexual appetite with her wits and her hands until her body had time to heal.

The months passed, and while Anton found that he enjoyed watching Sammy grow and witnessing the milestones that came to each baby's life…first words, first steps, he also realized he had become jaded with Star. She had gone from sexy siren to a mother figure, and he no longer desired her in that way. Just after Sammy's second birthday, Anton fired their personal chef and hired a new one—a woman named Lacey, who'd come highly recommended by a friend. Lacey was in her early thirties, short and stocky with black hair she wore combed into a Mohawk, and was as good in the kitchen as Star was in the bedroom. The only thing Anton didn't know about her was that she was an undercover Fed.

Anton Baba had long been suspected of being behind a large ring of human trafficking, but the Feds had never been able to prove it. Sending their agent in undercover was risky, but her skills in cooking gave her the edge she needed to get into his personal space.

It didn't take long for Lacey to learn Anton did not conduct business from his home. The only armed men on the premises were the guards who worked for him. During the two months she'd been there, she had learned nothing that would aid in building a case. Her superiors were considering pulling her out when Lacey picked up on some gossip among the staff. If what they were saying was true, she might have found a weak link in Baba's business—Star Davis, who was the mother of his child.

Star was in the nursery rocking Sammy to sleep for his afternoon nap. She loved this time with him, watching his long dark lashes as they fluttered against his cheeks while he fought to stay awake, and then the peaceful perfection of his little face after he finally fell asleep. She was about to put him to bed when she heard

Anton's voice. She thought he was upstairs looking for her but didn't want to call out and wake up Sammy. But when she realized he was on the phone, she relaxed.

It wasn't until she heard her name and how he was describing her that she realized he only considered her a product to sell.

Her life as she'd known it was about to explode. Learning that he wanted his son but he no longer wanted her was a death sentence. She would rather die than live a life somewhere else knowing her baby was growing up without her.

Anton's voice faded as he walked away, but what she'd overheard had been the warning she needed. As soon as she put Sammy to bed she grabbed his diaper bag and began packing it for a getaway, then left it inside his closet.

The hardest thing she'd ever done was pretend nothing was wrong as she went downstairs to the kitchen. Lacey, the chef, had been preparing vegetables for Sammy and then pureeing them for her, but she wouldn't be able to take food like this, and began gathering up jars of baby food from the pantry.

Lacey saw the tears on Star's face as she entered the kitchen, and when Star went to the pantry without speaking, she followed.

"Good afternoon, Miss Star. Can I help you in any way?"

Star shook her head and kept sorting through the jars.

"I'll be happy to make something fresh for Sammy," Lacey offered.

Star couldn't talk for fear she'd burst into tears, and

just shook her head as she set aside little jars of frui
and vegetables, and a box of teething crackers.

"Looks like we're packing for another trip. Want me
to get a small box?" she asked.

Star panicked.

"No, please. I just need…" Star took a deep breath,
trying to control the spreading panic, and started over.
"I just need to—"

A jar of applesauce slipped from her fingers and
shattered on the pantry floor.

Horrified, Star burst into tears.

"I'm so sorry."

"No problem, Miss Star. It'll clean right up!" Lacey
said. She grabbed a handful of paper towels and quickly
mopped it up.

But Star was beyond help. Once she'd started crying,
she couldn't stop, and that's when Lacey knew something more was going on.

"Come sit with me," she urged.

"I can't," Star whispered. "I don't want them to see
me cry."

"Who? You don't want who to see you cry?" Lacey
asked.

"The guards. They'll tell Anton."

"But Mr. Baba adores you," Lacey said. "I see the
way he treats you."

Star shook her head.

"Not anymore. He's going to sell me, just like he sells
the others," she whispered and then gasped at what she'd
done. "No, I didn't mean that. I just—"

Lacey's heart leaped, but she kept playing along.

"Sell you? But what about Sammy?"

And that's when Star's last defenses fell, and she took a chance.

"He'll keep Sammy. Sammy is his son, but he'll sell me to someone else, and I'll never see Sammy again. Please don't tell. Pretend you never saw me getting food. Just let me walk out of here. I have to get away before this happens. He'll be at his club tonight. It's the only chance I'll have to make a run for it. I can't lose my baby. I'd rather be dead."

"I'll help you," Lacey said.

Star's heart skipped a beat.

"How?"

"I have a friend here in the city. He'll help."

Star frowned.

"I don't believe you. You'll just tell Anton and then I'm done. If you do I'll swear you lied, and believe me, I'm good at lying. I've been doing it for seven years without getting caught."

Star made a grab for the food and was about to bolt when Lacey grabbed her hand.

"Stop," she whispered and pulled her back into the pantry, then leaned forward and whispered in her ear. "I'm with the FBI. Will you testify against him if I help you and Sammy escape?"

Star gasped, then stared at the woman, looking for the lie on her face, but she didn't flinch.

"You're serious?"

Lacey nodded.

"What do I do?" Star asked.

"Be ready to run. It'll be after dark."

"After Anton leaves," Star said.

Lacey nodded. "Go pack what you need for the baby and just be ready."

"Thank you," Star murmured. "Thank you."

"Go," Lacey said, and the moment the woman was out of the kitchen, she sent Ryker, her outside contact, a text.

We have ourselves a witness who'll testify. She's running tonight with a toddler. Pick us up at the back gate of the property.

She hit Send and then waited.

Drug the kid to keep it quiet. I'll have to disarm the alarm at the gate. I'll text you when it's done.

She sent back a thumbs-up emoji and stowed the cell back in her pocket beneath the chef's jacket and went back to prepping vegetables, but her thoughts were already locked into what she needed to do to get them off premises. She'd need to put the silencer on her weapon. There were at least three guards at all times between the house and the back of the property. She would have to take them out just to reach the gate.

Anton left to go to his casino just before 7:00 p.m., which was his habit. Since it was the Fourth of July, Las Vegas was packed with people on holidays. He got all the way to his office before it dawned on him that he hadn't told Star or Sammy goodbye, and then dismissed it as of no concern. It wouldn't be long before she would be gone, Sammy would be with a live-in nanny, and he would be giving full attention to the business of making money, again.

An hour passed and then another before the fireworks began. He got up and walked to the windows overlooking Vegas just as a shower of fireworks spread across the sky.

Entertainment.

That's what Vegas was all about.

He was still watching when his cell phone rang. He went back to the desk to get it.

"Hello."

"Boss, this is Ian. The security alarm just went off at the house. We found three guards dead in the back garden, and Star and the baby are gone."

Anton staggered.

"Gone? How? Who was supposed to be watching them?"

"I don't know, but it wasn't me."

"You and Dev know how to track runaways. Star has a chip as well and doesn't know it. Send out as many men as you need. I'm on my way home."

"Yes, sir," Ian said and disconnected.

Anton rang for his driver and then took the back way out of Lucky Joe's. He rode home in silence, mentally going over everything Star had said and done over the past week. He couldn't find one instance where he'd doubted he had lost control. He had enemies. It occurred to him that this might be the case, but whatever the reason, he wasn't too worried about getting her back. All of the procurers who worked for him, including Darren Vail, had one last duty before they turned the girls over to the men who took them out of state. They shot a tiny tracking chip just under the skin on the back of every girl's neck. It was done while they were unconscious, and they didn't even know it was there. It's also why no one ever got away.

Two

Boom!

Fire exploded in the night sky over the alley behind Pizza Rock, momentarily revealing the trio running through it. If someone had aimed a spotlight at them they couldn't have been more vulnerable. The car he'd picked them up in—the one he'd planned to make their getaway in—was stuck in traffic on a side street waiting for a parade to pass. Forced to abandon it so they wouldn't get caught, they were now afoot and running toward the backup plan—a second vehicle parked a few blocks away.

"Damn it all to hell," Ryker muttered and tightened his grip on the gun in his hand. "Fourth of July. This had to go down in Las Vegas on the Fourth of July? Keep moving. Whatever you do, keep moving."

Twenty-four-year-old Star Davis was behind him with her two-year-old toddler clutched tight against her chest.

"I'm sorry. I'm so sorry," she kept saying.

"Hush, Star! Just run," Lacey said and looked over her shoulder to make sure they weren't being followed.

Star stumbled and then screamed, thinking she and her baby were falling.

Lacey grabbed her.

"Stay with us, honey. It's not much farther."

The baby whimpered and then drifted back off to sleep. The medicine they'd given him earlier to keep him quiet was working, but it made Star anxious. What if they'd given him too much? What if he didn't wake up?

Ryker kept a continuous one-eighty sweep of the area in front of them, ready to take anyone down who got in their way while Lacey kept an eye out for who might be coming up behind them. He and his partner had been undercover too damn long to have this screw up now.

Boom!

The baby flinched in Star's arms but didn't cry.

A stray cat hissed from behind a Dumpster, then darted off into the shadows as they ran past.

Lacey was bringing up the rear without comment until she suddenly let out a low cry.

"Ryker! Runners coming up on our six."

Ryker paused and pivoted, his heart pounding. He heard them, too.

"Take Star and the kid and get to the Farmers Market parking lot. I'm right behind you."

Lacey grabbed Star's arm.

"We have to run now. Stay with me and don't look back."

"Oh, my God," Star moaned. "I'm—"

"Just don't fucking say that you're sorry again," Lacey said and grabbed her by the arm, pulling her closer into the shadows and lengthening their strides as Ryker darted behind a Dumpster into a crouch. He didn't have long to wait.

Three men were coming up the alley at a fast clip, but it was the silence they brought with them that was the tipping point for Ryker. If they had been tourists enjoying the fireworks they would have likely been drunk and noisy. Chances were more likely it was some of Baba's hired guns. He saw them from the side as they ran past the Dumpster and knew one man on sight.

He stood up and called out.

"Hey! Bergman!"

The trio turned in an orchestrated move that would have made the Cirque du Soleil proud, but Ryker was already firing.

Pop.

Bergman went down.

Pop.

Blood fanned out behind the middle man's head before he dropped.

Pop.

Blood flooded the front of the shortest man's shirt as Ryker's last shot tore through the carotid artery in his neck.

Three shots in three seconds without one fired in return. Efficient. Ryker prided himself on efficiency, and now he had to catch up. He ran past the bodies without looking down and caught up with the women just as they reached the car.

Lacey clicked the remote to unlock the doors, then tossed the keys to Ryker, who caught them in midair. He got into the driver's seat as Lacey put Star and the baby into the back. "Buckle up," she said and slammed the door, then jumped into the front passenger seat and grabbed her seat belt. "What happened back there?"

"Bergman and two others."

Lacey groaned.

"Our cover is blown. How did that happen?"

"Who knows, and it's too late to worry about it," Ryker said.

"You're right. Get us out of here," Lacey said.

Star was out of breath and trembling as Ryker started the car and drove away.

"Where are we going?" she asked.

"They're sending a chopper for us," Lacey said. "This might have worked better if the need for haste had not been an issue. Now we just have to get to the pickup site."

The toddler whimpered in Star's arms. Now that they were settled, she dug into the bag over her shoulder and pulled out a bottle, then smiled when the baby started drinking.

"My poor little Sammy," she crooned. "Mama's hungry little boy."

Lacey glanced over her shoulder at the young woman. At first glance, and in the darkened interior, she looked like a teenager. Lacey gave Star and the baby one last look, then turned around and buckled her seat belt. They were headed out of Vegas with fireworks exploding in the sky behind them. They had a date with an FBI chopper at a GPS location just off Highway 93, and time was wasting.

Lacey kept an eye on the headlights of the cars behind them while Ryker wove through the traffic with professional precision. The farther he drove, the less traffic they met, and the fewer cars trailing behind.

"How far now?" Ryker asked, knowing Lacey was keeping track of the GPS location for him.

"Looks like about six miles," she said.

He hit the accelerator, moving them faster, anxious to tie this up without anyone getting hurt. But he had a knot in his gut and a niggling concern that this wasn't over.

The night sky was beautiful, peppered with stars from a heavenly explosion a thousand light-years in the past, while the mountains to the north appeared as a ragged bulwark between the city behind them and the desert landscape around them.

Star glanced out her window and then looked up through the glass sunroof. Her pulse was as erratic as the trip they were on, and then she saw a shooting star.

"Look at that! A star on the run, like me."

"They burn out," Ryker reminded her.

The shock of his careless comment scared her, and she buried her face against her sleeping baby's neck.

Lacey frowned.

"Damn it, Ryker, that was harsh," she said.

"This whole situation is harsh," he muttered, then glanced up in his rearview mirror and frowned. "We have a tail."

Lacey turned to look.

"Are you sure? That seems impossible."

"See that right headlight on the car behind us? See how it's shaking?"

"Yes."

"I don't know how they found us that fast, but it's been behind us ever since we left Vegas."

"Oh no," Star moaned.

She started to turn and look when Lacey stopped her with a shout.

"Get down!"

Star lay down on the floorboard with the baby clutched against her chest as Ryker pushed the accelerator all the way to the floor. The engine vibrated like a roar in her chest. The high-pitched whine of tires against the highway was close to her ears as they raced off into the night.

"They're gaining," Lacey said and grabbed her cell.

Ryker's fingers curled even tighter around the steering wheel as the car began to vibrate, too.

"What are you doing?" he asked.

"Calling the chopper," Lacey said.

Ryker's jaw was clenched. The highway was a blur as he listened to her make the call.

"What did they say?" he asked, as she disconnected.

"They're still en route. Not even at the pickup site yet. What the hell's up with that?" Lacey cried.

"How far to the pickup site?" Ryker asked.

Lacey glanced at her GPS.

"Almost four miles."

"We aren't going to make it," he said.

Star started to cry. Softly, hopelessly.

"I'm so sorry," she cried, but she was talking to

Sammy, not them. She'd tried so hard to get him away. God only knew how this would end.

Lacey was on her knees, her gun drawn.

"Open the sunroof," she said.

Ryker frowned, but the headlights were closer and he didn't argue. The glass ceiling above them slid back, opening most of the roof to the night. The loud roar of the engine and the shrill whistle of the wind inside the car was shocking.

Suddenly glad they'd doped her baby to sleep, Star held him tighter and started to pray.

Someone in the car behind them got off the first shot, exploding the back window of the car, covering Star and the baby in shattered glass.

She screamed.

Ryker cursed.

Lacey popped up through the sunroof and fired two shots back in rapid succession before the force of the wind nearly blew her out of the car. She stayed up long enough to see their windshield shatter. The car behind them was now the one in trouble as the driver fought to stay on the highway.

She ducked back down but stayed on her knees, her gaze focused on the car behind them. For a few moments they had the edge and were putting some serious distance between them and their tail—until another car came up fast behind it, passing the damaged vehicle like it was sitting still. The new threat was suddenly at Ryker's side and swerved into them with such force that it threw their car into a spin.

"Hold on!" Ryker shouted, as the car spun backward, sliding off the highway into the desert.

He righted the spin and stomped the accelerator again, sending up a rooster tail of sand in a desperate attempt to get back onto the highway. But now both cars were coming at them fast.

"Where the hell is that chopper?" Ryker yelled.

Lacey was bleeding from her forehead and trying to focus as she reached blindly for her phone, but it wasn't in the console.

"I can't find my phone," she cried.

Star was on her knees on the back floorboard with the baby in her arms, praying the same silent prayer over and over. *Please, God, please, don't let Sammy die.*

Another round of bullets hit their car.

One tire blew, launching the car into a spectacular skid that threw them sideways into a roll.

Star closed her eyes and held Sammy tight, certain they were going to die. The first roll tumbled them from the bottom of the car to the roof and back down again. Just as they went into the second roll, Star and the baby shot through the open sunroof and up into the air. She felt the heel of her shoe hit the side of Lacey's head on the way out, and she hit the ground with such impact it slid her across the desert on her back. The blow knocked the air from her lungs and set her back afire. But none of that mattered, because she still had Sammy in her arms.

She was struggling to catch her breath when there was a deafening explosion. She gasped again and again until her lungs finally expanded, and was trying to get up when fire shot straight up into the sky behind her. She felt the heat as the car was engulfed in flames.

Sammy whimpered.

She panicked. Was he hurt or waking up? The fact that he still wasn't crying scared her, but if they found her now, they'd kill her and take Sammy. She couldn't bear to think of Anton Baba raising him as the heir to his criminal world.

There was always some traffic on this highway. Someone was bound to see this fire at any moment. If she could just hide Sammy and run, she'd let them take her. She was going to raise hell with Anton until he, too, believed their son died because of his orders. She'd lost her chance to get away, but she wasn't going to give up on someone saving Sammy.

His pacifier was still in her pants pocket, and she took it out and popped it into his mouth. Every muscle in her body was aching as she struggled to her feet and ran toward a small stand of scrub brush.

Both of the cars were driving toward the fire now. Her voice was shaking, her heart was breaking, but there was no time to waste.

"Sammy, my little Sammy. Mama loves you so much, but God is going to watch over you now."

She kissed him quickly, trying to imprint the feel of his soft cheek against her lips, then tucked him beneath the brush and ran. She was sprinting toward the highway when they saw her and gave chase.

"Help me, God," she muttered and kept running.

The night air was cooler now, the sand was in her shoes and her blouse was sticking to her bloody back.

Her footsteps were jarring as she ran, adding to the thunder of her heartbeat.

All of a sudden one car sped past her and then swerved, blocking her path. The other car came up behind her, skidded to a stop, and the driver, Ian Bojalian, took her down within seconds.

Star screamed.

"Where's the kid? Where's your son?" he yelled.

She was already crying now, as she pointed back to the fire.

"He's dead! You killed him! You killed him!" she cried.

She never saw the fist coming, but when he hit her, she dropped like a rock.

Dev Bosky, the driver who was now missing a windshield, frowned.

"Baba is not going to be happy about this."

"He told us to stop them. It's her fault for taking him away," Ian said, then gagged her and tied her up before tossing her into the trunk. "I'm going back to Vegas. You make sure nothing that would tie you to this scene blew out of your car. Without a windshield, there's no telling what shit you strung about out here."

"Someone is going to see this fire any second. I don't want to still be out here," Dev growled.

"Then make it snappy," Ian said from the front seat as he slammed his door and steered the car toward the highway. The moment his tires hit the pavement, he gassed it and disappeared.

Dev Bosky jumped in his car and put the headlights on bright, intent on making a quick sweep through the area for any evidence he might have left. He was on the back side of the fire and a good distance away when he saw a single light come into view out on the highway, heading toward Las Vegas.

"Damn it all to hell. A biker. If you wanna keep living, man, you better keep riding."

Quinn O'Meara was southbound on her Harley, heading toward Las Vegas on Highway 93, when she saw fire in the sky. At first she thought it was fireworks, but the flames weren't burning out; they were growing bigger. She sped up, topping the slight rise shortly afterward, and realized the flames came from something burning out in the desert.

The sight made her skin crawl, and the closer she came to it, the larger the fire appeared. It was on the northbound side, which was opposite to the way she was going, but her conscience wouldn't let her ride on without investigation.

She crossed the median and then the northbound lanes and rode out into the desert, only to realize it was a car that was burning. Horrified, she braked quickly and left her bike idling as she hung her helmet on the handlebars and jumped off.

She was walking toward the fire when the silhouette of a toddler moved between her and the flames.

"Oh, my God," she said and started running.

The baby was stumbling and falling and far too close to the fire. She ran up behind him, scooping him up in her arms. He was dirty and crying, but he didn't look injured in any way. When she picked him up, he surprised her by putting his arms around her neck and hiding his face against the front of her jacket.

"Oh, sweetheart! If only you could talk," Quinn said as she looked again toward the burning fire.

The car had rolled. That much was evident because the roof was crunched inward and flames were shooting straight up through the top. It took her a few moments to figure out they were streaming through what must have been the sunroof. Then she saw what looked like two bodies inside the car and groaned. The baby must have been thrown out as the car rolled. He could have internal injuries.

She started to take out her cell phone to call 911 and then saw headlights farther out in the desert coming toward the fire. She moved away from the fire for a better view, unaware that she'd just given a killer a clear view of her and the baby in her arms. One of the headlights was flickering in the distance while the other stayed steady. Help was coming. But her relief was short-lived when she heard a series of pops and saw the dirt flying up near her feet.

Shots? Were those gunshots?

Oh God, oh God, what had she walked up on?

She unzipped her jacket and stuffed the baby into it, his belly against her breasts as she zipped him back in. Within seconds she had her helmet on and was heading toward the highway as fast as she could ride. She was almost to the pavement when something hit her in the shoulder so hard she almost lost her grip. The ensuing pain was sharp and burning.

She'd been shot! The nightmare kept getting worse!

There was only one way to save both of their lives. She had to outrun the gunman. He was about a hundred yards behind her when she accelerated, crossing the median again and back onto the southbound lanes toward Vegas, riding without caution, desperate to stay far enough ahead to make shooting futile.

The baby was still now. She could smell the dust in his hair and feel the sweat of his little body. Her chin beneath the helmet was only inches away from his head when it occurred to her that the bullet might have gone through her into him. Now she had even more reason to get to Las Vegas fast.

When the highway flattened out into a straightaway, she could see the same shaky headlights behind her, but he had not gained any ground. The farther she rode, the heavier the traffic had become. She was closer to safety, but her shoulder was on fire and she was getting weak.

The car was closer now as she rode into Las Vegas. She saw the shaky headlight in her rearview mirror more often, but he hadn't gotten close enough to hurt her again. At the first stoplight she came to, she yanked out her phone and searched the address of the closest police station, then synced the directions to the mic in her helmet and followed them straight to the address.

There was a No Parking sign in front of the station, but she couldn't go any farther, and she needed to make it inside before the gunman caught up to them. Her legs were shaking as she got off the bike, hung her helmet and checked on the baby. He'd slipped farther down inside her jacket, but she could feel him breathing. He was asleep, though it seemed crazy to her that he could rest after such an accident. He was probably in shock. After one quick glance over her shoulder she ran inside, requesting to speak to someone in Homicide.

The officer up front led her to a separate area where three detectives were working. One was on the phone and two were doing paperwork. They all looked up at the same time, but Nick Saldano was the first to move as he hung up the phone. He was already taking her measure as he started toward the tall, dusty redhead. She was dressed in leather biker gear, and she looked strung out and—from a quick glance at her round stomach—pregnant. But she blew his first read all to hell when she put one hand under her belly and began unzipping her jacket with the other.

"Help me," she said.

All three saw the baby and the blood at the same time and bolted, running toward her as she began to fall.

Nick caught her and the baby before they hit the floor.

"Daniels, get the kid. Murphy, call 911."

He had her jacket off and was checking for an entrance wound when she moaned and opened her eyes.

"Tried to kill me," she whispered.

"Who tried to kill you!" Nick asked.

She grabbed his wrist so hard her nails dug into the skin.

"Help me."

"We've got you, ma'am. You're at the police station. What's your name?"

"The baby?"

"Your baby's okay," Nick said.

"Not my baby," she mumbled and passed out again.

"Daniels! Check for any kind of identification on the baby. She said he wasn't hers," Nick said, as he went through the pockets of the jacket they'd taken off of her. They were empty.

"I wanted this to be an easy end to this shift, but no. It's nearly midnight and the Fourth of July. Who was I kidding?" Daniels muttered.

"Paramedics on the way," Murphy shouted.

A few minutes later two medical teams came running into the room. One team headed for the sleeping baby while the other one began to assess the woman.

Nick stood off to the side watching them work, but every few seconds his gaze would go back to her face. He couldn't shake the feeling he should know her, but he couldn't think of her name.

He was still trying to place her when the medical teams loaded up both victims and headed for the ambulances.

"Hey! Where are you taking her?" Nick called.

"Centennial Hill Hospital," one of them said, and then they were gone.

Nick ran back to his desk, got his handgun out of the drawer and slipped it in the shoulder holster beneath his jacket.

"Someone tell Lieutenant Summers what's going down. I'll follow to the hospital," Nick said. "Maybe I can get some more of the story before they take her to surgery. Daniels, notify Social Services about the baby. They need to send someone to the hospital."

"Will do," Daniels said and headed for the phone.

Nick followed the paramedics down the hall and then out of the building. When he saw a big Harley parked in front of the precinct, he guessed it was hers. He called back to the office.

"Homicide."

"Murphy, it's me. There's a big black Harley parked in front of the precinct. Have it checked for ID and then have it towed. Their crime-scene analysts need to run it for prints."

"Will do," Murphy said.

Nick jumped in his car and, despite the noise of the ongoing holiday celebrations, ran lights and siren all the way to Centennial Hill.

Because of his missing windshield, there was no way Dev could drive into the city without getting stopped by local police. He cruised past a couple of bars on the outskirts of Las Vegas until he found one with a classier clientele. He pulled into the parking lot, ditched his car and within a few minutes found one unlocked and a man passed out in the front seat. He dragged the man out of the car, propped him up against the back of the Lucky Joe's Casino between two Dumpsters and took off.

By the time he got back on the streets, he'd obviously lost his target. There was nothing he could do but keep moving down the main drag and hope for the best. One minute passed into another, and just when he was beginning to think he was done, he saw the motorcycle weaving through traffic at a fast clip.

The knot in his belly eased. Pissing Anton Baba off

was never a good risk and not coming back with his son could be a deadly error.

He followed the biker through every twist and turn, hoping for a chance to get rid of her and grab the kid, but with the traffic he couldn't get nearly close enough to them. He didn't realize she was heading to the police station until it was too late to stop her, and she was inside by the time he parked. He picked a place where he could watch the front entrance, then made a quick call to Anton to let him know his son was still alive.

Ian pulled up to the gates at the Baba estate and keyed the number pad to let himself in. He could hear Anton's woman kicking and screaming in the trunk and was somewhat worried that he didn't have the kid, as well.

As the gates swung inward, he sped up the drive and around the mansion to the delivery entrance in back. He'd already called to let Baba know he was on the way and was not surprised to see the man himself standing in the doorway, silhouetted by the lights behind him.

"Well, where are they?" Baba asked, as Ian got out of the car and headed to the back of the car and opened the trunk.

Star had cried all the way into the city, so by the time the trunk was opened, her eyes were nearly swollen shut, her bloody back was visible, and she was screaming.

Anton was shocked at the condition she was in, and

the fact that the baby was missing was even more troubling.

"Where is my son?" Anton shouted, but she wouldn't stop screaming.

"Get her inside!" he said and strode back into the house.

Ian picked her up and followed his boss through the house to the library.

"Put her down," Anton said.

Ian dropped her on the floor at Anton's feet, ignoring her low moan of pain.

Anton looked at her in disgust.

"So she is here, but where is my son?" he asked.

Star was sobbing uncontrollably as she rolled over on her hands and knees and dragged herself upright.

"You killed our son!" she screamed and launched herself at Anton, hammering at his chest with her fists. "They shot at us over and over. We wrecked. Why? Why? If you didn't want us anymore, why didn't you just let us go?"

Anton reeled. Sammy was dead?

"No, no, that can't be," he moaned, then turned on Ian. "What did I tell you to do?"

"Find them and bring them back," Ian muttered.

Star was playing the grieving mother to the hilt and nailed Anton again.

"Why do you care? You were going to sell me. I heard you! I couldn't lose my baby, and then you let them shoot at us! Just because you didn't want him doesn't mean I didn't either. He was my life! He was a part of you! I thought we mattered. I thought we were a family! If you hadn't been such a miserable greedy bastard, none of this would have happened. I hate you, I hate you," she sobbed and then collapsed at his feet.

For one of the few times in his life, Anton Baba felt regret. He knelt beside her.

"What made you think that?" he asked.

"I heard you! I heard you making the deal! I curse you, Anton Baba. Your evil, ugly world is going to fall down around your ears."

She moaned, a sound so bereft and hopeless it cut to what conscience he had left. He put a hand on her back and then flinched when she screamed out in pain. He pulled his hand away covered in blood.

He looked up at Ian with a cold, emotionless stare.

"What did you do?" he asked.

Ian shrugged. "Only what you told us to do."

Star shrieked and began scooting backward away from Anton.

"You told him to shoot at us? He shot out the tires. I was thrown out of the car when it began to roll," she said. "I want to die. My baby died. I want to die, too."

Rage washed through Anton in waves, but he was calm as he stood up and turned around.

"Why did you shoot at them?" he asked.

Ian should have been warned by the quiet tone of his boss's voice.

"They were getting away."

"Where's Dev? Where's Bergman and his men?"

"Bergman and his crew are dead. Dev and I found them in an alley." He pointed to the floor at Star. "We followed her and your cook out of Vegas. I don't know who the man was with them. Dev was behind them. He shot at their car. They shot out his windshield. And then their car skidded off the highway and into the desert. We tried to stop them. The car rolled and caught fire. I left him behind to clean up."

All the color faded from Anton's face.

"You left my son."

"The car was burning. There was nothing we could—"

The roar that came out of Anton Baba was nothing short of terrifying as he pivoted and grabbed the dagger-like letter opener from the desk behind him.

At that moment, Ian knew he was done. He turned to run but was a couple of seconds too late. Anton leaped forward and stabbed the letter opener into the back of Ian's neck, cutting the spinal cord and the blood supply to his brain. He dropped without making a sound.

Anton pulled the little dagger out and wiped it on the back of Ian's shirt before dropping it back on his desk, then looked down again at the woman on the floor, at the blood and dirt on her body and the grief on her face.

"This should not have happened," he muttered, then reached for his cell phone and punched in the number to the wing where his hired guns stayed.

His call was answered on the first ring.

"Yes, sir?"

"Luis, I need the cleanup crew in the library."

"Yes, sir. Right away, sir," Luis said.

Anton disconnected, looked at Star one more time and then made another call. The phone rang several times before it was answered.

"Dr. Fuentes, it's Anton Baba. I need you."

"Yes, sir. I'll be there as soon as I can."

Anton disconnected and dropped his cell back in his pocket and then went back to Star. The moment he picked her up in his arms, she cried out from the pain.

"I'm sorry," he said softly and then carried her out of the library and all the way up to their bedroom. He could not put into words what he was feeling, but there was a pain in his heart and a roaring in his ears. His son was dead.

Anton laid her on the bed. He'd never seen her like this. Before, she'd been so passive, doing everything he demanded. He'd never looked beyond what she could do for him. But this woman…shattered, bloody, filthy, and so very broken in her grief. He saw her power and her rage and had never been attracted to her more.

His phone rang.

He took it out of his pocket, glanced at caller ID and then answered.

"Hello."

"Boss, this is Dev. Is Ian there?"

Anton thought of the dead man in his library and the blood spreading over the Persian rug beneath his body.

"Yes, he is here," Anton said.

"Okay, then you know what went down. I was still on site when a biker saw the fire and rode off the highway to where the car was burning. The moment the helmet came off I could see it was a woman. And then I saw her run toward the fire, and when she ran back toward her bike she was carrying the kid. I followed her to—"

Anton gasped.

"What did you say?"

"I said I followed her to—"

"No, no! You said someone took my son! He is alive?"

"Yes. I saw the biker pick him up and zip him up into her jacket. I tried to stop her but she got away. I followed her into Vegas but lost her in the traffic. When I caught up with her again she was already inside the police station."

"Where are you now?" Anton asked.

"Outside the police station waiting for her to— Oh, hell."

"What?" Anton shouted.

"Two ambulances just rolled up to the police station."

"What does that mean?" Anton cried.

"I shot at the woman as she was riding away. I might have hit her."

"She was holding my son in her arms and you shot at her?"

Dev realized what he'd just said.

"What do you want me to do?" Dev asked.

"Did she see you?"

"I don't know. It was dark. I doubt it."

"You doubt it? You fucking doubt it? Here's what I want you to do. I don't want a witness left who can identify you. Get rid of her and bring me my son."

Anton knew he'd just assigned an impossible task. One that would probably get Dev killed. He didn't care.

"Yes, sir," Dev said and disconnected.

Anton slipped his phone back in his pocket, sat down beside Star and took her hand.

"Star, Star, can you hear me?"

Star moaned.

He reached out, then drew back, uncertain of a safe place to touch.

"Sammy is not dead. Someone found him and took him to the police department. I will get him back for you. Do you hear me? I will get him back."

She opened her eyes.

"You lie."

He frowned. People did not accuse him in such a manner.

"I do not lie."

"You lied to me. You told me Sammy and I would always be safe with you, and then you made a deal to sell me. I will hate you forever."

He had no response to that. "I will find Sammy and bring him back. You will see," he said.

"Stop talking, Anton. Your words mean nothing to me anymore. I just want to die so that all of this will be over. I can't bear any more pain. I can't bear any more heartache. I'm sorry I didn't die. I'm sorry Sammy didn't die. Then we would both be free of you," she said and closed her eyes.

Nick followed the ambulances to the hospital. By the time he located the redhead in ER she was on an examining table, naked, bloody and unconscious. He could hear the baby crying a couple of doors down, but a toddler couldn't tell him anything he needed to know. He just had to wait, hoping the woman would wake up enough to tell him what the hell happened to her. And if that baby wasn't hers, who did he belong to?

Quinn woke up to bright lights and chaos, bathed in a pain she could feel all the way to her bones. Someone was trying to turn her over and someone else was talking in loud, staccato syllables. A part of her sensed the urgency in the voice, which was not a reassuring sound.

Where was she?

What had happened to her?

Was she going to die?

Someone was yelling in her ear. A woman.

She frowned. Why were they yelling? She wasn't deaf.

"Honey, can you hear me?"

Quinn moaned, struggling to pull herself out of the pain-induced fog.

"Yes."

"What's your name? Can you tell me your name?" the woman asked.

Quinn was struggling to stay conscious.

"Quinn."

"Thank you, Quinn. Do you know where you are?"

"Hospital."

"Yes," the woman said. "You've been shot."

Quinn felt someone running a hand across her midriff, pressing into the taut flesh. She reached out, trying to grab it.

"Police. Need police," she mumbled.

Nick's heart skipped.

"Here! I'm here," he said, as he moved to the foot

of the bed. "Detective Nick Saldano, Las Vegas Homicide."

"The car...on fire. Two dead inside. Found baby there."

"Where?" Nick asked. "Where did you see this?"

"93..."

Nick frowned.

"Highway 93?"

Quinn shuddered as a ripple of pain rolled through her and reached toward her shoulder.

"Ma'am? Quinn? Highway 93?" Nick asked again.

Her eyelids fluttered. The word came out on a sigh. "Yes."

"Who shot you?"

"Don't know. Someone...in the desert."

"Did you see what they were driving?"

But Quinn didn't answer. She was unconscious again.

"That's all for now, Detective. She's still bleeding. Must have nicked a vein. She's going to surgery."

Nick backed up and watched as they wheeled her out of ER. Something terrible had happened out in the desert, and he had a hunch Quinn was a witness someone had tried to kill. The fact that she was still breathing put her in danger all over again.

"Go with God," he said and left the examining room. He needed to call his lieutenant about the reported murder, and get a guard on this woman ASAP. And then check and see if someone from Child Welfare was here for the kid.

* * *

Quinn woke up again as they were moving her to the operating table. The simple act of moving her from the bed to the table was excruciating. Tears welled.

"Hurts. Please don't," she mumbled.

Someone patted her arm.

"I'm sorry, dear. We'll get you comfortable soon. Take a deep breath."

She didn't see the anesthesia going into her IV but she felt it. A fleeting thought went through her mind that if she died today, there would be no one to grieve her passing, and then she felt nothing.

The county authorities who were dispatched to find the crime scene drove several miles north on Highway 93 watching for signs of a fire off in the desert.

What they saw instead were floodlights and smoke. They drove up on a chopper parked near what was left of a smoldering car and a large number of vehicles parked a safe distance away.

Sheriff Baldwin frowned as they pulled up and parked. What in hell had they come up on?

Two men separated themselves from the crowd around the burned-out car and came to meet them.

"I'm Sheriff Baldwin." he said. "We're here to investigate a report of a car fire. Who are you and what are you doing with my crime scene?"

The man nodded at Baldwin, then flashed his badge as he introduced himself.

"Sheriff, Federal Agent Carl Gleason and this is my partner, Federal Agent Lou Powers."

Baldwin was noticeably surprised by Feds on the scene as Gleason continued.

"The victims in the burned-out car are two of our own, so we've taken control of the crime scene."

Baldwin frowned.

"Then you might like to know that the biker who reported this also found a survivor. The witness was shot leaving the scene but made it to the Las Vegas police precinct before she collapsed."

Gleason's pulse shifted gears.

"So the baby survived?"

"How did you know the survivor was a baby?" Sheriff Baldwin asked.

Gleason didn't answer. He just asked another question.

"Was there any sign of the mother?" Gleason asked.

"No one else was mentioned to me when they called this in," Baldwin said.

"Where is the baby now?" Agent Gleason asked.

"I have no idea, but why all the secrecy?"

"The kid is Anton Baba's," Gleason said. "The rest is on a need-to-know basis."

Baldwin frowned.

"This is my county, and I need to know why someone shot at a woman and a baby as they were leaving this wreck, understand?"

Gleason thought about it a moment and then decided he could let Baldwin in on this…to a degree.

"My agents had taken the woman and her baby into protective custody and were on their way to a pickup site. When they didn't arrive as scheduled, we started looking for them and found this. We assumed Baba took them back, but if you've got a witness on the scene who has the baby, then maybe there's still a chance to save him. We have to get to the kid before Baba does or he'll take that woman out for sure. For all we know, she may already be dead."

"Bad deal all around," Baldwin said. "You need to call the Homicide Division at the Vegas police department. They'll be able to fill you in with the details on the witness."

Gleason was already on the phone to the Las Vegas police as the sheriff and his deputies drove away, but Baldwin wasn't upset about losing this one to the Feds. He and his men had dodged a bullet by not being in charge of that crime scene. The last thing he wanted to do was start digging into the business dealings of Anton Baba.

Detective Saldano was in the hospital lobby getting an update from Summers.

"We've been contacted by the FBI regarding the woman and kid. This whole incident has taken on a darker, more dangerous aspect."

"How so?" Nick asked.

"Anton Baba is the father of the baby. They don't know where the mother is for sure, but they assume she's back in Baba's possession. The two victims in the car fire were Feds, and the FBI has taken over the crime scene and the case."

"Holy shit," Nick muttered.

"Exactly. The Feds already took possession of the

child from Social Services and are actively looking for the mother."

"What about the biker who found the kid? The one who was shot?" Nick asked. "Are they going to protect her, too?"

"They say they will interview her when she is able to be interviewed. If she has nothing new to add to their case, they're cutting her loose."

Nick frowned.

"Baba won't be that generous," Nick said. "Her life is in danger, sir."

Summers sighed.

"You're probably right."

"Are we going to put a guard on her? If they want her dead, they'll come to the hospital and try and finish the job," Nick said.

"I don't have the manpower to put round-the-clock guards on her."

Nick's frown deepened.

"Sir, if the man who shot her comes to finish the job, maybe we could link him to Baba and take him out of circulation that way."

"The criminal justice system has been trying to find a way to connect to that man and his crimes for years and hasn't done it yet," Summers said.

"There's always a first time," Nick said.

When his boss didn't answer, he feared the PD was going to leave Quinn hanging, too, and then Summers spoke.

"I'll get the guards set up. But once she leaves the hospital, she's on her own. We do not have the budget to put someone in a safe house who has no real bearing on a homicide case that we're not even working."

"Thanks," Nick said. "If it's okay, I'll stay here for the rest of the night. She went through a lot to get that little kid safe. I think we owe her, sir."

"Agreed. And there will be an officer there to replace you by eight tomorrow morning."

"Yes, sir. Thank you, sir," Nick said and disconnected.

His stride was long and hurried as he moved through the hospital lobby. By the time he got to the surgery wing, more than an hour had passed since he'd last seen the injured woman. He notified the nurses at the surgery desk that he was there on behalf of Quinn O'Meara and headed for the waiting room.

There was only one other person there when he walked in, a thirtysomething guy with curly black hair hanging well below his shoulders. He obviously spent more time in the gym than in the barbershop. The man looked up at Nick as he walked in, nodded and then looked back down at his phone.

Nick got a coffee from the coffee machine, a honey bun from the food dispenser, and sat back down to wait. He sent a text to his lieutenant to let him know he was on site and then opened the honey bun and took a bite.

The sugar was a much-needed jolt, as was the caffeine in the coffee. A quick glance at the clock on the opposite wall was a reminder that he'd been up for eighteen hours. It was a good thing tomorrow was his day off. He finished off the food, drained his coffee and went to the bathroom. When he came out, the dark-haired man was still there, still texting.

Nick sat, leaned his head back against the wall and closed his eyes, thinking again of the redhead. There was something about her that niggled at his memory. He couldn't imagine forgetting someone who looked like that. Bloody as hell, her beauty had still been obvious— and all that red hair. Maybe she just reminded him of someone else.

Dev Bosky knew the other man in the waiting room was a cop. His gut knotted when he saw him walk in, and the urge to leave was huge. But sitting in a room with a cop was still safer than going back to Anton Baba without his son. He'd already learned the kid was no longer in the hospital but didn't know where he'd been taken. He had contacts who could track the location of the kid later. First thing he had to do was get rid of his witness.

He'd been texting Ian for over an hour and still hadn't heard back. That alone was worrisome. It occurred to him that Ian's decision to go back without the kid might have been a deadly one. That fear alone was enough to keep him on task.

Three

Nick glanced at his watch. The woman had been in surgery a little over three hours, and he was beginning to worry when a doctor in green scrubs entered the waiting room.

"Who's here for Quinn O'Meara?"

Nick stood and flashed his badge.

"I am. Detective Nick Saldano, Las Vegas Homicide."

The doctor acknowledged Nick and then gave him the update he'd been waiting for.

"I'm Dr. Munoz. Miss O'Meara's surgery was successful. Barring complications, she should be fine."

"Where will you be taking her next?" Nick asked.

"She'll be in Recovery for a while and then up to her room. Fourth floor. You can check at the nurses' station for her room number."

"There will be a police guard on her room until she's released," Nick said.

"As you see fit," the doctor said. "But I don't want our other patients bothered or frightened. If need be, I can have her moved to a smaller facility that might be easier to secure."

"Understood, sir," Nick said.

They walked out together and parted company at the door with Nick heading to the elevator.

Back in the waiting room, Dev was too keyed up to sit still. The woman was so close, but there was no way he could get to her from here without getting caught. So, they were going to put a guard on her room. That meant his only chance to get to her would be when they were moving her to the fourth floor.

He wanted to go up now and get the lay of the area, but he didn't want it to appear as if he was following the cop, so he waited another ten minutes while he thought things out. He had a silencer. He could pop her and whoever was wheeling her to the room just as they exited the elevator, then make a run for it before anyone even noticed he was there.

After giving the cop enough of a lead, he made his way up to the fourth floor using the stairs. He noted which elevator they used to bring up surgery patients, but when he saw how close it was to the waiting room, and then realized the cop was already sitting within sight of the elevator, he knew he had to rethink his plan. He was going to have to go through the cop to get to her. Baba would be pissed if he killed a cop, but he also wanted the woman dead, so the way Dev looked at it, his job was to do what Baba sent him to do, regardless.

With a half-assed plan in place, he entered the waiting room and saw the cop on the phone. He headed for the coffee machine.

* * *

Dr. Fuentes wasted no time getting to the Baba estate, but had no idea it was Baba's woman he would be seeing. He'd been there enough over the past few years to realize she was something of a fixture and was horrified when he saw the shape she was in.

She was lying on her bed with her back to the door and made no attempt to communicate when he came into the room. Upon closer examination, he was shocked by the condition of her bloody back and the unkempt state of her hair and clothing. He'd need to be cautious of how he worded his questions. To his relief, Anton initiated the conversation.

"Star was in a car wreck. There are other factors concerning her condition that do not affect how you need to treat her, and we will not speak of these, do you understand?"

"Yes, of course," Fuentes said. "Where are her injuries? If she needs X-rays I will have to have her transported to an ER, and she might require hospitalization based on the results."

Anton frowned. It wasn't something he'd considered, but if she had broken bones, he couldn't ignore them. Regardless of what happened between them, having her healthy would either facilitate a cease-fire between them, or render her a whole and healthy product ready to move.

"She hasn't spoken of any specifics except that her back hurts, which is obvious."

Fuentes nodded, took off his jacket, gloved up and began his examination by cutting away what was left of her blouse. He hid his horror at the gouges dug into her slender back, tried to ignore the quiet sound of her weeping and kept going, checking for broken bones and anything that might indicate internal bleeding.

Anton knew the doctor was paying close attention to the change in Star's breathing, as well as the flicker of her eyelids when he touched on something painful, but when they began to turn her over and she screamed, Anton's heart sank. She was worse than he'd thought.

Dr. Fuentes shook his head.

"She needs X-rays for sure. There may be some cracked ribs and I fear internal bleeding. As for her back, just at a glance I see small rocks and sand in the wounds, which will require a very sterile setting to clean up. Will you please allow me to call an ambulance for her?"

Anton frowned, but he obviously had no other choice.

"Of course," he muttered.

Dr. Fuentes cleaned his hands and then stepped out into the hall to make the call.

Anton knelt beside the bed and ran a hand down the side of her cheek.

"Star?"

Her eyes opened, piercing him with a watery blue stare.

"Let me die."

"Then who will take care of Sammy?" he asked.

Rage flickered on her face and then disappeared.

"I am no longer his mother. You decided that. You have destroyed me. Let me die."

He stood abruptly. She'd nailed him on that. When

someone had no fear of death, he had no way to coerce them to his will. Then Fuentes stepped back into the room.

"There is an ambulance on the way. I will wait for them in the foyer."

Anton sat down in a chair beside the bed they shared and thought about the changes yet to come.

Star was shaking. Shock and pain were moving through her in waves. The fact that Sammy had been found was such a huge relief to her that the tears she shed were tears of gratitude. And she knew something Anton had yet to learn. The two people who died in that fire were federal agents. It was only a matter of time before the Feds made their move and took him down. However, if she was still under his control when he found out, he would kill her.

A short time later the ambulance came, and the paramedics loaded Star up and took her away. Anton called for his car and a couple of his men to go with him and followed, unwilling to let her out of his sight for long.

Quinn was struggling to wake up. She didn't remember going to bed and didn't know where she was. All she could hear was a woman trying to wake her up. She sounded like Mrs. Treadway. Quinn didn't like Mrs. Treadway. She wouldn't let them have butter or jelly on their toast.

"Quinn, can you hear me?"

Quinn moaned. She was so cold she couldn't stop shivering.

"Please, Mrs. Treadway, I don't feel like school," she mumbled.

The Recovery nurse smiled.

"No school, Quinn. You had surgery and you need to wake up now."

"Cold. Hurt," she mumbled and then tried to lick her lips. They felt swollen.

"I'll put another blanket on you," the nurse said.

As soon as Quinn felt the weight and the warmth of the added covers, she began to relax.

The nurse tucked the heated blanket around her and then laid a hand on Quinn's forehead.

"Quinn, open your eyes now!"

Quinn was trying, but her lids felt too heavy. After several moments more of struggle, she finally saw light and then the face of the woman beside her.

She wasn't Mrs. Treadway, and Quinn was no longer nine years old.

"Good girl!" the nurse said.

"Where...?"

"You're in Centennial Hill Hospital. You had surgery on your shoulder."

Quinn exhaled slowly as memories flooded.

"Someone shot me. There was a baby..."

"I don't know anything about a baby. We'll be taking you to your room in a few minutes. You can ask someone there, okay?"

Quinn let herself drift, wondering if any aspect of her life would ever get easy. This time of year, people would be chattering about holiday plans, going home to a block-party barbecue and having family over on the weekend. It all sounded so good—so ordinary. She had never lived an ordinary life.

And then the same nurse was back, patting Quinn's arm.

"We're going to move you to your room now. You just lie still and we'll do the driving," she said and giggled.

Quinn braced herself for motion, guessing it might hurt, and she was right. When they began wheeling her through the hall leading toward the elevators, she closed her eyes against the bright fluorescent light fixtures in the ceiling above and was drifting back to sleep when they suddenly stopped.

"Quinn, you're doing great. It was my honor to take care of you, and now Thomas will take you the rest of the way to your room."

All of a sudden Quinn was in the elevator with a stranger named Thomas. After what she'd been through, the thought unnerved her. Then she heard the orderly humming and relaxed as the car went up. When it stopped, Thomas put a hand on her shoulder.

"Are you okay, ma'am?" he asked.

"Yes."

"We'll get you comfortable soon," he said.

The doors opened as he began to push her out into the hall.

Nick had chosen a seat near the door so he could watch the elevator, and when he saw the elevator doors sliding open and the end of a bed emerging, he jumped up and went to see if it was his patient. He saw her red hair first and was about to speak to the orderly when he heard footsteps running up behind him.

The panicked expression on the orderly's face was all the warning he was going to get. He pulled his weapon even as he was turning around. It was the man from the waiting room. He was running toward them with his gun already aimed.

Nick jumped in front of the bed. "Get her back in the elevator!" he yelled and pulled the trigger.

Thomas reacted quickly, catching the door before it closed and pulling the bed back inside just as gunfire erupted.

Dev pulled the trigger as the cop was shouting. In his haste to get off the first shot, his aim was off.

Nick leaned just the least bit to the left as he fired and saved his own life. The bullet from Dev's gun grazed the side of his head instead of hitting him between the eyes, but for a moment Nick thought his head would explode from the pain. But it hadn't affected his own aim. Shot in the heart, the gunman hit the floor. Nick was still standing and the man was dead.

When the two gunshots sounded only feet away from her bed, Quinn screamed in terror, certain she would die. When the orderly slammed the side of her bed against the elevator wall, she cried out again, this time from the pain.

"I'm so sorry," Thomas exclaimed, trying to get around her bed to the button to close the door.

And then Quinn saw the cop from Homicide move into her line of vision. There was blood running down his face, and he was holding his gun in one hand and the elevator door open with the other.

"You're bleeding!"

Thomas turned, saw the blood running down the cop's face and leaped forward.

"You've been shot!" he said.

Nick's head was pounding. He ran a finger through the groove the bullet had left in the side of his head and shuddered. That was close. Too close.

"It's just a graze. Are you two all right?" Nick asked.

"Yes," Thomas said.

"Then get her to her room, *stat*," Nick said and began helping the orderly get the bed back out of the elevator.

Nurses were running toward them. They already knew he was a cop and that he was there to guard a witness in one of his cases, so there was no mistaking what must have happened.

Nick flashed his badge.

"Get her to her room and stay with her. Don't let anybody in but the police," Nick said.

One nurse grabbed Nick by the arm.

"Are you hit anywhere else?" she asked.

"No."

"You need to get to ER. I'll go get a wheelchair," she said, then hesitated when she glanced at the shooter and the blood spilling out onto the floor beneath him.

"What about him?" she asked.

"He's dead. Forget me right now and get her out of the hall. He may not be the only one after her."

Quinn was scared. The man standing at the foot of her bed was bleeding, and everyone was running madly around her.

"What's happening?" Quinn cried.

Nick heard the fear in her voice and turned around. Their gazes locked, and for a heartbeat everything faded. It was just him watching her eyes fill with tears.

"It's okay, Miss O'Meara. You're safe." He grabbed the orderly by the arm. "Move her now!"

After that, panic ensued as the RN on duty began issuing orders to put the floor on lockdown.

"Step aside!" Thomas yelled. "Coming through." He rushed her down the hall and into her assigned room.

Nick was watching them go when the thundering sound of running feet echoed up a stairwell. He turned with his gun already aimed, only to see a team from Hospital Security coming through the exit door and out onto the fourth floor with weapons drawn.

"Las Vegas Police!" he shouted and held his hands up with the gun in one hand and his badge in the other.

The first guard to reach him immediately took him by the arm.

"Detective, what happened?"

"You have a woman in room 424 who was shot earlier this evening out on Highway 93. Unknowingly, she rode up on a murder in progress and got shot for her troubles. That man followed her and just tried to finish the job."

The guard nodded. "We need to get you to ER, Detective. Wilson, escort him down, and the rest of you start a room-by-room check to make sure there aren't any gunmen on site. I'll wait here with this one's body until the police arrive."

"I need a guard on room 424 or I'm not going anywhere," Nick stated.

"Go. We're on it."

Nick was reluctant to leave, but he also knew he needed some first aid. He called in to his lieutenant again as they were going down in the elevator to tell him what happened.

"Lieutenant Summers."

"Lieutenant, this is Detective Saldano. Someone tried to take out the O'Meara woman as they were bringing her up from surgery. I shot him."

"Is she all right?" Summers asked.

"Yes, sir. The shooter is dead, and I'm on my way to ER to get some first aid."

"You're wounded?"

"Head wound, sir, but nothing serious. It's going to be a big headache and nothing more."

"Write up your report and consider yourself off duty."

"Sir, seriously, I'll be—"

"That's an order," Summers said, leaving no room for argument.

Nick sighed.

"Yes, sir."

The security guard glanced at Nick.

"Pulled you, didn't he?"

"Yeah," Nick said and leaned back against the wall as the elevator took them down to ER.

Anton was standing in the doorway of the bedroom, watching as the EMTs were preparing Star for transport. He didn't like what was happening, but he'd made the decision to keep her alive, and this was the consequence.

His phone rang, and he frowned when he saw the name on his caller ID.

It was his snitch in the Las Vegas PD. This was a call he never ignored. He backed out into the hall and lowered his voice.

"This is Baba."

"Mr. Baba, this is Alicia Alvarez. We just got word that a man named Dev Bosky was killed in a shoot-out with a homicide cop in the Centennial Hill Hospital."

Anton stifled a curse. So much for getting his son back the easy way.

"Thank you."

"Yes, sir," she said and disconnected.

Anton shoved a hand through his hair in abject frustration. What the hell was going on? All the people he normally depended on were failing him miserably. He was just superstitious enough to wonder if he'd brought it upon himself by betraying the mother of his son.

At any rate, he couldn't go after the witness from the desert at the moment. Dev was already dead, and if he did anything more it would surely tie him to that crime. He was going to have to step back for the time being and see how this played out. The Feds would come, that he was certain of, and he would be questioned. His best bet now was to remain patient and, as always, deny, deny, deny. After all, Dev hadn't worked for him in months…

Star cried out as the EMTs loaded her faceup onto a stretcher, bouncing her repeatedly on her injured back as they took her downstairs to the ambulance. She could hear Dr. Fuentes talking to Anton as they followed her down, but she wouldn't open her eyes.

Her back was miserable, but she didn't think she had any broken ribs or internal bleeding. Still, she was going to stay quiet and allow the paramedics to take her to the hospital. The only way she was going to survive any of this was to get away again, and right now the best chance she had to get away was on this stretcher. Her mind was focused on one thought: Sammy. The only hope she had of getting him back was to testify against Anton Baba—and to do that, she had to escape and stay alive.

When they transferred her to a gurney and loaded her into the ambulance, she moaned. She heard the back doors closing and then waited until it was moving before she dared a quick look.

There were two EMTs with her and then the driver up front. These two were strangers to her, but she knew enough about Anton's world to understand that didn't mean they weren't in his pocket.

One of them was swabbing the inside of her arm.

"Just a small stick," he said, as he slipped a needle into a vein to establish an IV.

Star felt nothing but the constant throb and burn of

the wounds on her back. The ride was rough, and by the time they reached the hospital, tears were running down her face.

The EMTs were running when they wheeled her into ER. She knew because she could hear the rapid slap of their shoes against the tile. She heard one of the men giving out her stats and heard a woman ask her name.

"Her name is Star Davis," the EMT said. "She's Dr. Fuentes's patient. He's on the way to the hospital, too."

"Star, my name is Dr. King. Can you tell me where you hurt?"

Star moaned softly.

"My back, my back. Please turn me over," she begged.

The doctor frowned as she pointed to two of the nurses.

"Help me roll her... Not much. I just need to get a quick look at—"

The doctor froze. It was only for a second, and then she began issuing orders quickly and loudly.

Star sighed. The relief of lying on her side, if briefly, was huge. Her tears turned into soft, choking sobs.

"What happened to you?" Dr. King asked.

"I was in a wreck," Star said.

X-ray techs wheeled the portable X-ray into the room.

"I'm sorry, Miss Davis. I'm going to need you to lie flat for these X-rays," the doctor said.

"No, no. Not again," Star moaned.

She felt hands on her shoulders, at her waist and at the backs of her legs trying to ease her back down, but when they rolled her down onto her back, the pain was so intense she passed out.

Dr. Fuentes came into the exam bay, recognized Dr. King and nodded.

"Dr. King."

"Dr. Fuentes," she replied, giving him a hard look. "What can you tell me about your patient?"

"That she lives with Anton Baba and she was in a wreck."

Dr. King guessed the rest of what he wasn't telling, which meant not asking too many detailed questions.

Seconds later, Anton and his two bodyguards entered the room.

"Wait outside," Anton told the men and then aimed his questions at the doctor he didn't know. "What is her condition?"

"Mr. Baba, I'm Dr. King. We're just about to x-ray her, but she's unconscious at the moment—the pain is quite intense. As soon as we're finished, we'll focus on the wounds on her back," Dr. King said.

"Did she say anything?" Anton asked.

The doctor frowned.

"That she was in pain. If you will step outside long enough for us to get the X-rays we need, you will be allowed to return until we take her to surgery."

Anton glanced at her, startled by this news.

"She needs surgery?"

The doctor folded her arms across her chest.

"I assume you saw her back?"

Anton nodded.

"Then you understand the severity of her injuries.

She'll need to be under anesthetic and in a perfectly sterile environment when we begin removing the debris embedded in her back and closing the wounds."

"Yes, of course," Anton said. With one last look at Star's unconscious body, he stepped out of the room.

He was pissed all over again. Now she was damaged goods, which would definitely bring down her worth in a sale. She was still the best woman he'd ever had in bed. Maybe this accident was the nudge he needed to keep her with him. All he had to do was get their son back, and he knew she would stay.

Still, what a fuckup.

He would kill Ian all over again if he wasn't already dead. It was just as well that the cops took Dev out, too. Saved him the trouble of doing it.

Nick was sitting on an exam table in the next bay waiting for a doctor to come back with the results of his X-rays. They had already cleaned and dressed his head wound, and his head was throbbing to the point of making him nauseous when he noticed the chaotic sounds of an emergency in the room next to his.

He heard the soft cries of a woman in pain and couldn't help but hear what the EMTs were saying as they discussed her injuries. He heard the word "wreck" and then "in the desert" and frowned. But when he heard she was one of Dr. Fuentes's patients and the name Anton Baba, Nick's heart skipped a beat.

Could this possibly be the mother of the little boy Quinn O'Meara had found?

There was more shuffling in the room next door,

and then he overheard Anton Baba introduce himself. He held his breath as he leaned close to the wall separating him from one of the most wanted criminals he'd ever known, not wanting to miss a word of what was being said. He didn't dare make a phone call and take the chance of being overheard. He inhaled slowly but grabbed his phone and sent Lieutenant Summers a quick text.

Get word to the Feds. Anton Baba is in ER. I'm not certain, but I think the woman getting treated in the room next to mine might be the Feds' missing witness. She said her name was Star.

Then he hit Send.
An answer came quickly.

Do nothing. They've been informed. Go home.

Nick sent back a final text, Will do, then slid off the table, slipped his handgun back into the shoulder holster and put on his jacket.

The moment he stood up, the room began to spin. Damn it. Most likely he had a concussion to go with that bullet wound, but after knowing Baba was so close, he didn't care about orders or his injury. He wasn't leaving the O'Meara woman alone when the man who wanted her dead was in the same hospital.

He tentatively fingered the bandage on his head and then slipped out of the exam room, stopping at the nurses' desk long enough to tell them he would be on the fourth floor if anyone needed him, then walked out despite their protests that he had not been released.

The ER staff didn't want him to leave, but his boss told him to go home. Since he couldn't do two things at once, he decided to do his own thing. He'd stay with Quinn O'Meara until real backup arrived. Just in case.

Nick got back to the fourth floor, but was stopped at the elevator by a Las Vegas cop. After showing his badge, they let him pass. He made his way down the hall in his bloody clothes, fielding comments about his welfare until he got to Quinn's room. Another cop was outside her door. He recognized Nick, eyed the bandage on his head and the blood all over his shirt and jacket, but stepped aside to let him in.

The room was quiet but for the machines hooked up to the woman's body. The nurse stood up as Nick walked in.

"How's she doing?" Nick asked.

"She's doing well. Resting comfortably. Are you all right, sir?" the nurse asked.

"I will be," Nick said. "I'll be staying here with her."

The nurse frowned, then scooted an overstuffed chair close to the bed for him to use.

"It reclines. If either of you need anything, press this red button," she said, pointing to the call button fastened to the side of Quinn's bed.

"I hate to ask, but if there is a clean scrub shirt in an extra-large anywhere around, I sure could use it. And… could someone bring me a cup of coffee? My head is killing me. Oh, and if any ER doctor comes looking for me, tell him where I am."

"I'll see what I can find," she said and left.

Nick moved to Quinn's bedside, still trying to figure out why she looked so familiar. She was pretty in a wild, unharnessed kind of way. Long red hair, with slightly darker eyebrows that framed her deep-set eyes, which he remembered as being a vivid shade of green. He turned her hand palm up, felt some calluses and wondered if it was from riding the Harley or something else that she did.

He brushed a flyaway strand of her hair from her forehead and then eased himself down into the recliner. From where he was sitting he had a clear view of her and the door. He patted the shoulder holster, making sure his phone and gun were in place, and then leaned back.

A few minutes later the nurse returned with a clean blue scrub shirt, his doctor-ordered meds, a cup of coffee and a sweet roll.

"From the break room," she said and handed them over with a sympathetic smile.

"Thank you so much," he said softly.

She nodded, then checked Quinn's IV and heart monitor again before she left.

Nick changed into the clean shirt, and by the time he had finished the food and coffee, the sick feeling was gone from his stomach. His head wasn't throbbing as much as it had been. He got up to throw his garbage into the trash can, and as he was washing up, he heard Quinn's voice.

He hurried back to the bed, but she wasn't awake, just talking in her sleep—and crying.

"Where is he? Where's my Nicks?" she mumbled, then turned her head and slipped into a deeper sleep.

His heart skipped a beat. He hadn't heard that name in nearly twenty years.

He backed up and sat down in the recliner again, and sent a text to one of the other detectives in Homicide.

Run a background check on Quinn O'Meara. Get license tag info off her Harley. It's in police impound. Send it to my phone.

Then he put the shoulder holster back on over the scrub shirt and leaned back in the chair to wait. Thirty minutes turned into an hour as he drifted in and out of sleep, awakened occasionally by the sound of Quinn's mumbling and crying.

When his phone finally signaled a text, he scrolled through the information quickly. He couldn't believe what he was reading. He leaped to his feet, looking down at Quinn in disbelief.

"Oh, my God! Queenie!"

She was crying in her sleep again.

He stroked her cheek, then wiped the tears.

"Queenie?"

She sobbed, still caught in whatever nightmare she was having.

"Nicks is gone," she murmured.

"Oh, my God, my little Queenie. What happened to you after they took me away?"

Four

Induced by pain and drugs, Quinn was caught up in a very vivid dream of her past. He was cursing her with every breath, beating her on the back with one fist while he pushed her head under water with the other.

Quinn was kicking and thrashing, needing to breathe, trying desperately to get away, but the hand on the back of her head kept pushing her down, farther and farther into the water.

Help me, God. If you're real, make this stop.

She woke abruptly, trembling and gasping for air. She heard the heart monitor before she saw it, and when she opened her eyes, she was shocked that it was hooked to her.

My things! Where are my things?

Everything she owned was on her Harley. Then she noticed the man sleeping in the recliner beside her bed, recognizing him as the cop from Homicide. Why was there a bandage on his head and why was he—

Her pulse jumped.

The elevator. The shooting! Blood all over the side of his face as they rushed her past him. Shouldn't he be in a bed somewhere, too? Why was he still here?

She found the buzzer and rang for a nurse.

Nick sat up with a jerk and then grabbed his head as the room began to spin.

"Oh, crap," he mumbled, then eased himself upright and moved to the side of her bed. "Are you okay?"

She pointed at the bandage on his head.

"Are *you* okay?"

Before he could answer, a nurse's voice came over the intercom.

"Good morning, Quinn. What do you need?"

"To go to the bathroom," she said.

"We'll be right there," the nurse said.

"I'll step out of the room," Nick said.

"No need," Quinn said. "Sit back down before you fall down. Do you know what happened to my bike? Everything I own is on it."

"Your Harley is in police impound. It's safe and so are your things," he said and eased back down in the recliner just as a nurse walked in, saw Nick and pointed toward the door.

"Detective, would you mind stepping out for—"

"No!" Quinn interrupted. "Please! I've been shot at twice in the last twelve hours. He and his gun stay."

"Okay by me," the nurse said with a smile, then lowered Quinn's bed and let down the guardrail.

Quinn glanced over her shoulder, giving Nick an awkward smile.

"But, um…maybe you want to turn around so you don't get flashed?"

Nick nodded, then winced as his head rang with pain.

"I'm closing my eyes," he said.

Quinn groaned as she eased up from the bed, then grabbed the nurse's arm to steady herself and headed for the bathroom.

"Call if you need help," the nurse said, closing the bathroom door behind Quinn as she went inside.

Quinn eased herself down on the commode and then had to talk herself out of crying. Twenty-four hours ago she had been in Alamo, Nevada, doing a favor for a friend by filling in at her restaurant after her regular hostess took time off to get married.

If she had not just lived it, she wouldn't believe all that had happened to her since leaving Alamo. Her shoulder was throbbing right along with her head. She was scared of what might happen next and still unsure of why any of this had happened to begin with. How had a simple trip to Vegas gone so wrong?

By the time she was through in the bathroom, she was shaking from the exertion and pain. She called for the nurse, then grabbed her arm to steady her steps, stopped at the sink long enough to wash up and didn't relax until she was stretched back out in bed.

"They'll be bringing breakfast soon," the nurse said, with a wink at Nick. "We had them send a tray up for you, too."

"Many thanks," Nick said, following her to the door, then looking outside to make sure the guard was still there.

He recognized the officer, gave him a nod of recognition, then shut the door and walked back to her bedside. There was no use beating around the bush anymore.

"So, I guess we have a lot to talk about, don't we, Queenie?"

Quinn's heart skipped a beat.

"What did you just call me?"

Nick smiled and repeated, "Queenie."

All of a sudden she was a child again, sitting up in bed and waiting for the boy who slept in the room across the hall to come read her a story—the only person who'd ever called her by that name. She stared at the man in front of her, trying to picture the boy's face, but it had been too long.

"What's your name?" she said.

"Detective Nick Saldano, Las Vegas Homicide, but you used to call me Nicks."

Quinn's eyes widened at that. Oblivious to the pain, she threw back her covers in excitement.

Nick got a flash of her long bare legs, and then her good arm was around his neck.

"I can't believe this. I never thought I'd see you again," she said and buried her face against his shoulder.

Nick was surprised by her reaction and then touched by it as he eased her down to the side of the bed and took her in his arms.

"Don't cry, Queenie. You're breaking my heart," Nick said, his voice shaking from emotion.

Quinn leaned back, still searching his face for recognition.

"I never would have known it was you. How did you—"

"You talked in your sleep," Nick said.

"I did?"

"You asked for Nicks. That was a name from the time I was in foster care, so I ran a background check."

Quinn was trembling as she touched his face, then the bandage covering his forehead.

"That man you shot. He was shooting at me, wasn't he?"

Nick nodded.

"He came close to killing you," she said, taking his hand. "I would never have realized who you were. This is all so— Why is this happening? Who was that baby I found? What hell did I stumble into?"

"You're shaking," Nick said. "This has been a lot for one day. You need to lie down."

Quinn let him tuck her back in, but refused to turn loose his hand.

"You were my guardian angel…my touchstone in that house. Where did you go when you left our foster family?" Quinn asked.

"I didn't know I had any other family until my mother's sister and her husband found me. They adopted me and brought me to Nevada. Didn't they explain why I left?"

Quinn sighed.

"All our foster mother said was that your family took you home. I was little. I didn't understand. I just felt… abandoned." She shook her head. "It was my fault for getting attached. After you, I didn't let anyone get close to me again."

Nick felt a pang of regret for the little girl she'd been.

"So no adoptive parents?" he asked.

He saw her expression go blank and her eyes narrow.

"It didn't work out," she finally said.

He sensed something dark behind those words but decided this wasn't the time or place to press it.

"Where do you live now?" he asked.

"Nowhere."

He frowned. "What do you mean, nowhere? Are you wanted somewhere? Are you on the run from someone?"

She didn't much like what he'd asked, but she understood the reason why he'd asked. He was, after all, a cop.

"I'm legal. I work for a while and then I move on. No ties or traces of me left behind."

Nick felt sick. Something bad *had* happened to her.

"Then I guess it was fate that our paths crossed once more," he said.

She wanted to know everything about him but was afraid to find out he already belonged to someone else, so she shifted the conversation from their briefly shared history to the present hell she'd brought down upon herself.

"Whose path did I cross before I stumbled into Las Vegas Homicide?" she asked.

"The Feds were helping a woman and her baby escape in return for her testimony against the man she was being held by."

"And? Where are they now? It didn't look like anyone other than the baby survived that crash."

Nick shrugged.

"The way we figure it, you rode up on the aftermath of the murder of two federal agents. They didn't survive the accident. The baby's mother was in the car, but she and the baby survived. We don't know how. We have nothing but guesses as to why she was with the Feds except that he's someone they've been after for years. Maybe she was going to testify against him…maybe not. I can't say. The main thing is that the baby is safe, thanks to you. What you did—that was amazing."

Quinn's stomach knotted.

"Who is this man? What's his name?"

"Maybe it's best you—"

Quinn jammed her finger into his chest.

"I have the right to know who wants me dead," she snapped.

Nick took her hand. She was right.

"Anton Baba."

All the color went out of Quinn's face, her anger turning to shock and then fear.

"Oh, my God. He's notorious."

"And yet has never been convicted of anything," Nick added.

"I'm dead," Quinn said and closed her eyes.

Star woke up in a hospital room and never remembered coming out of surgery. The first face she saw was Anton standing at the foot of her bed talking to a doctor. She felt instant despair. Her life was a joke. Her future was doubtful.

Then Anton saw she was awake and rushed to her.

Even though he was smiling, there was a flash of anger in his eyes.

"My darling, the worst of that terrible wreck is over. Now all you have to do is heal. I will leave a guard on the door outside…for your protection, of course." He brushed a thumb across the softness of her lower lip, then pressed it inward against her teeth just enough to remind her she'd displeased him greatly. "Dream of me as you sleep," he whispered, then leaned over and kissed her forehead before he left.

There was nothing she could do as she watched him leave. She was helpless to defend herself, and her life— and the life of her baby boy, wherever he was—was in the hands of fate.

The pillows wedged against her back kept her from rolling over onto the bandages, but it still felt like someone was holding a torch to her back. When a nurse came in to inject meds into her IV, she was shaking from the pain.

"Bless your heart, honey," the nurse said. "This medicine will give you some relief. Don't fight it. Just close your eyes and sleep."

"Thank you," Star said and closed her eyes.

The nurse was right. She could immediately feel a heaviness sliding through her body, limb by limb, pulling her conscious self back into the darkness. The last thing she remembered as she was going under was the look in Anton's eyes and the tone in his voice. It was a warning: *don't run from me again.*

Star was dreaming about home—something she hadn't done in years. Maybe it was because she was separated from her baby and now understood the loss her mother surely must have felt when she disappeared She woke up in tears and rang for the nurse, then waited for her arrival. She needed to go to the bathroom and was dreading making a move.

The nurse came in, turning on lights as she moved toward the bed.

"Good morning, Star. How're you feeling this morning? What would you rate your pain level on a scale of one to ten?"

"Probably a seven or eight," Star said, as she swung her legs over the side of the bed, then moaned. "Oh, my God, my back! Is it time for my pain meds?"

"I'll find out," the nurse said, helping Star to the bathroom and then back to bed. As soon as the nurse got her settled down, she left to check on Star's request for pain meds.

Star looked for a phone and noticed it was gone and then rolled her eyes. Who would she call? There was no way to know who Anton had in his pocket, but she knew he had snitches everywhere…in every facet of the government. She looked at the closed door, imagining what it would be like to have the freedom to just walk out and never look back. She was crying quiet tears when the nurse came back, injected pain meds into the IV and adjusted her covers.

The dreams faded.

The meds dragged her under.

Federal Agents Gleason and Powers were elated to know where their lost witness was, but by the time they reached the ER of Centennial Hill Hospital, Baba and his men were already there. Forced to change their plans, Gleason left Powers in ER to keep an eye on them while he headed for the hospital administrator's office. It would be signing Star Davis's death warrant if they confronted her in Baba's presence, so they needed to find a more subtle way to question her.

He learned from the office that Star would be taken into surgery shortly, but that Baba had already appointed an armed guard at the door of her room. He'd be there waiting when she got back from Recovery, so there would be no way to get to Star alone. With the help of the hospital administration, they organized a small undercover approach—they'd return the next morning posing as a doctor and his nurse making rounds, which would allow them to check on Star's "recovery" without drawing any alarms from Baba's guard.

When they got to Star's room early the next day, Gleason was dressed in scrubs, clipboard in hand as he approached Baba's man. He frowned at the gun he could see in the shoulder holster under his jacket.

"Who are you and what are you doing here?" Gleason asked.

Luis stuttered a moment, trying to think how to answer without antagonizing the medical staff.

"I am Luis Alvarez. I work for Mr. Baba, and at his request, I am guarding this woman while she's healing."

Gleason glared at him. "He thinks she's in danger from the people who are healing her?" he snapped.

"You'll have to speak to Mr. Baba as to why I am here. I'm only doing what I was ordered to do," Luis said.

Gleason gave the guard a disgusted look, then stormed past him with Powers, his "nurse," right behind him, into Star's room, making sure the door was firmly closed behind them.

Star was awake but clearly uncomfortable. Powers positioned himself at the door to keep watch, while Gleason approached Star's bedside.

"Good morning, Star. How are you feeling today?" Gleason asked.

"Like all the skin has been flayed from my back. How are you?"

Gleason blinked. The rage in her voice was so subdued he almost missed it.

He flashed his badge, hoping that would reassure her they were there to help, but she slapped it away.

"Doctors don't use nurses as guards at the door. I knew who you were. Where is my son?"

"He's safe," Gleason said.

"I'm sure you will understand when I say I don't believe you. If Anton finds out the two people who died in that fire were Feds, I'm dead. You know that, right?"

Gleason nodded.

"That's why we're here. We're ready to put you under protective custody and—"

"I don't trust you. I can't. You people already promised to help me once, and that cost me my son. You nearly got us both killed! You were supposed to protect us. Where the fuck was that damn chopper when we were getting shot at?"

Gleason understood her pain, her anger. This was his job, but it was her life they were talking about. Still, he tried to remain objective. "We got a late start to the pickup site. We deeply regret what happened. We weren't aware you were in that kind of danger."

"You lie. I heard Lacey calling you."

Gleason bowed his head. *Damn.* That wouldn't help her ability to trust them.

"Not in time. She didn't call in time," he said, lowering his voice. "Star, I'm sorry. We're all sorry. But please keep your voice down—Anton's man is still out there."

Star took a breath, then looked Gleason in the eye angrily. "Where is my son? I want to see him. I have to know he's okay or this conversation is over."

Gleason pulled out his phone and sent a quick text.

"Okay. They're getting him to the phone. We can FaceTime. You can see him…talk to him for yourself."

Star's heart almost burst with relief, tears rolling down her face as they waited. But she wouldn't let herself believe until she saw him.

The phone rang, Gleason answered, and then he moved to the side of her bed and leaned over, holding his phone in front of her face so she wouldn't have to move.

"There's your boy. Talk to him, but keep it quiet. That guard outside can blow this whole thing wide open."

When Star saw her baby, her breath caught in the back of her throat. He didn't have a scratch on him, and he was chewing on a teething biscuit. It was one of his favorite snacks. The sight of him and the crumbs on his cheeks made her heart ache. Instead of weeping, she waved.

"Sammy? Hi, baby, it's Mommy."

The toddler's eyes widened, and then he was slapping at the phone and saying "Mama" over and over.

"I love you, Sammy. We'll be together soon," she said and blew him a kiss.

He put a fat little hand on the phone, blocking her sight, but she knew he was trying to touch her.

Gleason ended the call and dropped the phone back in his pocket.

"Where is he?" Star demanded.

"Like I told you, he's safe."

"That's not good enough. I want out of here. You have to get me out now," she said.

"We're working on it," Gleason said. "Just trust us. We'll get you out of here before Anton checks you out."

"Why are you waiting? You don't know him. If he wants me dead, it could happen anywhere…even here."

"Just stay calm and trust us," he said. "We'll be back in a couple of hours. We need to get people in place so that if Baba tries to run after he knows we have you, he won't get away. Do you want to have to go into witness protection for God knows how long while we try to find him? If he leaves the country, you could be hiding all your life. Do you want to chance that?"

Star groaned. "Oh, my God, this hell is never going to end."

"Try not to be afraid. We'll have someone undercover on the floor at all times, and we'll be back before nightfall."

"And I'll get Sammy back when we leave?"

"As soon as we get you settled in a safe place, yes. You don't want him in any danger, right?"

"He was born into danger," Star said. "I need him with me."

"Okay, yes…just rest and heal. We'll be back, and soon," Gleason promised.

He gave what he hoped was a reassuring smile and nodded at Powers to follow him as he exited the room, glaring at the guard again for good measure as they left.

Star was relieved to know Sammy was safe. She'd been given a reprieve, of sorts, but she was impatient and deathly afraid of the timing. And her pain was getting worse, not better. When the nurse came in a few minutes later with her pain meds, Star closed her eyes and thought of her son as she drifted back to sleep.

Anton sent a text to Luis, asking if all was well with Star. Luis sent a quick text back saying she was in her room and had no visitors other than medical personnel. Anton nodded in satisfaction and sent back one more text.

Make sure she stays there.

The threat was implied, but Luis understood. His life was at stake if anything went wrong.

Now that Anton had Star back in his grasp, he began to send out feelers to all his snitches, trying to find where the police had taken his son. They likely had him in some kind of foster home at the moment while they tried to work out who his family was, and if that was the case, he'd get word soon. If he didn't get Sammy back, there was no way to know what Star would do. Her mothering instinct was strong. As long as she was still alive but without her baby, she would try to destroy Anton. But if he got rid of her before he got his son back, Anton was sure he would never see Sammy again. Now that he'd publicly tied himself to Star, he would be the prime suspect if she died under suspicious circumstances.

He went to the bar, bypassing his usual shot of whiskey and picking up a bottle of Grey Goose instead, a nod to his Slavic roots. He poured himself a stiff drink and took it to his office, sat down to check the stock market, then moved to email, cruising through the messages as the vodka in the glass slowly disappeared.

He was getting up for a refill when his cell signaled a text. He frowned as he read the message—this was not the news he wanted to hear. His son was in federal custody, and the woman who'd found him in the desert was in the hospital on the same floor as Star, and under police protection.

Was this fuckup ever going to end?

Nick was on the phone with his cousin Santino when two doctors entered Quinn's room, but the moment he saw them, he knew they were Feds and told his cousin he had to go.

Gleason was surprised by the man's presence. He'd been given to understand she had no family and was a stranger to the city. He motioned to Powers to stand guard at the door and then approached the bed.

Quinn saw the doctors enter and then saw the look on Nick's face. She reached for the bed controls and raised her bed to a sitting position, unwilling to be flat on her back if she needed to run.

When one of the doctors started toward her, Nick walked between them, preventing him from coming any closer, and Quinn nearly lost her composure. It had been a long, long time since anyone stood between her and trouble.

Nick wasted no time flashing his badge.

"Don't insult my intelligence by trying to pass yourself off as doctors. May I see some credentials?"

Gleason frowned but did as he'd been asked.

"And your friend by the door?" Nick asked.

Agent Powers flashed his badge.

"Thank you," Nick said. "Keep in mind Miss O'Meara is recovering from surgery."

Gleason nodded.

Nick stepped aside to let him pass, then moved to Quinn's side.

"Miss O'Meara, I'm Special Agent Gleason. That's Special Agent Powers by the door. I need to speak to you about the night you were shot."

"Okay," Quinn said.

"We were told you saw the fire from the highway and rode up on the scene. Is that true?"

"Yes."

"What did you see once you were there?"

"At first just a car on fire. I had just realized there were bodies inside when I saw the silhouette of a toddler walk between me and the fire. I grabbed him before he could get burned."

"Is that when you were shot?"

"No. The baby was crying and then I saw headlights coming from out of the desert driving toward the fire. I thought it was someone else like me. Someone who would help."

"Can you describe the vehicle?"

"It was after midnight. All I saw were headlights coming out of the dark. I guess one of the headlights kept shaking—bouncing up and down—although the other one was steady. Not sure if that's any help."

"What happened then?"

"I was heading toward the vehicle for help, and then they started shooting at me. I zipped the baby up inside my jacket as I ran for my Harley and headed for the highway. I kept hearing gunshots, so I knew they were still shooting at me. I thought I was getting away until I took one in the back. Nearly lost it in the sand on the shoulder of the road, but then caught concrete and gunned it."

"So you have no idea who was shooting at you?"

"No."

"Did you see anyone following you? Did they get close enough you could get a make on the car?"

"I already told you I didn't see anything. I caught a glimpse of the car once in the distance on the outskirts of the city, but like I said, it was dark. I couldn't make out the driver, but I did notice one weird thing. The car was missing a windshield."

Gleason frowned. This woman wasn't going to help

their case in any way. "Really? But you didn't see the driver?"

"No, but Detective Saldano saw the one who tried to kill me here as they were bringing me up from surgery. I don't know if it was the same man or not."

Gleason glanced at the bandage on Saldano's head.

"Did you recognize him, Detective?"

"No, but his body has probably been identified by now. You can check with my boss for details. Lieutenant Summers, Las Vegas Homicide."

"Is there anything else you can think of that might help us?"

"No, sir," Quinn replied. "All I saw with any detail was the fire and the baby."

Gleason sighed.

"Thank you for your time. If you do happen to think of anything, notify Detective Saldano here. He can get in touch with us."

Nick held out his hand to stop the agent from walking away.

"Wait a minute. Are you just writing her off?"

Gleason shrugged. "I'm sorry she was hurt, but her incident is separate from our case."

"Like hell," Nick said. "We both know Baba's men shot at her out in the desert, and it was one of Baba's men who tried to kill her here."

"Which would put her case in your hands, Detective. Not ours."

Quinn had been listening, slowly coming to understand that since she had nothing they wanted, the Feds didn't care what happened to her. It didn't surprise her, but it made her mad as hell.

"Stop, Nick! Stop now. I don't want their protection. They already got two of their own murdered and left a baby to die alone in the desert. I'll take my own chances."

Gleason flushed at the accusation and then flinched as the woman pointed straight at him.

"You! Take your buddy over there by the door and get out."

The men turned and walked out without another word.

The moment the door closed behind them, Quinn's defiance disappeared, and the fear began to catch up with her.

"Oh, my God," she muttered.

"Don't," Nick said abruptly. "You haven't been abandoned. I'm still here. I won't leave you, Quinn. I won't walk away from you again."

"I need to ask you something," Quinn said.

"Ask away," Nick said.

"Are you in a relationship?"

"No."

Quinn sighed.

Nick's eyes narrowed intently.

"Was that the right answer?" he asked.

She looked up at him, studying the man he had become, then looked away, embarrassed.

"I just wondered," she said.

He cupped her cheek, making her look at him again.

"It's too soon to go there," Nick said.

Nick lifted a stray lock of hair away from her eye-lashes with his forefinger, then ran it down the side of her face.

"You were my baby girl when we were little, re-member?"

His voice was hypnotic, drawing her gaze back to his face.

"You always were the Prince Charming, weren't you?" Quinn said with a smile. "I remember wanting to be a princess, and you made me a cardboard crown covered in foil and told me I was a queen."

"Yes, I did." Nick perched on the side of her bed and took her hand. It was still hard to believe that this woman—this strong, brave…beautiful woman—was the little girl he'd grown up with so long ago. "Between us, we have a lot of life to catch up on. There's a lot about you I'd like to know."

Even this hint of exploring a future scared her, be-cause the worst part of a relationship was waiting for it to end.

"I have to survive Anton Baba first," she said.

"You'll survive. I promised you that. When you're cleared to leave here, you're coming home with me," Nick said.

Quinn couldn't believe what he'd just said. She took care of herself. Hard times and bad times, she'd never had anyone to depend on. The thought of Nick at her side, ready to defend her against these men who wanted her dead… It was enough to bring tears to her eyes.

"My things are all on my bike. I need my bike," she whispered.

"I'll get it moved to my garage, okay?"

Quinn's voice shook as she spoke. "I don't know how this happened…what the odds are of us meeting again like this after all these years, but I want to believe it means something more than a coincidence."

"It's our full circle moment, Quinn. I loved being your big brother when we were kids and I admire the woman you have become. I want to get to know you again. Are you good with that?" He smiled at her, and she saw something else in his eyes when he looked at her. He lifted her hand to his lips.

She could feel the warmth of his breath and the softness of his mouth against her skin. If this was a dream, she didn't want to wake up.

Five

Anton was in Caesars Palace having lunch at Nobu with a man he knew only as Mr. Stewart. In the past two months, Anton had lost ten girls from a three-state area and needed replacements. It wasn't uncommon. In his line of work, deaths were usually attributed to suicide or drugs, and Stewart was also another supplier for replacements.

Stewart had flagged down a waiter to ask for more sauce for his food, so their conversation was on pause when Anton caught two pretty young things staring at him from a few tables away. He lifted his glass to them in a toast, which made them giggle and look away. He looked good and he knew it. It was moments like this that fed his vanity. He took another bite of his yellowtail tuna and returned his attention to his lunch partner.

The waiter left, and Stewart resumed their conversation about the time line for the new shipment when Anton's phone rang. When he saw the number pop up, he stood quickly and picked up the phone.

"My apologies, Mr. Stewart, but I need to take this," Anton said and walked into a hallway leading toward the restrooms, talking as he went.

"Alicia? Go ahead."

Alicia Alvarez was Luis's sister. He trusted Luis to guard Star, but having his sister as a plant in the Las Vegas Police Department was also proving to be worthwhile.

"I have information for you," she said.

"About my son?"

"No. Something you need to know about the people who died in that car fire."

"What about them?" Anton asked.

"They were federal agents."

Anton's heart skipped a beat.

"You're sure."

"Yes, sir. There's no mistake."

"Thank you, Alicia."

"Yes, sir."

He disconnected, dropped his phone back in his pocket and then lifted his chin and returned to the dining area. His stomach was in knots now, wondering what the Feds already knew.

And that's when the final link of the enormity of this situation hit him. His chef. The one who'd left with Star the night she escaped. He'd just assumed she was a do-gooder who had taken pity on Star's situation and helped her get away. But this changed everything! She'd been a plant, he realized—a mole in his home who had cooked his meals, lived under his roof, even banking the money he paid her with full intentions of taking him down. He was furious that he had been taken in. God only knew what she had learned while she was there or what Star had already told her. The smartest thing to do would be to cut his losses right now and get out of the country. He could run the business from anywhere. But the longer he thought about it, the more he hesitated. What could she have learned, really? Nothing they could convict him with, surely. He didn't do business at home, ever. Even if Star already told the Feds how she came to be with him, she wasn't going to tell it again on a witness stand, thinking she would be sending her family to certain death. As soon as he got his hands on her he was going to end her conversations permanently.

The one thing he knew he had to do was to back off the woman who'd taken Sammy to the cops. Sending Dev after her had gotten him killed. The police clearly understood his involvement, and if he made another mistake, they'd be able to pin it on him. He needed to regroup. The most immediate goal was to get Star out of the hospital. Once she was gone, the Feds' case would be back to square one. He returned to his lunch meeting and slid back into his seat with a nod to Mr. Stewart.

"Duty calls," he said apologetically. "I'm afraid I'm going to have to forgo dessert, but please, order anything you want. Lunch is on me."

Stewart shook his head.

"That's very generous of you, but I'll pass." He patted his bulging belly to make his point. "It was a pleasure to see you again. I'll be in touch with a firm delivery date soon."

Anton nodded, dropped a handful of hundred-dollar bills on the table and left as Stewart finished eating his meal.

It was afternoon at the hospital, and the nurses were making the rounds picking up lunch trays. Visitors were coming and going. Some old man was shouting for help over and over at the far end of the hall, and the door to Star's room was ajar enough that she heard everything. She could tell her back was beginning to heal because the pain had lessened. But the rub to her situation right now was the guard outside her room. He was blatantly leering.

It pissed her off that she felt so vulnerable when all she wanted to do was go to the bathroom. What he needed was an attitude adjustment. So she got out of bed, purposefully letting the top of her hospital gown slip just enough to reveal a good portion of her right breast. She held on to her belly as she moved, trying not to hurt her ribs, and paused at the doorway and stared back.

He seemed startled that she was challenging his rudeness.

"Your name is Luis, right?" she asked.

He grinned.

"On the money, honey."

"Just wanted to make sure I thank Anton for your… services," she said shortly and then stepped back and pushed the door closed enough that he could no longer look in, leaving him to wonder what damage she might do to his status with the boss.

Then she heard his phone ring, and instead of going to the bathroom, she stayed to listen.

Luis answered immediately, and when he began saying "yes, sir" and "no, sir" in rapid-fire answers, she knew he was talking to Anton.

"Yes, sir. She just had lunch. No, sir, she's up and moving around. Okay…yes, I'll be here. Are you coming to get her yourself, or are you sending someone?"

Star's knees nearly went out from under her.

Sweet Mother of God, Anton was coming. Why the sudden rush? He must have learned about the Feds.

She turned away in panic. There was no way to contact Gleason, and she had no idea who their plant was on the floor. She should have known not to assume she was safe, but what the hell could she do? She slipped away from the door and began going through the drawers and closets in a panic to find her clothes, only to remember they'd cut them off of her in the ER.

She had to get out, but how? Then she spotted her lunch tray and had an idea. She palmed a plastic knife, grabbed the tray and threw it to the floor, scattering dirty dishes and leftover food everywhere. The glass that had held her iced tea shattered on the tile, and she gritted her teeth before purposefully stepping on the broken glass. Then she let out a cry just loud enough to alert Luis, as a shard pierced the bottom of one foot.

Within seconds he was inside her room, his hand on his gun.

"What happened?" he asked.

She was doubled over and pointing at the blood seeping out between her toes.

"I knocked my stupid tray over and stepped on the broken glass. Can you help me get to the bed?"

"Yeah, sure," Luis said, putting his handgun back in the shoulder holster under his jacket and scooping her up in his arms.

She winced as his grip tightened on the bandages on her back. Her hospital gown had slipped even more, revealing most of one breast. Her cheeks flushed as he leered at her and grinned.

"Nice tits."

Her eyes narrowed. It was the only warning the man would get before she plunged the plastic knife into the softest portion of his throat.

He gasped, unable to scream. His eyes were wide with shock and pain as he began clawing at the knife. She landed on her feet, grabbed his gun from the holster and swung the butt of it at his face before he even knew it was gone. His nose shattered beneath the impact.

Luis dropped to his knees and grabbed his nose, moaning as blood from both wounds spilled between his fingers.

She grabbed the empty food tray off the floor and broke it over his head. He crumpled to the floor, unconscious and bleeding.

Frantically she tore off his jacket and shirt, pulled the belt from his pants, then emptied his pockets.

The first thing she went for was his wallet. She removed all the cash, then dropped the hospital gown at her feet and pulled the piece of glass from her foot and tried not to think of what she was doing.

Standing stark naked on the far side of her bed, she

put on his shirt. The shirttail barely brushed the top of her knees, but it was long enough to hide her bare body beneath. She wrapped the belt around her waist twice then fastened it off. It was a poor excuse for a dress but it worked. The blood splatters on the collar and down the front were obvious but she hid them with the jacket. She put the gun in one jacket pocket and zipped it up, then dropped the money into another. His boots were way too big for her to wear, so she was going out of here barefoot in the fastest way possible.

But how to do this without being caught?

The moment she focused on the cigarette lighter, she knew what she was going to do. She pulled a section of newspaper from the trash, wadded it up and lit it on fire, then dropped it back into the metal can, knowing the rest of the trash was going to catch fire, too. She took off out the door, keeping her head down as she headed for the stairs.

She made it as far as the Exit sign by the stairwell when the sprinkler system went off on the fourth floor. A spurt of panic made her move faster. She had to get out before the fire alarm sounded and the staff shut down the floor. She pushed through the door into the stairwell at a run, stumbling down the stairs. Seconds later the fire alarms activated. With one hand gripping the handrail and her other flattened against sore ribs, she leaped, taking the steps down two and three at a time.

She reached the ground floor and came out into a lobby that was in total chaos. Firemen came running in the front doors as she was running to get out. From the corner of her eye, she saw a pair of slippers in the gift shop window and darted into the shop, grabbed the shoes from the display and ran. There was so much panic around her that no one saw it happen.

Nick had been smelling food out on the floor for a while now and guessed they were making the rounds delivering lunch. A few minutes later the door opened and Quinn's nurse came in with a tray.

"Hey, Betty."

"Hello, Detective... I have a tray for you, too," she said and glanced at Quinn. "Sleeping, is she?"

"I appreciate the food, and yes, she's been sleeping awhile. I'll wake her up and help her to the bathroom," he said.

Betty went back for the second tray and set it on the ledge below the window.

"It's meat loaf, one of our better efforts. Enjoy."

"Thanks," Nick said. Then he popped a pain pill and washed it down with a drink of iced tea from his tray.

Betty quickly checked Quinn's vitals and then left as Nick leaned over to wake her up. Asleep, and with no makeup, she looked like the little girl he'd once known. Only this woman was no longer a child, and he wondered what it would take to bridge the secrets in the darkness in which she lived. Her skin looked so soft, her lips so tempting— Whoa, where had that come from? Spending all this time by her side, protecting her again—he somehow felt connected to her, as though they'd been destined to find each other after all this time. But it would be taking advantage of her helplessness if he gave in to this sudden yearning, so he settled for a gentle stroke of his fingers on the side of her forehead instead.

She sighed.

He ran the back of his finger down the side of her cheek and thought how the little Queenie he'd known had done a fine job of growing up.

"Wake up, Your Majesty. Lunch has been served."

Quinn roused, then winced as she rolled over.

"What did you say?"

"Lunch is here. Want to go to the bathroom first?"

"Yes."

He let down the guardrail and pulled back the covers as she struggled to sit up.

"Let me help," he said and eased her into a sitting position and then out of bed.

"I don't need—" she started to say.

Nick winked. "But I do. Hold on to my arm."

She moaned when the room began to spin.

"I guess I need help after all," she said and grabbed his arm.

Nick waited as she steadied herself, and then he walked her to the bathroom door. After she went inside, he moved a distance away to give her privacy. As he was waiting, he remembered another time when they were together just like this. She'd gotten sick and wound up in a hospital, dehydrated from constant nausea. He had been afraid she was going to die. When she finally came home, he sneaked into her room after lights were out and slept on the floor beside her bed, afraid to leave her on her own.

Although he hadn't thought of her in years until she

rode back in his world, that same feeling of responsibility and devotion he'd had for her then had come back in spades.

Moments later the bathroom door opened, and he let go of the past and went to meet her. She was pale and trembling, but the tentative smile she gave him made his heart thump.

"Thanks," Quinn said and made her way back to bed with his help.

She was super conscious of his body looming beside her. She was tall, but she had to look up to see his face. His shoulders were wide and his strength was evident. She wondered what it would feel like to be held within his arms. She still couldn't believe she'd found him again, and while life had taught her not to believe in happy endings, she was glad he was here for her now.

Quinn wrinkled her nose as she removed the cover from her food. It didn't look any better than it smelled, but Nick's palate was obviously not as picky. He was already chewing his first bite.

He noticed she wasn't eating and grinned.

"Wait until you taste it. Kudos to the cooks for saving the salt for another day."

She smiled at his joke. He seemed to be such a happy man. She forked a green bean and put it in her mouth, then wrinkled her nose again. He was right. It needed salt, but she'd been hungry too many times in her life to quibble about seasoning.

They ate in mutual silence for a couple of minutes, and then Nick paused to take a drink and caught Quinn looking at him.

"What?" he asked.

"Nothing," she said quickly, poking at the meat loaf and taking a small bite.

"Then I'll start," Nick said.

Quinn looked puzzled.

"Start what?"

"Asking the questions that fill in the blanks."

But Quinn didn't want to talk about her life and headed him off in another direction.

"No, I'll ask the questions," she said with a smile. "Have you ever been married?"

"No, but engaged once," Nick said and took another bite of meat loaf.

"What happened?" Quinn asked.

"She changed her mind and joined the army. She chose Uncle Sam over me."

Quinn smiled.

"You're a funny one, aren't you? I don't remember that about you."

"I figured out early on that if I made the jokes and laughed first, then it didn't matter what anyone else said or did. I was the one calling the shots. And my aunt and uncle helped. They gave me confidence. Knowing they'd come looking for me made me feel wanted. And when they took me home with them, I took heart from the fact that I'd been chosen. I finally mattered to someone."

"I know I was just a little kid, but you always mattered to me," Quinn said, then quickly reached for her glass and took a sip of iced tea to keep from tearing up.

"Thank you," Nick said. "Now it's my turn. What are you running away from?"

He saw her flinch, and then her head came up, her eyes narrowing before she looked away.

"The devil," she muttered and shoved her tray table away.

"Who was he to you?"

"My last foster father."

Nick realized almost instantly that she didn't want to talk about this. As much as he wanted to know, to understand, he didn't want to upset her.

"Do you still like peanut butter and honey sandwiches?" he asked.

She blinked. Where had that come from? Then she saw the compassion in his eyes and was instantly grateful he'd backed away from the tough questions.

"Yes, on white bread."

He grinned. "I think I remember, the gummier the bread was, the better you liked it."

She laughed.

"As long as it's white, I'm good," she said.

"Where did you graduate high school?" he asked.

"Still in Chicago, just a different suburb. Is your family close by?"

"Yes. They live here in the city. They're finally retired and spend all their time and money spoiling their four grandkids."

Quinn was staring again, fascinated by the changing expressions on his face as he talked.

"How many children do they have…counting you?"

He scooped up a spoonful of some kind of fruit pie and aimed it at her mouth.

"Open," he said, and she did. "Four…counting me," he added. "Santino is just older than me. He and Lara have two little boys who look and act just like him. Melina and her husband, Aidan, have one baby girl, and Francisco and Donita have a girl. She's about three, I think. I can't wait for you to meet everyone, especially Aunt Juana and Uncle Tonio."

Quinn's chest tightened. Meet his family? *What will they think of a woman like me?*

"They won't approve. I'm wired all wrong," she said and then picked up her spoon and took another bite of his dessert.

"Bullshit. You don't know them, so don't go getting yourself all worked up for nothing." He handed her his dessert and took hers. He scooped up a bite and popped it in his mouth, then winked, trying to tease the shadows from her eyes. "Ha. Got the first bite from both of them."

Quinn paused, watching how laughter lit up his face, then finished the dessert.

Once they were done, Nick stacked their trays and set them aside to be picked up later. Another nurse named Trina came in to check Quinn's wound, which changed the mood in the room.

Quinn reached for Nick's hand, clenching it as the nurse began removing the bandage to be replaced. She grimaced at the spots where it was stuck, mutely bearing the pain.

The nurse was finally through and getting ready to

leave when out of nowhere the sprinkler systems came on and began to soak the room. A few seconds later the fire alarm went off.

"Stay here," Trina cried and ran out of the room.

Before Nick could react, Quinn came out of the bed like she'd been shot all over again and ran for the door.

Nick caught her in his arms.

"Wait, honey, wait! She told us to stay here."

But Quinn was frantic. The water in her face had triggered the panic. Her heart was pounding; her breath was coming in gasps. She'd lost all sense of reality and in her mind was trying not to die.

"Let me go! Let me go!" she screamed. "You're going to drown me!"

Shocked, Nick immediately turned her loose and stepped back, holding his hands up in the air while the water rained down upon them.

"Look at me, Quinn! Look! I'm not holding you. I'm not touching you."

She covered her face.

"Make the water stop. Please make the water stop."

He had no idea what had triggered this panic in her, but ran into the bathroom, yanked the plastic shower curtain from the hooks and came back to find her squatting in a corner of the room with her hands over her head. He crouched down beside her and pulled the shower curtain over the both of them as the water continued to pour.

"It's okay now. There's no water on your face. You're safe." But Quinn just moaned and kept rocking back and forth.

"Damn it," he said softly and pulled her into his arms. To his surprise, she didn't resist but collapsed against him, her face buried against his chest.

Just as suddenly as the sprinklers had come on, they went off. Nick tossed the curtain aside, then picked her up and took her to the recliner.

He didn't talk as he held her close. There was nothing to say. He'd seen enough PTSD to recognize a flashback. He didn't know why she reacted to water in her face, or who was responsible for the trauma, but he would find out. He was damn good at finding the bad guys.

Six

The sprinklers were still raining water down on the fourth floor, and nurses were hurrying door by door down the halls, making quick bed checks to assess the condition of their patients and move people where necessary. The firemen had just arrived and were looking for whatever had triggered the sprinkler systems and alarm.

Betty, the RN, was in a rush and counting heads when she saw thick smoke snaking out from under the door of Star Davis's room. She ran toward it, calling for the nearest firefighter as she went, then pushed the door inward. A cloud of gray smoke billowed out, and she coughed and dropped to her knees just like she was trained. Once the initial cloud had escaped the room, the smoke wasn't so bad. She passed the source of the issue as she crawled through the doorway—the wastepaper basket must have caught fire somehow, though the water seemed to have put it out.

A short distance into the room she froze, horrified

by what she saw. A body spread out in front of her and the contents of a lunch tray scattered about brought her to a sliding halt on the wet floor. She recognized him as the man who'd been guarding Star's door, but Star was nowhere in sight. As more smoke escaped the room, the scene became clearer, as did the plastic knife in the man's throat and the blood running out of his nose and scalp. The nurse gasped and reached for his wrist, searching for a pulse. It was there, but weak. Relieved, she dashed to the bathroom, hoping against hope that Star might be in there, but the room was empty. She ran back to the door, shouting for help.

Within minutes the room was full.

The wounded man was put on a stretcher and was on his way to surgery, while the firemen agreed this was the source of the fire that triggered the alarm, then shut down the sprinkler system and took a report, leaving the rest to the police and hospital staff.

Hospital Security was on the scene until the police arrived, knowing they would be working with two possible scenarios. Either Star Davis had been abducted by whoever attacked her guard, or she'd attacked him herself and set the fire to escape. Security put a guard on her room to protect the evidence, although there was probably little to gather since everything was water-soaked, and went to check security footage.

When Anton's driver pulled into the hospital parking lot he was immediately denied access to go farther.

"What's happening?" Anton asked from the back seat.

"I don't know, sir, but it appears there's been an

emergency at the hospital. There are fire trucks and police cars everywhere."

"Get me as close as possible," Anton ordered.

"Yes, sir."

They parked at the back of the lot, and then Anton and his bodyguards got out and headed toward the front entrance. They didn't get far before they were stopped again by the police barricade and a trio of officers.

"Sorry, sir. Emergency entries only at this time," one officer said.

Anton frowned.

"Why not? What's happened here? The mother of my son is a patient on the fourth floor, and I need to see her. I need to make sure she's okay."

"The fourth floor?" the officer said.

"Yes."

"What's her name?"

"Star Davis."

The officer frowned.

"Sir, I need you to come with me."

Thinking he was being personally escorted in, Anton was surprised when the officer swerved to the right a few yards from the front entrance.

"Hey!" Anton yelled.

The officer turned.

"This way," he said.

Anton ignored him and stormed toward the front doors, determined to get to Star while he had the chance. But when he veered back toward the entrance, cops came running.

Despite Anton's best arguments, his bodyguards

were sent back to the limo, and he was marched toward a trio of men in suits standing beside an ambulance.

Anton didn't know what was going on, but he was no longer willing to argue. The fact that they were not in uniform made him anxious. If they were FBI, maybe all his careful planning was already too late. Maybe they had what they needed on him. This could be the moment he was put under arrest.

A bald man with a sheen of sweat on his head flashed his badge.

"Mr. Baba, I'm Detective Pitney with the Las Vegas Police. We were told you were with Star Davis when she was admitted. Is this correct?"

"Yes," Anton said. "She is the mother of my son. I came today to take her home. What's happening here? Why am I not allowed to go inside?"

"There was a small fire on the floor she was on. They're cleaning up now," Pitney explained.

"Did Miss Davis know you were coming?" the second man asked. He had thick, curly hair cut close to his head and looked like a miniature version of Arnold Schwarzenegger.

"Who are you?"

"Special Agent Gleason, FBI," he said and pulled out his badge.

Anton's heart skipped a beat, but his best defense had always been offense, and so he immediately challenged the Fed.

"I'm not answering another question until someone tells me what's going on. I want to see Star."

"What about your son? Do you want to see your son, too?" Gleason asked.

Anton's gut knotted, but he didn't let them know they'd touched a nerve. He'd do what he'd always done: deny, deny, deny.

"What does Sammy have to do with anything?" he asked, feigning surprise at the question.

Gleason looked at him sternly. "If Sammy's mother is here in the hospital, and you're here in front of me, where is Sammy?"

"I don't understand what's going on. Sammy's with the nanny! What does this have to do with anything?"

Agent Gleason was watching Baba's face and couldn't tell if the man was lying or truly ignorant of the fact that the law had his son secreted away. But he was about to find out.

"There was a fire on the fourth floor that started in Star's room. They found a man—the guard you apparently paid to stay outside her room—unconscious on the floor and bleeding from multiple wounds."

Anton gasped. "Luis? No! Oh no! Where is Star? Is she okay?"

"We were hoping you could tell us," Gleason drawled.

"You what? What does that mean? She's not here?" Gleason nodded.

Anton didn't have to pretend anymore. His shock at this news was real. He couldn't believe that she'd done it again, that she would betray him twice this way, but he couldn't let them know she was running from him. Obviously the Feds now had his son; that much was clear to him by the way they were talking to him, but he didn't have to let on that he knew it. He could still play the role of panicked father if it came down to that.

"None of this makes any sense," Anton said. "Luis is one of my more experienced bodyguards. He was supposed to be keeping her safe. You're telling me he was injured, that there was a fire in her room? How did that happen? And why isn't she here? Was she abducted?"

Star Davis had not been abducted—not by anyone but Baba. She'd obviously run, just like she'd run from Baba before. Gleason wasn't going to tell him they'd already seen her making her escape on the security footage, though.

"We don't know yet. We're still viewing security footage."

Anton began to pace nervously.

"I want to see the tapes. I might recognize the abductors!"

Gleason smirked at that.

"If we run into trouble, we'll keep that in mind."

Anton covered his face as if hiding his despair, when in fact he had to compose himself so as not to give away his rage. When he finally lifted his head he had managed to work up a few tears.

"What can I do?" he asked.

"Just go home for now. We'll keep you abreast of our investigation, and if you hear from Star—or from anyone who might have her—you notify us."

"Yes, yes, of course," Anton said, and he walked away slowly with his shoulders stooped, as if overwhelmed by what he'd learned.

He grabbed his phone and called the house.

"Yes, Mr. Baba, this is Jorge."

"Jorge, alert the trackers. Star's on the run. Find out where she's at, now. I'll hold," he said, as he headed for his limo.

A few moments later Jorge was back on the phone.

"Mr. Baba, she is not on the radar at all."

Anton gasped.

"What do you mean? Of course she is. She's chipped like the rest of them."

"Yes, sir, I understand, but it is not registering at all."

And then it hit him. The wreck in the desert. All those wounds. It either came out in the desert or was picked out as debris in surgery and discarded.

Son of a bitch.

She really was gone.

"What do you think?" Detective Pitney asked, watching Baba go.

Gleason shook his head and glanced over at his partner.

"What do you think, Lou?"

Powers shrugged.

"If I was a betting man, which I'm not, I would never bet against Anton Baba. He knows far more than he's telling, and he knows Star Davis wasn't abducted. She's running from him."

"What about his kid?" Pitney asked. "Do you think he knows we have him?"

"Yes, or he would have pressed us for more reasons why *we* were asking about him," Gleason said. "But we need to take precautions, just in case. As for Star

Davis, this has been a cluster-fuck ever since the night of the wreck, and it keeps getting worse. We need to find her before Baba does, or she's dead and so is our case against him."

Star's stolen slippers were a size too small for her feet but they were stretchy and so she coped. Years ago when she'd first been kidnapped, she'd made a plan for herself in case she ever got a chance to escape. Then she'd given it up once her family's life was threatened.

Seven years later, here she was on the run. The plan was the same, but her options had changed. Because of her injuries she was going to need medicine, different clothes and the means to change her appearance. She no longer had an ID and wasn't about to go to the police for help. Anton had too many snitches inside the organization, so she just kept walking, staying within the busy foot traffic. A few blocks farther down she turned a corner and saw a secondhand clothing store and darted inside.

The interior was just the teeniest bit shabby like the merchandise, but she was way past being picky. And the girl sitting at the checkout register barely looked up from her phone.

"Help yourself," the clerk mumbled. "If you have questions, let me know."

"Right," Star said and went for a table full of folded T-shirts. They were three for five dollars. She picked two with elbow-length sleeves and one long-sleeved T. Even though it was hot as blazes outside, she didn't want to advertise her scrapes and bruises.

She moved on to a table with jeans. They were two pairs for ten dollars. She looked back at the clerk and called out.

"How about three pairs of jeans for ten dollars?" she asked.

The clerk shrugged.

"Yeah, okay."

Star sorted through the jeans, found three pairs, all of which were distressed styles. Then she found a bin of used lingerie and tried not to think about the fact that she was about to wear someone else's underwear. She sorted through the bin until she found a few pairs in almost new condition. She would need a bra, but feared it would cause her healing wounds to break open. Then she saw a pile of sports bras, found two in her size and headed toward the dressing room.

The mirror was cracked at one corner and the silver was coming off on the back, leaving the mirror with a pocked reflection. She shed the jacket, the bloody shirt, and then turned to the mirror to see how her back looked. The bandages were still in place, and she didn't see any fresh blood. Satisfied, she began to get dressed. The simple act of wearing underwear again gave her a strange sense of security, as if she was no longer as vulnerable to the world as she'd been only minutes before. The sports bra was uncomfortable but a necessary evil if she didn't want to draw more attention by the size of her unfettered breasts. She chose the gray T-shirt and a pair of faded jeans to wear, and by the time she was through she almost felt human.

She took the gun out of Luis's jacket and stuck it in

the back of her waistband, then left her oversize T-shirt untucked. As she began counting the money that was in Luis's wallet, she was surprised to find a trio of one-hundred-dollar bills along with the rest of it, coming to a total of just over five hundred dollars. She stuffed it in her front pocket. Now all she had left to do was get rid of the old jacket, belt and bloody shirt, but where?

Then she realized the answer was in front of her. She folded the shirt up neatly and, when she went out, slipped it beneath a stack of folded shirts on a nearby table. She hung the jacket on a rack filled with other coats and jackets.

"Hey…do you have any tote bags?" she asked the girl at the counter.

The clerk didn't look up, but called out, "If we do, they'll be hanging on the back wall."

Star wound her way through the long, narrow room, wrinkling her nose as she went. She doubted any of these clothes had been washed before they were donated, and no one had bothered to wash them before putting them out. It smelled like stale cigarette smoke and old houses back here. She couldn't wait to get back into fresh air.

She saw a little bit of everything hanging from hooks on that wall and had to search awhile to find any bags. Then she spied an old backpack and pulled it down, checking to see if all the zippers and snaps still worked, and if it was clean enough inside. Relieved to find it worn but clean, she took it with her. She spotted the shoes on her way back to the register, picked out a pair of used tennis shoes in her size and added them to the pile.

"I'm ready," she said, as she plopped the stack down at the register.

The clerk laid down her phone, glanced up at Star briefly and then began checking her out.

"I'll need to pay for the bra, panties, T-shirt and jeans I'm wearing. And I'm going to put those tennis shoes on as soon as you ring all of this up," Star said.

The clerk nodded and totaled up the purchases.

"That will be thirty-eight dollars and twelve cents," she said.

Star pulled out two twenties and slid them across the counter, then pocketed her change.

"I don't need a sack," Star said. "I'll put everything in the backpack."

"No problem," the girl said and watched Star stuff her purchases into the bag.

A phone rang. The clerk turned around to answer it, and when she did, Star slipped the gun into the bottom of the pack with her bloody slippers, put on the tennis shoes and walked out of the store.

She caught sight of her reflection as she walked past a store window and felt better. As soon as she got rid of the long blond hair, she would be much harder to recognize.

She'd made it a few blocks down when a pair of cop cars came flying past, running with lights and sirens. Her heart thumped, but she just moved away from the curb and kept on walking.

Stay with me, Lord. I'm going to need all the help I can get.

Traffic was crazy as usual, almost as many people

walking on the sidewalks as there were driving up and down the streets. She was trying not to look nervous, but she knew Anton's people would still recognize her if they saw her this way. One more stop and she'd be set. When she finally saw a pharmacy, she breathed a quick sigh of relief. Her back was burning, her muscles were stiff and aching, and the bottom of her foot ached where she'd stepped on the glass, but she was met with a blast of cool air as she walked into the pharmacy, and she knew she was almost safe. As good as it felt to be in out of the sun, there was no time to waste. She grabbed a shopping cart and headed down the aisle, but soon came to a halt.

Everything looked different than she remembered. There were products she'd never seen before and updated versions of the ones she knew. She hadn't had the freedom to shop for herself since Anton had kidnapped her, and that's when it finally hit her—she was actually *free*. She rubbed a shaky hand across her face to keep from crying and started grabbing what she needed.

She left the store as abruptly as she'd entered with a disposable phone, a pair of scissors, hair dye and bandages, snacks, some makeup, a big bottle of water and meds that would ease the pain. Now all she needed was a place to finish up her transformation—a cheap motel would work, preferably one that charged by the hour.

She tore into the painkillers and read the directions. Take two every eight hours. She shook four out into her palm and downed them with a swallow of water, then opened a bag of chips and ate as she walked.

An hour later she opened the door to her motel room.

For the grand sum of fifty bucks it was hers for the night. She locked herself inside, shoved the table in front of the door and sat down, every muscle trembling. She wanted to sleep, but there was too much yet to be done. She read the directions for her burner phone and then set it up before pulling out a candy bar and finishing it and the bottle of water off in front of the air conditioner.

The tears came without warning, welling and running down her cheeks.

"Oh, my God, oh, my God," she said and buried her face in her hands.

In the hours after the fire alarm sounded, the fourth-floor patients were temporarily moved to empty beds all over the hospital and orderlies were pulled off other floors to help with the moves. It was a lot of work, but necessary so that the cleaning crew could get the water-soaked rooms back in order.

Because Quinn O'Meara was under police protection, she was one of the first to be moved. A nurse wrapped Quinn's long wet hair into a towel, removed her wet hospital gown and gave her a dry one, then redid the bandage on her shoulder.

Nick had a wheelchair waiting, and when she was ready to leave the room, the nurse laid a copy of Quinn's orders in her lap for the nurses on the new floor. With Nick wheeling the pole with her IV hookup and an orderly pushing the chair, the three of them headed for the elevator.

Quinn's heart was pounding every step of the way, afraid that whoever wanted her dead might use this opportunity to try again. Even though Nick was armed and right beside her, it didn't help. Leaving her room was terrifying.

Nick kept an eye on Quinn's face as they went. It was obvious she was rattled. She was pale and her skin looked clammy, and when the elevator door closed she reached for his hand.

"Easy, Queenie…you've got this," he said.

With tears welling, Quinn closed her eyes. The car went up, and she opened them the moment it stopped.

Nick stepped out first. Once he was satisfied all was clear, he went back for the IV pole and walked them out.

There was a nurse waiting at the door to Quinn's new room who had already been briefed on the dire situation this patient was in, and when she saw them coming she went out of her way to make the transition smooth.

"I'm Elena. I'll be your nurse for the rest of this shift. Welcome to Casa Cinco Dos Tres," she said.

Nick grinned.

"Nice. Five two three it is."

Quinn was shaking as she handed Elena the orders.

"Thank you, Quinn. Let's get you inside and back in bed. You'll feel better soon."

As soon as they got her settled, Nick pulled up the recliner. Another nurse came in with a cup and a pitcher of ice water and then paused at the foot of her bed.

"You aren't due for any pain meds for another couple of hours. Can I get you anything else?" she asked.

"No, thank you," Quinn said.

She watched the nurse leave, and, even though she had Nick beside her, she felt like she was coming undone. These last few hours had reinforced the feeling that she had no control over her life whatsoever, and for someone as independent as Quinn, that was frightening to admit.

"Sleep if you want," Nick said.

She felt a sense of shame creep over her. Nick was going out of his way for her, putting himself right in the face of danger, and all she could do was curl up like some baby and cry? It was all because of that flashback. It scared her to lose control.

Nick started to say something, but then thought better of it and instead sat down in the recliner and held her hand.

She grasped it like a lifeline and closed her eyes.

The silence lengthened inside the room to the point that Nick began hearing things he normally would have ignored, like the water dripping from the showerhead in the bathroom and the squeaky shoes of some nurse out in the hall. His head was throbbing, and he was so damned tired. When they'd shut down the fourth floor for cleanup, the officer who'd been standing guard outside her door went back to headquarters for dry clothing. With no one watching the door, Nick was afraid to close his eyes for fear someone might come after her up here.

He got up and pulled another blanket over her and then eased back down. He thought she was asleep until her quiet, quivering voice broke the silence in the room.

"His name was Vester Whitlaw, but he made us call

him Pappy. He was a sadistic bastard, and I used to pray every night that he would die. I lived there seven weeks before I ran."

Nick was surprised she wanted to open up, but he was more than ready to listen. "What did he do to you?" Nick asked.

"Drowned me."

Nick came out of the recliner so fast it made his head spin.

"What the hell do you mean, he drowned you?"

"He pushed my head down in the toilet, and when I tried to fight back he punched me in the back over and over, trying to knock the breath out of my lungs. He wanted me to take a breath, and when I finally did, I drowned. Then he dragged me out of the toilet and performed CPR, timing himself to see how long it took to revive me."

The horror of what Nick was hearing was unbelievable, but it made sense when he looked at the woman in front of him. She'd been running from the devil for so long she didn't know how to stop.

"Oh, my God, Quinn," Nick said. He pulled down the guardrail, climbing into bed beside her, and she immediately curled up to him. He wrapped his arms around her, wishing he could somehow form a barrier between this amazing woman and all the pain she'd had to experience.

She was limp against him, as if the telling of it sapped all her strength.

"I'm so sorry," Nick whispered. "I will find him and make him sorry for the day he was born."

"Last I knew, he was on death row somewhere in Illinois. He did it again to another girl after I ran, and he couldn't revive her. Then they found videos."

"Just when I think I've seen and heard it all," Nick said.

Quinn cried quietly in his arms.

"He broke me, Nick. I still have nightmares. I can't go swimming or take a bath. Even showers freak me out to the point that it's all I can do to wash my face and hair. No matter what I do, it just brings me right back to that moment. And besides all that, I don't trust people. I can't."

He laid his cheek against the crown of her head.

"You are the least broken woman I ever met," Nick murmured. "You are a freaking warrior, that's what you are. You rescued a baby out in the middle of the desert and rode miles into Vegas with a bullet in your back. You do just fine when the need arises, get that?"

"Please don't be nice to me just because you feel sorry for me," she whispered.

"I'm being nice because I'm a nice guy," Nick said. "And when you get well enough, I might just show you how nice."

She looked up at him then, needing to see if he was making another joke, but he wasn't smiling. Instead, he leaned down and kissed her, and she felt a warmth spread through her at his touch.

He pulled back gently, tucking a stray hair behind her ear and then leaning back so that she could rest against his chest. He felt the tension in her body easing with every breath, and finally, finally, he looked down to see she'd gone to sleep.

Only one thought was on his mind.

Please, God, help me keep her safe.

Seven

Anton Baba was in the back seat of his limo with a burner phone, setting the dogs in his world on to Star Davis's trail. From so-called bounty hunters to guns for hire, to every hard-up loser he knew that would sell his mama for a hit of cocaine. For five hundred thousand dollars, he'd set them all on the hunt.

It was unfortunate for him that Star had a good two hours head start on her escape before he knew she was gone. He didn't know where to start and couldn't guess where she might go, because the truth was he had no idea where she'd come from. All he knew of her past was that she was a virgin when he took her off the auction block, and that she was part of a shipment from the Southern states.

He didn't think she would go far without Sammy, but she'd surprised him so many times now that he couldn't be sure. The Feds couldn't legally use Sammy to force her to testify. But she was pissed, and there was no telling what she would do. What he did know was that the

Feds were far too close up his ass. As soon as he hung up from the last call he lowered the window between him and the driver.

"Ivan, I'd like to take a drive out to the Hoover Dam now."

"Yes, sir, Mr. Baba," his driver said and moved into another lane to loop back in the other direction.

Anton broke the seal on a bottle of whiskey, added a couple of ice cubes to his glass and poured a double shot in the tumbler. The whiskey was aged and smooth as silk until it hit his belly with a welcome kick. Tired of the day and all the repercussions, he took another sip and began a mental countdown of what had yet to be done.

It wasn't like he'd never had issues before. In his line of business there were always issues. The difference now was that he'd let things get personal. It had been pure ego to want a son, and Star was as good in bed as he'd ever had. He'd let both of them get under his skin.

With the current state of things, his gut said it was time to get the hell out of Vegas. But he'd underestimated Star before, and these were the consequences. She'd seen too much. She knew too much. She threatened his safety and everything he'd spent his adult life creating. He did not want to spend the rest of his life looking over his shoulder. He needed to see her take her last breath before he could disappear. As for the son they had, maybe it would be best to leave him behind. If the boy became too important in his life, he would be vulnerable to his enemies. He'd have a weakness. That was always a mistake.

"Sir. We're coming up to the dam," Ivan said, interrupting his thoughts. "Is there any place in particular you want me to park?"

"I want you to stop at an overlook," Anton said and downed what was left of the whiskey in one gulp.

A few moments later the limo began slowing down. As soon as they stopped, Anton slid across the seat toward the door.

"Stay here. I won't be long."

"Yes, sir," Ivan said, looking straight ahead as Anton exited the limo.

The sun was white-hot, the rays refracting on the water like floating diamonds. Anton felt the heat all the way through the soles of his shoes as he walked up to the railing. A small group of tourists were a few yards down taking pictures, but they were of no consequence to him. He palmed the burner phone he'd used to make the calls relating to Star's bounty and slipped it through the railing. Then he opened his hand and let it go, watching until it disappeared into the water below.

Satisfied there was no way to trace the calls back to him, he was on his way back to the limo when one of the tourists hailed him.

"Hey! Hey, buddy!"

Anton paused, then turned around to see the man jogging toward him with his iPhone.

"Are you speaking to me?"

"Yes! Would you mind taking a picture of us? I'd like to get the whole family in one together to commemorate our last day here."

Taken aback by the innocence of the request, Anton accepted the phone.

"Thanks so much," the man said. "I'm George, by the way."

"Anthony," Anton said.

George grinned.

"Nice to meet you, Anthony. Really nice of you to do this for us." He pointed at an icon on the face of the phone. "Just press here when we're ready, okay?"

Anton watched them pushing and shoving to get in place, but still laughing as they settled. A big blond man with a sunburn. The woman with mousy brown hair who needed to lose thirty pounds. Two teenage boys with the same face, and a short, skinny girl with big boobs and purple hair. If they were representative of an all-American family these days, he was not impressed. But then the silliness ended, and he watched as they leaned in together shoulder to shoulder, and wondered if it was an accident that the woman was dead center in the group, or if it was instinctive. A woman in the family was always the heart of a home.

The moment he thought it, his gut knotted. He wouldn't describe the setup he'd had with Star and Sammy as family, exactly, but their presence had been a routine he usually enjoyed. Looking back, he couldn't recall exactly why he'd decided to send Star with the next shipment to Dubai, but it had thoroughly fucked up his little nest.

"We're ready!" George shouted.

Anton snapped six shots in succession, and then George came running.

"Really appreciate that, Anthony."

"Sure," Anton said.

"Have a nice day!" George said and then ran back to his family and began herding them toward a big white SUV.

Anton noticed the Iowa license plate—right out of the heartland, he thought—then got into his limo and closed the door.

Both the air-conditioning and the plush interior brought him back into the moment as he poured himself a second drink.

"I'm ready to go home now," he said.

"Yes, sir," Ivan said.

Anton closed the window between them, then added a fresh ice cube to the glass. Star was on the run, and his future depended on her demise. Hopefully his hunters would bring her in soon, but in the meantime he needed to get the hell out of town.

Star had been cutting her hair for over an hour, and now she paused to stare at herself in the mirror. Most of her long blond hair was in a trash can…and in the sink and on the floor. Butchered was a better description than cut, really, because the scissors she'd purchased weren't meant for cutting hair. The longest hair left on her head were the bangs. Every time she blinked they got caught in her lashes. The rest of it ranged from three to four inches long, leaving her with the appearance of having fallen headfirst into a Weed eater.

She had looked at the boxes of hair color at the pharmacy, pretty shades of chestnut brown and sunset red. But she'd decided that this transformation needed to be much more dramatic. She sighed, then opened the first can of color spray and put streaks in her hair that were a vivid shade of purple. Then she opened the second and third cans of color spray and finished off what was left with streaks of pink and a few streaks of neon green.

She stepped back to look at herself again.

The pink-and-green bangs were resting just above black lashes. The purple spray was in her ears.

"Shit," she muttered and went for a wet washcloth, removing the excess, including what was on her hands.

She dug through the makeup she'd purchased, turned her black lashes gold, put a ring of black eye shadow around each eye and swiped a lipstick called Black Heart on her lips. As a finishing touch, she hung the skull and crossbones earrings through the piercings in her ears, then stepped back to get the full effect.

Startling was the kindest adjective she could think to use.

"If Beetlejuice and My Little Pony had a baby…"

She grimaced, thinking of how horrified Anton would be to see her like this.

"How do you like me now?" she muttered, then raked everything left over into her backpack and started wiping up the hair from the floor and then out of the sink. Everything else she washed down the drain.

It was past time to deal with her injuries, but she was dreading this. She took off her clothes, grabbed a bottle of alcohol and stepped into the shower because she needed to make sure she was washing off any germs or bacteria from the used clothes she'd put on. She scrubbed bath soap all over one of the T-shirts she'd bought and began scrubbing, washing every inch of it clean. Then she rinsed it twice, wrung it out and tossed it in the bathroom sink before tending to her back.

Her hands were shaking as she removed the bandage from her back and tossed it on the floor. She removed the lid and emptied the contents onto her wounds, letting the antiseptic properties of the alcohol wash through every raw and healing cut in hopes it would kill anything from the clothes that could infect her wounds.

Tears were a reflex of the burn. She was shaking so hard by the time the bottle was empty that she slipped on the puddle beneath her feet. In a panic, she grabbed on to the shower curtain with both hands, barely catching herself before she fell. She stepped out of the tub onto the bath mat and dropped to her knees, sobbing.

Tears ran down her face in black streaks as she made herself rise. She got the wet shirt out of the sink, shoved the shower curtain aside and threw the shirt over the shower bar to dry, then picked up her clothes, staggered out of the bathroom and sank down onto the side of the bed.

In the midst of the pain, her belly began to rumble. She was surprised that her hunger could actually surpass the danger and pain she was in, but eating had to wait. There was something else she needed to do first.

Anton had always told her that if she ever betrayed him, he would find everyone she loved and kill them. She'd believed him until the federal agents who were helping her escape told her different. Anton didn't keep track of where his girls were from. It was all a ruse to keep them from running. All these years she'd stayed with him because she'd believed the lie. She got sick to her stomach thinking of how many times she could have called for help and didn't.

But things were different now. If Anton killed her and got away with it, the authorities might give Sammy back to him. A DNA test would confirm his paternity, so everything she was doing now was to make sure that never happened.

She sat on the side of the bed, wrapped in a towel and staring at the buttons on her phone. Her hands were shaking as she started entering the number. She still hadn't forgotten, even after all this time. As she hit the first digits, her fingers shook with doubt. What if the number was no longer valid? What if something had happened while she was gone and all of her family really was dead or had moved away?

Then she thought of Sammy.

To hell with "what if."

As the call began to ring, she noticed the clock on the bedside table. It would be after seven o'clock in Tennessee. The phone rang twice, then three times. Now her gut was rolling, and she was struggling hard not to cry. On the fourth ring, she heard someone pick up.

"Hello?"

The voice was familiar…and sounded like everything Star remembered as home.

"Mom…? Mom…it's me."

The outcry of disbelief on the other line was not unexpected.

"Starla? Starla, baby, is that you?"

"Yes, it's me."

Her mother screamed and then started crying so hard Star could barely make out the words.

"I told them you weren't dead. I told them. Oh, my God, John! John! Get on the other line!"

Star heard an extension pick up, then heard her dad's gruff voice.

"I'm here. What the hell's wrong? Who's talking?" he asked.

"Daddy, it's me!"

She heard him gasp and then heard the tears in his voice.

"Sweet Mother of God," John Davis said. "Where are you? I'm coming to get you."

"No, no, listen to me, both of you. I don't have time to explain the past seven years over the phone. I just need you to know what's happening right now because I finally have the chance to be free—but I need help. I'm on the run. I'm hiding from the man who's been holding me captive, and if he catches me, he'll kill me because of what I know about him."

Connie Davis moaned.

"Oh, my God. My baby, what has he done to you?"

"None of that matters now. Just listen. The FBI is involved in this. Two of their agents were helping me escape when they were killed. The FBI has Sammy, and I need you and Daddy to know that if anything happens to me, you have to get Sammy. Contact the FBI and tell them who you are. That's all you have to do."

John interrupted her.

"Wait, Starla—who's Sammy?"

"He's my son, Daddy. He's two years old. He is my world and the only thing that matters."

Connie began to cry all over again. "We have a grandson? John! We have a grandson!"

"I heard her, but what I want to know is what does the FBI have to do with this, and why haven't they helped you all this time? Call the police right now, baby. They'll help you until we can get there."

"No, Daddy, you don't understand. The man who had me is a very powerful man. He has people everywhere. If I tell the cops where I am, someone in the precinct will tip him off before anyone can help me, and the next time I disappear it will be for good."

Her father went from tentative to outraged in a matter of seconds.

"Don't tell me I can't come get you. We searched nearly two years straight for you before everyone else gave up. Now I hear your voice and know you're alive, and I'm coming! Tell me where you are! Do you understand? I will find you, Starla."

Star was crying now. Wishing it would be just that easy.

"I will never be safe until Anton Baba is behind bars or dead."

There was a long moment of silence in which Star realized she'd just said his name. She froze, terrified at what this mistake might cost her—and her family.

"The Anton Baba who owns the Lucky Joe's Casino in Las Vegas?" her mother asked in a small, shaky voice.

Star was shocked. How did they know about Lucky Joe's Casino in Vegas? But regardless, she figured it was too late to lie about it.

"Yes."

Connie began sobbing.

"Your father and I were there Christmas before last. Are you in Las Vegas? Have you been there all this time? I can't believe we were so close to you."

"Yes, but I won't be here for long. I have to get out of the city before he finds me. I just need you to promise you will take care of Sammy."

Again, John interrupted.

"We'll get your Sammy, but you're the one I'm saving first. All I need right now is for you to tell me where you are."

"You can't do that, Dad. You're too far away and I need to be gone. Now."

"Oh, but I can. The reason we were in Vegas at all is because Justin is an officer with the Nevada State Police. Give me your address, baby girl, and your brother will be at your door within an hour…do you hear me? One damn hour. Don't run anywhere."

She was stunned, but unable to speak. Was it possible? Could this nightmare really be over in only an hour?

"The address, Starla. Give it to me now."

Star was too shocked to argue. After all this time, maybe fate was finally rolling things her way. She recited the name and address of the motel she was staying in.

"Okay, I've got that," John said, writing down everything she said. "Call us again after you've been picked up. I can't believe we're getting you back after all this time!"

"One other thing, Daddy. Warn Justin that he won't recognize me. Anton has people hunting me, so I had to change my look completely. Lingering too long in one place is dangerous, but I have this place for the night."

"Yes, we understand, and I'll tell him what you said. I love you, Starla, honey. Thank God for this call."

"I love you, too, baby," Connie said. "Just don't leave there, whatever you do. Wait for Justin. He'll come get you."

"I love you, Mom. I love you, Dad. I promise I won't leave."

The moment the connection ended Star jumped up and began to dress. Her hands were shaking, but for the first time in years she felt hope. She'd just about given up on God, but she was beginning to realize He hadn't given up on her.

It was way past time to pray.

The hunters Anton had set on Star's trail began their search on an equal basis from the same location— Centennial Hill Hospital.

After that, money was flying fast and loose as they paid people off to let them look at the security cameras at their businesses, checking with the locals who lived on the streets, trying to be the first one to get that hit on her trail.

It was a female bounty hunter who was the first to think of checking resale stores where Star might have changed her clothes. A good two hours had passed before she found the used clothing store where Star Davis had made her purchases. At that point she no longer had a description of what she was wearing. The clothing store didn't have a security camera, so she only had the clerk's description to go on, and it was pathetically random. A T-shirt, pants. No details at all. Star Davis would be even harder now to find.

A different bounty hunter found a pharmacy clerk who said he recognized Star's description, and that she was in the store earlier that day. But he couldn't remember what she'd bought, and the store would not give them access to the security cameras without ID, no matter how much money they offered.

Most of the hunters assumed Star would try to transform her appearance beyond clothing. They began scrambling, looking for motels where she could hide out long enough to make the changes.

They were racing the clock and each other, when word spread that someone had found her. But disappointment quickly turned to elation when it turned out to be a false alarm.

The bounty hunter had captured a Star look-alike, but he realized he'd forgotten to check her back for wounds until too late, and when he found perfectly smooth skin instead, he'd had to let the girl go with a warning to keep her mouth shut. No one had to tell the hooker twice. The hunt was still on.

Cops soon heard from their snitches that there was a bounty on Star Davis's head, and that Anton Baba had conveniently disappeared from the city. When the

FBI found out about the hunt, they upped their game, as well.

Gleason was already kicking himself for not heeding the girl's earlier warning. They should have taken her straight out of the hospital and to hell with worrying about letting Baba know they were building a case against him. Now that she was gone, there was no more pretending. And unless they found her, there was no more case.

It was almost sundown when Nick found out Star Davis was responsible for setting off the sprinklers after taking out the guard Baba had on her door. And, if what his partner texted him was true, Baba had put out a half-million-dollar bounty for her safe return, which meant every bounty hunter and creep in the city would be on her trail. But what if Star actually got away? No way could Baba stay in Vegas if he knew the Feds had her again. But would he leave the country immediately, or play it safe and eliminate all the loose ends beforehand?

Quinn was one of those loose ends. Baba would assume she could tie one of his men to what happened out in the desert.

Nick was still reeling from the shock of knowing what her life had been like, and since she had no one to speak up for her, he'd already made it his business to take care of her before the world fell down around her again. He needed to talk to his lieutenant. Despite the late hour, he quickly made the call, and when his lieutenant answered with less than enthusiasm in his voice, Nick was braced for the worst.

"Saldano, something better be on fire again for you to be calling me at this time of night."

"I'm sorry, sir, but there's a situation here. Is it true Baba has put a bounty on Star Davis's head?"

"That's what I was told."

"Am I still ordered to be off duty?" Nick asked.

"I'd ask you if you're home in bed resting like you were told, but I suspect you aren't. But, yes, you are *officially* off duty."

"Thank you, sir," Nick said. "And just for the record, I am going home."

Nick hung up, buzzed the nurses' station to ask for help, then stood in the hall outside the door, waiting for someone to show up.

It wasn't long before a nurse was hurrying over to him.

"Is everything okay?" she asked.

"I'm checking Miss O'Meara out tonight. The situation regarding her safety has escalated, and I need to move her. Unfortunately, I can't wait for her doctor's permission, so I'm just letting you know. What I need right now is for you to show us the quickest way out of here without being seen."

"She doesn't have any clothes. If she's walking down the street in an open hospital gown, that's going to be pretty conspicuous," the nurse said, tapping her foot for a moment as she thought. "We're pretty close to the same height. I'll be glad to donate a set of scrubs if it would help?"

"That would be great," Nick said. "You're helping me save her life."

"I'll be right back," the nurse said, then turned and ran.

Nick went back inside to wake Quinn. He hated to disturb her because it had taken so long to get her settled down after she'd cried herself to sleep, but necessity took precedence.

He leaned over her bed and gently shook her.

"Quinn, honey, I need you to wake up," he said.

Quinn's eyes fluttered open. "What's wrong?"

"I'm checking you out of the hospital. There's been a change in the case, and I want you gone from here with as few witnesses as possible."

She didn't ask what was happening. She didn't panic. She just reached for his arm, and he was relieved at the sense of trust she seemed to place in him.

"Put down the guardrail for me. I want to go to the bathroom."

"All your stuff is still with your bike, but a nurse is bringing you a set of scrubs so you'll have something to wear," he said as he lowered the safety rail.

Quinn finger-combed her hair and then swung her legs over the side of the bed and let Nick help her down.

"I've got this," she said and slowly made her way to the bathroom.

By the time she came out, the nurse was waiting with the change of clothes, and Nick was on the phone with Hospital Security.

Quinn was trying to get dressed when Nick got off the phone. She had the pants on, but because of her shoulder wound she couldn't get the top on over her head.

"Just put your hospital gown back on over the pants,

Queenie. We're not stopping anywhere, so you'll be fine until we get where we're going."

Grateful for the reprieve, she reached for the gown and let the nurse tie it at the back of her neck and at her waist again.

Nick grabbed a blanket from her bed, draped it over her head and shoulders and helped her into the wheel-chair.

"Now pull the blanket around your face, lower your head as if you're asleep and don't talk. We need to hide that pretty red hair—it's too easy to identify you."

She gave him a thumbs-up, dropped her head and pulled the blanket tight beneath her chin.

The nurse pushed Quinn out of the room with Nick matching her pace as she quietly moved them to an elevator the public wasn't allowed to use. They rode down in silence. When the car doors opened, they were met by four hospital security guards. She pushed Quinn out, gave Nick a thumbs-up as he took control of the wheelchair and then took the elevator back up.

"Detective," one of the security guards said as he nodded at Nick. "My name's Walker. My boys and I have got your back. Get your car. We'll bring her out that door as soon as we see you pull up."

Nick hated to leave her alone, but there was no other way to make this happen.

He knelt in front of her.

"Okay, Queenie... I'm going after your coach. Hang with the royal guards for a few, and I'll be right back."

In spite of a new wave of panic she felt at having him leave her side, he'd made her smile.

As he exited the building, the security guards encircled her.

Eight

Star was anxious. It had been forty-five minutes since she'd called her parents. She wasn't sure how her rescue was going to happen, but she had to believe they wouldn't let her down. This would likely be her last chance at freedom.

She pulled the curtain aside, but saw nothing except city traffic and a few pedestrians walking on the street beyond the motel.

Her heart was beginning to thump erratically. The fear of failing to get away again was overwhelming. The skin on her back felt as though it was pulling, almost like it was shrinking. She knew the sensation was a result of the alcohol she'd poured on her wounds, but it was better to be uncomfortable than get an infection that would slow her down.

She went back to the bathroom to see if the wounds had dried up again. She couldn't see all of her back but what she could see wasn't pretty. There were scabs trying to form and staples on a half-dozen different places—they'd told her forty in all. That Nevada desert shit was almost as mean as Anton Baba. She would be scarred for the rest of her life, but it wouldn't matter if she and Sammy got to safety.

Deeming her back dry enough to get dressed again, she slipped into the sports bra and pulled the well-worn T-shirt over her head. The fabric was soft, close to threadbare in places, and would do as little damage to her back as possible. She put her shoes back on, got Luis's gun from the backpack and turned out all of the lights except for in the bathroom. She sat down in a chair against the wall where she'd be out of the line of fire if someone came through the door shooting.

She took a deep, shaky breath and glanced at the clock beside the bed. The hour she was told to wait had come and gone.

Her heart was thumping harder.

"God, please let this be okay."

They came into Las Vegas in a convoy. Eight dark blue Chevrolet Impalas with Nevada Highway Patrol insignia on their doors driving bumper to bumper, but devoid of flashing lights and sirens, down the main drag. In spite of the high energy and the myriad of colored and flashing lights from businesses and Lucky Joe's Casino, their dark and silent presence was obvious.

Inside the cruisers, the radios were silent. The officers driving the cruisers had volunteered for this rescue mission. They knew there was a connection to Anton Baba with this case, and that the mission could go sour at a moment's notice. But they'd been told a brother officer was going to rescue his sister who'd been missing for the past seven years, and that was all they'd needed to hear.

Officer Justin Davis, a four-year veteran of the force, was in the lead car, following GPS directions to get to the address his father had given him.

He was still in shock from the phone call, and like his parents, he had pretty much given his baby sister up for dead long ago. He didn't know what was waiting for them upon arrival, but he was ready for it. It would be the ride of his life if Starla was really at the end of it—waiting for someone to take her home.

The night she disappeared was as fresh in his mind as if it had happened yesterday. He'd had nightmares for over a year afterward, imagining her crying out for help and no one coming. He didn't remember when the family began to act as if she was dead, but for years now she was always spoken of in the past tense. If this rescue played out, it would be nothing short of a miracle.

The GPS told him to take the next right, and as he did, he glanced up in the rearview mirror, grateful for the backup behind him. He took a left turn at the next stoplight. The motel would be four blocks down on his right. He could hardly believe his sister was really this close. When he finally saw the neon light of the motel sign, his gut knotted.

He flipped the turn signal, and as he drove into the parking lot, he began reciting the details his dad had given him in his mind. Seven doors down from the office, window facing the street, room 107. There weren't any parking spaces, but that didn't matter. Justin wheeled his cruiser behind the car parked in front of 107, while the other seven officers fanned out beside him and parked.

Justin checked the rearview mirror again. Their abrupt and silent arrival had caught the interest of people walking the streets. Some were slowing down; others had come to a complete stop, curious as to what was happening. That many patrol cars in one place was unusual, especially since highway patrol territory was the roads and interstates. He couldn't do anything about their presence, but as long as the curious kept their distance they'd be fine.

He got out with his weapon drawn, slipping between the cars, as did the officers behind him.

Justin motioned for two patrolmen to stay outside as guards, then pounded the door with his fist and called out loudly, "Nevada Highway Patrol. Open the door!"

Sitting alone in a darkened room would normally have made Star sleepy, but she was too sore and scared to close her eyes. When she heard the knock she nearly flew out of her chair, but then she heard her brother's voice and felt an instant flood of relief and hope. One quick glance through the peephole was all it took. Her knees went weak.

Justin!

Forgetting she still held the gun, she unlocked the door and seconds later the room was flooded with police, all yelling at her.

"Drop your weapon! Drop your weapon!"

She had not even remembered she was still holding it and immediately laid it on the floor.

Her brother's voice sounded cold and angry as he grabbed her by the wrist.

"Where's Star Davis? What have you done with her?" he yelled.

She was shaking so hard her body was swaying.

"Justin, it's me! I told Daddy to tell you I was in disguise. Didn't he tell you?"

Justin stared at the woman standing before him in disbelief.

"Starla?"

She nodded and held his gaze firmly, waiting for some sign of recognition.

"Oh, my God," he whispered suddenly. Then he pulled her into a hug.

But the moment his arms slid against her back she screamed out in pain.

Justin immediately let her go, then turned and pointed at his team.

"Close the door and hit the lights!" he ordered, then grabbed Star by the arms. "What's wrong with you?"

She shrugged out of his grasp as the lights came on, then turned her back to the room and pulled the old T-shirt over her head.

She heard the officers gasp. One cursed softly beneath his breath. One cleared his throat.

When Justin spoke, his voice was shaking. "Sweet Mother of God! Sis...what happened to you?"

She lowered her shirt and turned back to face him. "I was in FBI custody when Anton's men caught up to us. They shot at the car we were in. It started rolling and... Sammy and I were thrown out of the open sun-roof. I guess I slid across a lot of desert."

There was a muscle ticking at the side of Justin's eye, the only outward sign of his distress.

"We need to get you out of here *now*. I'm going to cuff you and take you out as a prisoner. We want this to look like a regular arrest, in case any of Anton's hunters are out there. We don't want anyone to realize we have you. So keep your head down. Don't look up no matter what."

"I need my backpack," she said.

Justin handed it off to one of the officers as she turned and let him cuff her.

She was in tears.

"Thank you—all of you. I've dreamed of this moment for seven years, and there aren't enough words to express what this means to me."

Each of the officers nodded in respect as Justin led her past them. One touched her arm, another her hand, simple gestures to let her know they heard and understood.

Then the door was open, and they were on the move. With no wasted motion, he put her in the back seat of his cruiser, buckled her in as he would have any suspect they'd taken into custody, but before he backed out, he quickly unlocked the cuffs and closed the door.

"Let's do this," he said to the men, and within moments they were all back in the cruisers.

The sound of eight high-powered vehicles starting up at once echoed within the confines of the parking lot.

Justin led the way out, back through the streets of Las Vegas and then out of the city. The moment they passed the city limits sign, they hit their lights and sirens and were doing eighty miles an hour when they disappeared into the night.

Nick gave Quinn a quick glance as he slid behind the wheel. His head was pounding. He patted his pocket to make sure he hadn't left the bottle of pain pills behind, then turned up the air conditioner to cool off the car a little faster. She was sitting so still...almost too quiet. He had yet to explain why this was happening in the middle of the night and guessed she was nervous.

"Are you okay? I can recline the seat if you'd feel better lying down?" he asked.

"No, I'm okay. Just uneasy about this. What's going on?"

Nick put the car in gear, and as he drove away, he began to explain what he'd learned about the fire alarm and the sprinklers, and the bounty on Star Davis's head.

Quinn was quiet for so long after Nick stopped talking that he was wondering if he'd said too much. As he stopped for a red light, he absently noted a convoy of Nevada Highway Patrol cars passing through the intersection and was wondering why so many were in the city at this time of night when Quinn finally spoke.

"She's tough, isn't she, Nick?"

"Who? Star?"

"Yes. She knew testifying for the Feds would be dangerous, but she loved her baby enough to take the chance to make a new life for them. And she's still taking chances, willing to do anything to change her life. I hope she gets away...far, far away. And I hope Anton

Baba winds up in prison somewhere…or dead. Preferably dead. People who do what he does don't deserve another chance."

"It's my job to find and capture the bad guys and bring them in…but I'm not going to argue," Nick said.

"I've been afraid. I ran," she said.

The quiet tone in her words reminded him of what she'd said about her past. Some horrors could only be talked about in whispers. He reached across the seat and gave her hand a quick squeeze.

"It took you a while to do it, but you ran straight into my arms. I'm still trying to come to terms with the odds of this happening, although I probably shouldn't be surprised. This *is* the city for luck and playing the odds."

Then the light turned green and he drove on.

Again she stayed silent as he steered into the flow of traffic. After a few minutes more of trying to stay awake, Quinn leaned her head back against the headrest.

"Are we far from your home?" she asked.

"No, not far at all."

"Do you live in an apartment?"

He smiled.

"No. I have what's called a Spanish-style bungalow. Three bedrooms, with some bells and whistles. You'll have your own room with a private bath."

"It sounds like heaven, but I don't want to wear out my welcome."

"That's not going to happen unless you snore. I'm the only one allowed to snore in my house."

She smiled.

"You make me laugh, Nick Saldano."

"You will learn that I have a full repertoire of amazing skills."

Her laugh was soft, but he heard it. It felt good to know he'd taken her mind off the fact that Anton Baba knew her name.

It wasn't until he finally turned onto his street that he began to relax. When he saw his house, he tapped the remote for the garage door, and it was already going up as he turned into the driveway.

Quinn was wide-eyed now and taking notice of all the houses on the block. They all had some kind of security light on except for his. Seeing Nick's home by moonlight gave it a hint of secrecy.

The light from the garage door opener was dim as he pulled into the garage, but light enough to see her Harley up against a wall and the duffel bag still tied down on the back.

"My bike! Oh, thank you for taking care of it. It's basically my whole life right there."

He hit the remote to close the door, and as it was going down, he brushed the back of his finger along her cheek.

"Hey… I said I would. Don't doubt the cop in the car beside you. Sorry everything is so dark, but I haven't been home in days…actually, not since you walked into Homicide and turned my world upside down."

"I'm not afraid of the dark," Quinn said. "Besides, you're light enough for me."

Nick was so moved by the declaration that it took him a few moments to speak. Then he reached for her hand.

"You were always special to me, and nothing has changed that. I know you're scared. I'm scared for you. But it's no longer just you against the world. You have me, and we have the entire Las Vegas police force on our side. I can't promise the rest of this is going to be smooth sailing, but I can promise you won't bear it alone."

Quinn nodded. Blinking back tears, she unbuckled the seat belt and grabbed the blanket in her lap.

Nick aimed a remote and deactivated the security alarm, then hit another button that turned on a few lights inside.

"I'll show you to your room and then come back for your things while you get settled in, okay?"

"Yes."

Shaky and exhausted, Quinn let him help her into the house.

She caught glimpses of dark wood and warm red tiles on the floor as they moved through the kitchen, and overstuffed leather furniture in the living room off to her right as he led her down a hall.

The energy in the house was calm. She would be safe within these walls. When she was a child, Nick and safety were synonymous. Despite their unexpected reunion, it seemed nothing had changed.

"This is my bedroom," he said, pointing to the open door on the right. "Yours will be the next one on the left."

The lights in this room were not programmed into his remote, so he flipped the switch on the wall and then stepped aside for her to enter.

"I have a great cleaning lady, so I trust everything in here is in good shape. The bathroom is through that door. There's a shower and a tub, plus a linen closet with towels and washcloths."

He led the way into the bathroom, opening drawers to show her where extra toiletries were kept and where the night-light was so she wouldn't be stumbling around in the dark.

And all the while was watching Quinn's face. Her silence was unnerving, and he was hoping she wasn't suddenly uneasy about being alone with him.

"There's also a lock on your bedroom door," he added in case it might reassure her.

Quinn looked up at him then, and he realized there were tears in her eyes.

"I'm not afraid of you," she said quietly and then walked into his arms and laid her head on his chest. "Thank you for this…for a safe place to be while I heal."

"Anytime. Always," he said and kissed the top of her head. "I'm going after your things. I'll turn down the bed as I go so it's ready when you are."

He gave her a gentle hug, careful not to hurt her shoulder, and left her in the bathroom, closing the door behind him as he went. She heard him moving around the bedroom, then heard him walking away. She had washed up and was already in bed when he came back with her duffel bag.

"I'm going to put this on the desk so you won't have to bend over to get to your things in the morning. I have my pain pills if you need one, and I'll call the doctor tomorrow to get your meds."

"Thank you," Quinn said, watching as he moved about the room adjusting the curtains and lights.

She couldn't get over the fact that they were back in each other's lives, or that she was in the guest room in his home.

Nick leaned over and lightly kissed her on the cheek.

"Welcome to my home. Sleep until you're ready to get up."

She wanted to hug him, but didn't.

"I am so grateful," she said.

"I'm the one who's thankful to be able to help you," he said and headed for the doorway, only to pause at the foot of her bed.

"You are a very beautiful woman, Quinn O'Meara," he said, and then he turned out the light and closed the door.

Quinn shivered. Part of her wanted him to come back and explain what that meant but was too afraid it meant nothing. She nestled down into the pillows beneath her head, eyeing the room again. This time it was in shadows, lit only by the night-light in the bathroom. After years of apartment hopping, she couldn't remember the last time she'd slept in a real home.

The house was quiet. A neighborhood dog was barking somewhere down the block. The glow from the streetlights coming through the closed blinds left thin slashes of light on the darkened walls. She was in Nick Saldano's house and she was safe. She took a deep breath and closed her eyes.

After the constant bustle of the hospital and the messages on the nurses' intercom interrupting her sleep, the silence wrapped around her like a hug. She touched the place on her cheek where Nick had kissed her and let go.

The next time she woke, the sun was up and the comforting scent of coffee filled the room.

Anton had gone to the TomCat Club, one of the houses he ran outside of Vegas. He'd availed himself of one of the new girls and spent the whole time thinking Star was better than this and sent her away after he tired of her. He was still asleep when his cell phone began to ring. He rolled over, saw that it was already almost 9:00 a.m. and frowned. He never slept this late. The phone rang again but without an ID. He wasn't going to answer it, then remembered his life was not stable enough to ignore anything and reached for the receiver.

"Hello."

"Your girl's not in Vegas."

"Who is this?" he snapped.

"Just a guy doing you a favor. Star's gone. Word is she got picked up."

"And you're telling me this, why? Because you're such a Good Samaritan?"

"I'm telling you this so you won't hurt Luis Alvarez for letting her get away."

"Who is this?" Anton snapped.

"Just another Alvarez who appreciates your generosity toward my siblings."

"Okay, I hear you and thank you for the info," Anton said.

The line went dead.

Anton's belly was in knots. He guessed she'd been

picked up by the Feds, and this time there was no chasing after her. It was time to leave the country.

A couple of hours later he was packed and ready to go, with just a few loose ends to tie up. He called the hospital to check on Luis's condition and learned he was still in ICU. He left info with the billing office to send the charges to him as a signal to Luis that they were okay with each other. Now it was time to check in on the one person other than Star who could do some real damage to him right now. The woman who'd witnessed the car crash.

"Transfer me back to the main office," he told the woman on the phone. "I need to inquire about another patient."

"Yes, sir. One moment, please," the billing clerk said.

Anton got a couple of minutes of music and then another voice in his ear.

"Centennial Hill Hospital. How may I direct your call?"

"I need to get the current status on a friend who is a patient there," he said.

"One moment," the operator said, and again Anton got the hold music.

"Centennial Hill Hospital. How can I help you?"

"I would like the current status of a friend. Her name is Quinn O'Meara."

"Yes, sir. Let me check," she said, then moments later, "Oh… I'm sorry, sir. We don't have anyone here by that name."

Anton's heart skipped a beat. "Check again," he demanded.

A moment of quiet, and then the clerk confirmed what Anton already suspected—she'd been discharged.

"Damn it!" he yelled, throwing the phone down on his bed and shoving a hand through his hair in angry frustration. "Son of a bitch. I bet the Feds have her up, too."

Now the urgency he felt to leave was overwhelming. The car he'd called from home to come pick him up was outside, waiting to take him to the private airport where he kept his jet, and he was digging his passport out of the briefcase when the phone rang again. This time there was a name on caller ID, and it made him groan.

"For God's sakes! Will this shit ever end?" he muttered, then took a deep breath to collect himself and answered the call.

"Good morning, Mr. Stewart."

"Good morning, Anton. I have a firm delivery date for the products you needed."

"Right…about those products. It appears I won't be here to take delivery after all, so I won't be wanting them at this time."

"What do you mean, you don't want them?" Stewart snapped.

Anton's voice rose in unchecked anger.

"Exactly what I said. I have a situation I'm dealing with, and I don't want to mess with a whole new delivery right now."

"That's all well and good for you, big shot. But that's not good for me," Stewart snapped again. "You've just proved to me that I can't trust you to keep your word."

Anton frowned. He didn't like to be challenged like

this, but Stewart was a man of mystery, and Anton didn't know enough about him to push any further.

"All I can say is I'm sorry," Anton said. "I'll let you know when I'll be available."

"We're not done here," Stewart said and hung up.

A niggle of concern pushed at Anton's conscience, but he let it go and called to have his luggage taken to the limo.

He called his home, left word with his housekeeper to tell people he was on a business trip, and then he was off.

But the trip to the airport became yet another issue—they got stuck behind an accident and were trapped in a long line of traffic while ambulances removed the injured and tow trucks removed the wrecked vehicles. Finally one lane was opened to traffic, and the line slowly began to move.

Anton kept looking over his shoulder the whole time they were there. The impending hand of the law was far too close on his ass.

By the time they reached the airport he was short-tempered and shouting even though there was no need. His pilot, Paul Franklin, met him at the top of the boarding ramp.

"Welcome aboard, Mr. Baba."

"Get me in the air ASAP," Anton muttered.

"Absolutely, sir," the pilot said. Then he added, "There was a situation here. As I was driving in I saw a man staked out watching this airport. He's still there, up on the ridge as you drive in. I'm sure he saw this car and probably you getting out. I just thought you should know in case…"

Anton tossed his briefcase onto a section of seating along the wall and grabbed his phone.

"Thank you. I'll take care of it," he said.

The pilot nodded and left as Anton sat down in his flight seat beside his dining table and buckled up, then waved away the flight attendant.

"Not yet," he said.

She turned and walked away as he made his call.

"Hello, Mr. Baba."

"I have a problem at my airport. Get out here ASAP. There is a man in an old green Jeep up on the ridge as you drive in. I want him gone."

"Yes, sir."

"How soon can you get here?"

"Within the next ten minutes."

"We won't take off until it's done. Call me."

"Yes, sir."

He disconnected, then buzzed the pilot, who'd already fired up the engines.

"Don't take off until I say so."

"Yes, sir," he said.

Anton wiped a hand across his face in frustration. All of this shit was getting on his nerves.

"Linda! Bring me a drink."

The flight attendant entered within seconds, bringing Anton his usual in-flight drink of choice—two shots of whiskey, neat—and mini-Bavarian pretzels, heavy on the salt, in a cut-glass crystal dish.

Anton eyed the woman who'd been serving him in

this capacity for as long as he'd been in Las Vegas. Logic told him she must be in her midforties by now, but she still looked like the young, vivacious girl she'd been when he hired her.

"Thank you, Linda."

"You're welcome, sir. Would you like me to bring you something to eat? We have the Gulf shrimp on ice that you like and some rare roast beef with horseradish sauce."

Anton took a sip of the whiskey and leaned back with a sigh of relief.

"Shrimp cocktail and a roast beef sandwich. Sounds perfect."

"Yes, sir. I'll have it to you soon after the pilot reaches flight altitude."

"We're not leaving yet, so hold off for a bit."

"Yes, sir," she said and walked out.

Anton sipped on his whiskey and nibbled at the pretzels while waiting for that text.

Five minutes came and went, and then ten. He was getting antsy when his phone suddenly dinged, signaling a text.

It is done.

He buzzed the pilot again.

"Take off now, please, and hurry."

"Yes, sir, Mr. Baba."

Anton buckled up.

"This is your captain. We are getting ready to taxi for takeoff. Take your seats and buckle up, please."

Linda made sure Anton was situated and then went to her seat and buckled herself in.

Anton had visions of the Feds somehow stopping takeoff and boarding his plane, then hauling him away in cuffs. It wasn't until he felt the plane go airborne that he finally relaxed.

Nine

Nick was in the kitchen making breakfast when his doorbell rang. He glanced at the clock and frowned: 8:04 a.m.

"Who the hell comes visiting at this time of the morning?" he muttered, then set the skillet of bacon off the fire and went to find out. He glanced down the hall as he passed, looking to see if the sound had awakened Quinn, but her door was still closed.

The doorbell rang again.

"I'm coming, I'm coming!" he said to himself and then looked through the peephole and groaned.

He was about to catch hell. Might as well start off with a smile.

"Hey! Aunt Juana… Uncle Tonio…just in time. Coffee's done, and you must have smelled the bacon cooking. Come in, come in!"

Juana was just a little over five feet tall, but she came across like a Titan when she was upset, and today her voice was high-pitched and scolding.

"Look at you with this bandage on your head! You get shot and you don't call us? Who does this?"

"Your nephew the cop does this," Nick said, then swung her off her feet and into his arms until she started laughing and begging to be put down.

He did so, with a kiss on her cheek.

She spent a couple of minutes fussing with her dress and patting her hair.

"You are a *loco popo!*" she said, wagging her finger in his face.

Nick threw back his head and laughed. *Popo*, the slang word for cop, cracked him up. Crazy cop fit him far better than he would have cared to admit.

"Good morning, Uncle Tonio! You knew she was going to chew me out, and you brought her anyway?"

His uncle, who wasn't a whole lot taller than his wife, chuckled and gave Nick a big hug.

"It looks like that was a close call, *mi hiho*. So glad you are okay."

Nick ran a finger along the bandage.

"So am I, but you've both fussed enough. Come to the kitchen with me. I need to finish cooking bacon. I have a convalescing houseguest to feed."

"Someone else is shot besides you?" Tonio asked.

"Yes, but not at the same time. She was shot first. Then I was shot when the bad guy came to the hospital to finish her off."

Juana made the sign of the cross.

"*Madre de Dios.* Who is this person?"

"Just a thug and he's dead. Let it go. It's part of the job, and I'm fine and she's healing."

Juana's dark eyes flashed.

"Why do you have a stranger in your house? Why is she not healing in a hospital where she belongs?" she asked.

Nick was turning bacon as he talked. He needed to explain this right. It mattered to him that they like her.

"She's not a stranger, and she isn't safe in the hospital. And she has no one in the world to belong to, Aunt Juana…except me."

Juana frowned. "This is the first I'm hearing that you have a woman in your life."

"It's not like that. She's an old friend…from my life before. We were foster kids together in the same family for almost two years. The one where I lived when you guys came for me."

"And she just found you?" Tonio asked.

"Not like you mean. It was about as random as a chance meeting could be. She staggered into Homicide with a bullet wound in her back and a toddler zipped up inside her jacket. She fainted in my arms. Look, the less you know about this case, the better. Just know that she was way out in the desert when she saved a baby's life and got hurt in the process."

"She sounds like quite a hero. When do we meet her?" Tonio asked.

"Here I am. Look all you want," Quinn said.

They all turned in unison to see the leggy redhead in scrub pants and a wrinkled shirt standing in the doorway.

Juana and Tonio were a bit taken aback. She was very tall, and all that red hair gave her something of a wild, exotic look. She had a sling on her arm, but she looked less like a victim than anyone they'd ever seen.

Nick was eyeing her too, but with appreciation.

"Good morning, Quinn," he said.

"Morning. Sorry to interrupt. I could just really use a cup of coffee and one of those pain pills."

Nick could tell by her narrowed eyes and the way she was cradling her arm in the sling that she was hurting.

"You got it, honey. Oh… Aunt Juana, Uncle Tonio, this is my friend Quinn O'Meara. Quinn, my aunt and uncle, Juana and Antonio Chavez."

Nick handed the kitchen tongs to his aunt.

"Aunt Juana, would you please finish the bacon for me? Uncle Tonio, if you would pour Quinn a cup of coffee, I would appreciate it."

He led Quinn to a seat at his kitchen table. "You sit. I'll be right back with the pills." Then he loped out of the kitchen, leaving the trio to deal with the awkward moment.

But Juana also saw the pain on the woman's face and her mothering instincts kicked in.

"Tonio! *Andale!* Get her coffee…and a napkin. Don't forget a napkin."

Tonio smiled as he set a cup of hot coffee in front of Quinn.

"It is good to meet you, Quinn. Do you take sugar or cream?"

"No, thank you. Just black," she said and smiled.

Nick hurried back into the kitchen with the pill bottle in his hand, shook one out and handed it to her, then set the bottle on the counter as Juana took the last pieces of bacon from the skillet.

"Thank you, Aunt Juana," Nick said and set her down at the table with a cup of coffee before she took over his whole kitchen.

"Hey, Quinn…want your eggs scrambled or fried?" he asked.

"I'll have mine however you eat yours," she said.

Juana rolled her eyes.

"Then that would be by the dozen."

Quinn grinned.

"Two will be sufficient," she said.

"Good. That leaves the rest of them for me," he said and began breaking eggs into a bowl while his aunt grilled him about his head wound.

Quinn was taken by his family. It was obvious how much Nick meant to them and how much they meant to Nick. She was glad they'd taken her presence so matter-of-fact and weren't asking her questions she didn't want to answer.

"Uncle Tonio? Aunt Juana? Do you want some breakfast?" Nick asked.

"Thank you, but we already ate," Juana said.

"I would eat some toast and jelly," Tonio offered.

Juana glanced at his belly and frowned, but he ignored her.

Quinn hid a smile. It was obvious both men adored the little woman no matter how loud and fussy she became.

Nick set a plate of bacon on the table and then absently pushed a long curl away from her eye. He started to pull his finger away and then chuckled.

"What's funny?" Quinn asked.

"Your hair is alive. It's curling around my fingers."

"You should see it when it rains. It becomes this red monster, impossible to tame."

"I like my women wild," he said beneath his breath, then quickly turned to get her food before she could respond.

The toast Tonio wanted popped up in the toaster on the counter. He slid them onto a plate and carried it to the table. Quinn saw him eyeing the bacon and quietly pushed the plate to where he could reach it.

He winked when he saw what she was doing.

She grinned and then tuned in to the fuss going on at the stove. Nick was arguing on her behalf.

"Aunt Juana, Quinn might not like my eggs if they are too hot."

"Don't worry about the heat on my account," Quinn said. "I lived a whole year in Mexico. As the old man I worked for used to say, 'It can't get too hot for me. I done burnt the hair off my tongue years ago.'"

Laughter followed, but what was funnier to Quinn was watching Juana take the bottle of hot sauce out of Nick's hands and shake more into the eggs. The byplay between them was adorable. Their love for each other was obvious. She kept thinking what a stroke of luck it was for Nick that they found him when they did.

Unaware he was the object of Quinn's attention, Nick dished up the eggs, added toast on both plates and took them to the table.

As soon as he was dressed, he called headquarters to see who was staked out at Baba's private airport, then got contact information and put in the call.

He was walking to the kitchen to get a coffee to go as he waited for the call to pick up. Instead it went to voice mail. He frowned, got in his car and drove in to the office and then made the call again—again it went to voice mail.

He told himself there were any number of reasons why the agent wouldn't answer, but this was Anton Baba they were dealing with, and it bothered him. He thought about sending someone out to check on him, but then decided, *what the hell, I'll do it myself.* He called his boss to tell him where he was going, grabbed his coffee and left the building.

The day was already hot, and it was barely past 8:00 a.m. when he drove out of the parking lot and back into traffic. He kept thinking back through the entire case, from the time they put Agent Lacey Lane under-cover, to the night she and Agent Ryker were murdered. Losing them and the witness they needed had been a blow to the whole team. It was another home run for Baba, an out for them, and downhill ever since.

He took the exit off the highway that led out to the private airport and then grabbed his sunglasses as he turned east into the sun. It was still glaring on the hood of his car and into his eyes when he topped the ridge above the airport.

He saw the old green Jeep, which was what he'd expected, but he didn't see a driver sitting in the seat. He pulled up behind the Jeep and parked. He was getting ready to get out when he happened to look up through the windshield and saw a buzzard circling overhead and another one higher up.

It doesn't have to mean anything.

The moment he opened the door, he smelled something dead. The hair rose on the back of his neck as he reached for his gun and began to approach.

"Chalmers! Agent Chalmers! This is Agent Gleason. Are you there?"

No answer.

The Jeep was empty. The keys were still in the ignition, and binoculars were lying in the seat beside a cell phone and a notepad and pen.

"Son of a bitch," Gleason muttered and started walking up the slope.

Chalmers's body was facedown in the sand and crawling with ants. Gleason turned away before he threw up and contaminated the crime scene, then turned his face to the breeze as he called it in.

Star's night had not passed as calmly as Quinn O'Meara's. While Quinn had been settling in at Nick Saldano's home, Justin Davis and his men parted company as soon as he hit the city limits of Henderson. They drove off in their respective directions without breaking radio silence. As far as they were concerned, this night never happened.

Justin was riding an emotional high and had yet to wipe the smile off his face. His wife, Donna, had seen past Star's clown-colored hair and makeup the moment they met and went into her angel-of-mercy mode. As

nurse, it came natural to her. She cried when they
were introduced, then asked Star what she wanted to
do first. Sleep or eat?

Star couldn't stop shaking. She needed pain meds,
but all she asked for was someone to let her parents
know she was safe.

"They already know," Justin said. "I called them on
the ride home after you fell asleep. What do you need,
honey?"

"Something for pain and a fried egg sandwich."

Donna frowned.

"Where do you hurt?"

"My back," Star said.

"Show her," Justin encouraged.

Star took off her T-shirt and turned around.

Donna gasped.

"Oh, my God! You just had surgery. So many staples. Antibiotics! You need antibiotics as badly as you
need pain meds."

Star pulled her shirt back over her head. She didn't
know what they were thinking and didn't much care,
but they needed to understand where she was coming
from, and this was as good a time as any to explain.

"I survived the last seven years by prioritizing. I have
a son because I chose not to kill myself. I finally saw
a chance to escape with him and trusted the Feds, but
it nearly got us both killed, and it put me back under
Anton's thumb anyway. When I found out he was coming to check me out of the hospital, I knew he intended
to eliminate me so the Feds can't use me as a witness
against him. Since the Feds failed me miserably the

first time, this time I chose to rescue myself. I stabbed my guard in the throat with the plastic knife from my food tray, broke his nose with the butt of his own gun and set a fire in the wastebasket of my hospital room to get away. I've suffered worse pain than what's going on with my back, and with nothing to deaden it, and I'm serious about wanting that sandwich. I'll happily settle for over-the-counter pain pills until I can get to a doctor."

Justin felt like he'd been sucker punched. The self-centered teenage sister he remembered had morphed into a warrior.

"I'll get those pain pills," Justin said.

Donna's hands were shaking.

"I'll fry the eggs. How do you like them?"

"Well-done, please, with mayo."

"You've got it," Donna said and left the room.

For a few moments Star was alone, trying to come to terms with the fact that her brother was a highway patrolman, that she'd just met his wife and was sitting in their living room like any relative who'd just come for a visit. Except that she was on the run and scared to death she might bring Baba into their world because of her presence.

She looked up as Justin came back with a glass of water and a bottle of over-the-counter pain pills. He shook some out in her hand, and she downed them with the water. When she glanced up, she caught Justin staring at her again.

"I'm sorry for staring," he said. "I'm just trying to see you beneath the disguise."

"If you'll show me where the bathroom is, I'll wash it off," she said.

"Sure thing," Justin said, then helped her up and led her down the hall to a bedroom. "This is our guest room, and you've got your own bathroom in here, too."

Star gazed in awe at the four-poster bed with a cream-and-gold bedspread, the thick fluffy rug over gold-flecked tile, and the big windows, now shuttered against the dark.

"This is wonderful. I keep saying thank you, but the words aren't big enough."

Justin shook his head, too close to tears to speak.

Star sighed.

"Tell Donna I'll be there soon. Don't want that sandwich to get cold."

Justin gave her a thumbs-up and left.

Star went to the bathroom, decorated with the same color scheme, and looked through drawers until she found some wet wipes and began cleaning the makeup from her face. Once the bulk of it was gone, she got a washcloth and scrubbed it clean. She couldn't do much about the color on her hair right now. It would have to be shampooed out.

As soon as she was finished, she looked at herself in the mirror. Once again she was naked to the world.

Justin grinned when she walked back into the kitchen, and Donna gasped again.

"Oh, my word! You look like a younger version of your mother."

Star blinked back tears.

"I haven't heard that in years."

"Don't cry! I'm sorry. Here's your sandwich. Would you like milk to go with it?"

"That would be great." Star sat down and pulled the plate close. "Both of you...sit with me and talk."

"What do you want to talk about?" Justin asked.

"Anything but the danger you're in for bringing me here," she said.

"No danger, little sister. We all had permission to participate, but this whole rescue was on the down-low. There isn't a record of it anywhere, and I trust the officers who came with me with my life. As far as their families will be concerned, they were at work as usual. It will never be discussed among them."

"Really?"

Justin heard so much in Star's voice, including a desperate need to believe.

"Yes, honey. Really. And just so you know, Mom and Dad are on their way here. They'll be here tomorrow by midafternoon."

"Oh, my God...that doesn't seem real," she said. "I used to dream about them finding me. I can't believe this is all coming true."

"You'll settle in during the days to come. Right now just eat your sandwich before it gets cold," Donna said.

"I used to dream about these, too," Star said and took a big bite.

"Mmmmm."

Justin grinned.

"I think she likes it."

"I think you're right," Donna said.

Star chewed and swallowed.

"If I ignore the pain on my back and close my eyes, I can almost believe I'm still home in Mother's kitchen eating my after-school snack."

She ate in silence and then went back to her room, crawled between the sheets and tried to sleep, but all she heard was her baby calling for Mama. It was a long night.

She woke the next day, unaware of the ongoing drama back in Las Vegas.

After finding Chalmers dead and getting a phone call from Lou telling him Quinn O'Meara was no longer a patient at Centennial Hill Hospital, he was trying to wrap his head around what that could mean. The thought went through his mind that Anton Baba might have both Star and Quinn. But he remembered the Las Vegas cop in her room, how dedicated he'd seemed to protecting Quinn. He was breathing a little easier as he drove back into Vegas, and waited until he was back at the office before he called the police precinct.

He asked to speak to Detective Saldano, only to be told he was off duty for the time being. That's when he remembered the cop was wearing a bandage on his head. So if the cop was home and the redhead was missing, even if they weren't still together, he was betting the cop knew where she was.

It took one phone call to Dr. Munoz, Quinn's doctor, to get prescriptions ordered, but it took a couple of hours before Nick's local pharmacy called to let him know they were ready.

Tonio and Juana were just getting ready to leave when Nick got the call, and he ran to catch them at the door.

"Uncle Tonio, please do me a favor. Quinn's prescriptions are ready. Would you pick them up for me?"

"Sure!" Tonio said. "Down at the CVS in your neighborhood?"

"Yes. There will be two. I don't know how much they'll be, so take my wallet."

"You got it," Tonio said. "We'll be right back."

"Not that fast. We will be observing the speed limit," Juana snapped.

Tonio shrugged.

"What she said," he muttered, and then they were gone.

Nick shut the door and then paused in the foyer, listening. Quinn had disappeared soon after breakfast with an excuse about brushing her hair, but he had suspected she just wanted to be alone. When he walked into her room and saw she had fallen asleep with the covers down around her waist, he pulled them up over her injured shoulder. He didn't know if she was in pain or if she was dreaming, but there was a slight frown between her eyebrows.

He noticed the duffel bag was no longer on the desk, which meant she'd already settled in. The thought of her in his home made him happy, and he reluctantly left the room.

About a half an hour later Tonio was back with his wallet and the prescriptions.

"Did I have enough cash to cover the meds or do I owe you?" he asked.

"You had enough with some left over."

"Thanks again, Uncle Tonio," Nick said and gave him a quick pat on the shoulder.

"You are most welcome. Call anytime you need me to run another errand. It will give me an excuse to get away from Juana's constant need to keep me busy."

Nick grinned. He already knew the story. Juana had read an article about retirees passing away soon after their retirement because of sudden inactivity, and she took it upon herself to make sure her husband was not another statistic.

A car horn sounded.

Tonio frowned.

"*Madre de Dios*, that woman! I better go."

Nick walked him to the door and waved as they drove away.

He paused as he turned, looking at his house anew—wondering what Quinn thought about it, hoping it would become the place of peace and shelter to her that it was to him.

Ten

It was midafternoon when Anton leaned across the arm of his seat to look out the window of the plane, admiring the geography of what was below him. Nestled between the vast sea of jungle green and the clear blue of the coastal waters was the whitewashed Moroccan-style palace that was his vacation home. The tear-shaped swimming pool was the centerpiece of an elaborate courtyard surrounded by a lush landscape of palms and the vibrant colors of blooming plants.

Seeing it from this angle always gave him a sense of pride. He'd come from nothing to wielding great wealth and power. The fact that his wealth came from young women caught up in a hell not of their own making didn't matter to him. Life was for the strong—for the ones who dared.

The plane tilted slightly as Captain Franklin began to circle for landing at the private airstrip, and Anton leaned back in his seat, momentarily closing his eyes.

He was now officially out of the FBI's reach. His

heartbeat accelerated with anticipation as the plane touched down. In his mind, he imagined he could already smell the ocean.

The plane taxied to a full stop.

Captain Franklin came out of the cockpit and lowered the steps onto the tarmac while Linda began gathering up Anton's things.

He was in a good mood as he began to deplane, and the good mood continued when he saw Jorge Ramirez, the caretaker of his estate, waiting a short distance away with the car.

The sun was brutally hot and, as always, so bright it almost hurt. He adjusted his sunglasses as he started down the steps to the luggage Franklin had placed below.

Jorge was driving toward the plane. He pulled up and got out, moving fast for a man his age as he circled the car to open the door for his boss.

"Welcome, Senor Baba," Jorge said.

"Thank you, Jorge," Anton said as he slid into the back seat into air-conditioning comfort.

"Miss Star and the baby do not come this time?" he asked.

Anton frowned.

"No, not this time," he said.

Franklin loaded the luggage into the trunk, and Linda handed Anton's briefcase and jacket to Jorge.

Anton rolled down the window.

"Paul! I'll be here indefinitely. If I need the plane, I will text you."

"Yes, sir. Thank you, sir," Franklin said.

Anton saw Linda standing in the doorway of the plane. She smiled and waved.

He rolled up the window as Jorge got into the front seat.

"Do you wish to go directly to the main house, sir?"

"Yes," Anton said.

The airstrip was a couple hundred yards from the estate, giving Anton time to admire his empire from the ground.

His massive estate was whitewashed yearly to keep the exterior the blinding white color he preferred. It had been built over two hundred years ago, and the first time he'd set foot on the premises it had given him a strange sense of the past, as if he'd been here before, maybe in another lifetime.

He couldn't help but remember this was also where Sammy was conceived. A slight frown creased his forehead. He still couldn't quite believe Star had betrayed him this way. It was her fault that he would have to hide here now, her fault that his carefully structured life was beginning a downward spiral.

His eyes narrowed angrily.

To hell with that deceptive bitch. It was time to make new memories.

Justin had left the house almost an hour earlier to pick up their parents at the airport, which meant they would be here any minute, and Star was worried about how she looked. Last night she'd washed off all the makeup she'd applied to hide her face, and by the time she'd sat down with her egg sandwich she'd already been starting to feel more like herself. But the wild colors she'd chosen for her hair practically screamed at her in the morning when she'd looked in the mirror. The first thing she wanted was to get rid of the hair dye, but showering it out on her own was impossible. She couldn't take a chance on getting whatever was in that cheap dye into her open wounds. So she took her shampoo and towel and went looking for Donna to ask if she could use the kitchen sink.

"Absolutely!" Donna said. "In fact, you just lean over the sink and I'll do it for you. How's that?"

"Much appreciated," Star said, following Donna into the kitchen.

"Okay… I think that's got it," Donna said after the third wash, and she wrapped a big towel around Star's shoulders to catch the drips as she straightened up.

"Justin picked a winner with you," Star said. "You've been so patient with all of this chaos coming into your lives."

"You're my sister. It's my pleasure," Donna said.

Star swallowed past the lump in her throat.

"I still appreciate it," Star said.

Donna towel-dried Star's hair and then began trying to finger-comb it into place.

"Want me to even up your haircut? I'm pretty good with a pair of scissors," she offered.

"That would be great," Star said, relieved she wouldn't have to wait for the damage she'd done to grow out. "At least make me presentable for my parents."

Donna pulled out a kitchen chair.

"Sit here. I'll go get my scissors and cape."

Star sat as Donna left on the run and came back the same way.

"You have the real deal," Star said, eyeing the hair-cutting scissors and black plastic cape.

"Told you I was pretty good," Donna said. "I made extra money for nursing school by cutting hair for interns and nurses at discount rates."

She fastened the cape around Star's neck, combed through her hair and then began telling stories about nursing school as she cut and clipped and the intern who passed out on top of a body during an autopsy. By the time she was through she had Star laughing. She handed Star a mirror and then stood back to await her opinion.

"What do you think?" Donna asked.

"It's perfect," Star said, and it was—a perfect pixie cut for the shape of her face. "I'm going to get dressed now. It's secondhand chic, but I bought it fair and square with the money I stole off my guard when I rolled him."

Donna's eyes widened. Then a big smile spread across her face as she burst into laughter.

"You have just knocked Scarlett O'Hara off my personal pedestal as favorite heroine. Starla Davis...modern-day warrior. Has a nice ring to it, don't you think?"

Star grinned and was surprised that she *could* smile about all this.

"Not bad at all. I'm going to get dressed. Yell at me if they get here while I'm gone," she said and went to change.

Less than fifteen minutes later Star heard Donna call out.

"They're coming up the drive!"

With one last glance in the mirror, she had to accept she'd done the best she could with what was left of her, and she hurried out of her room to see her family.

She made it as far as the living room, before her nerves stopped her in her tracks. Her heart was pounding so hard she felt faint. Donna gave her a thumbs-up as she walked past Star for the front door to let them in, but Star couldn't move. This was her dream. It was happening, finally, and yet she couldn't move for fear she'd wake up and find out it wasn't real.

She heard footsteps and voices outside the door and reached for the back of the sofa to steady herself.

The door swung inward. Justin was carrying luggage, and she could hear her daddy's voice behind him.

The lump in her throat became a sob.

She got a glimpse of her mother's face, and then everything became a blur of joyful cries and arms reaching toward her.

All of a sudden Justin leaped between them.

"Wait! Mom! Dad! You can't hug her!" he said. "She's hurt!"

The horror on their faces broke Star's heart.

"I don't care if it hurts," she said and walked into her mother's arms and cried.

John couldn't bear it. The two women he loved most in the world were in tears. No way in hell was he just going to stand there. He pulled them close and cried with them.

The Davises talked all the way through the dinner hour and late into the evening before Star's stamina eventually gave out. Everything she'd told them about her recent life had been glossed over or edited down. She could never give voice to all of it. It was enough that she'd survived it.

Her father had been mostly quiet. She guessed it was because he felt guilty that he hadn't been able to find her—he'd hinted at it throughout the evening.

It wasn't until Justin and Donna got up to go make coffee that John moved to a seat on the sofa beside his daughter. Tears welled as he forced himself to meet her gaze.

"I'm…I'm so sorry," he said, his voice catching in his throat.

"You have nothing to be sorry for," Star said.

"I quit believing," he said.

"Oh, Daddy, so did I."

"We thought you were dead."

Star shrugged. "There were many times I wished it…until Sammy. After that, my sole purpose was to stay alive for him."

Connie scooted closer.

"How do we get him back?" Connie asked.

"He's in FBI custody. I have to let them know where I am, and they will bring him to me."

"What about this man… Anton Baba? How can we keep you safe? What if he's trying to find you right now?" John asked.

Star's cheeks reddened in anger.

"I'll testify against him—that's what the FBI has wanted all along. They'll bury him so deep in a federal prison that he'll never see the light of day again. And then I will take my son and live happily ever after."

Nick was at the door paying for the pizza and salads he'd ordered for lunch when a black SUV pulled up in the driveway beside the pizza delivery car.

The hair rose on the back of his neck as he recognized the two men who got out.

Son of a bitch. What are they doing here?

He gave the delivery boy a generous tip, and even though the Feds were halfway to his house, Nick closed the door and took the food into the kitchen, fully aware he'd literally and symbolically shut the door in their faces. He was on the way back to the living room when the doorbell rang. He swung the door inward, then stood blocking their entrance.

"What?" he snapped.

Agents Gleason and Powers blinked. So, they hadn't misread the fact that he'd shut the door on them. It was not the greeting they were expecting.

"May we come in?" Gleason asked.

"Why?" Nick asked.

"Is Quinn O'Meara with you?"

"Yes."

"Well, that's good news," Gleason said.

"Why?" Nick asked again.

"Because it turns out her testimony will help us build a stronger case against Baba after all."

"Shit," Nick muttered.

"Now may we come in?"

"She's asleep. I was just about to wake her up for

lunch. You have five minutes with her, and then you will leave, understand?"

Gleason nodded.

Nick stepped aside to let them in, then led them to the living room.

"Have a seat. I'll go get her."

"Thank you for—"

Nick walked off, leaving Gleason talking to himself. Powers looked at his partner and grinned.

"Pissed off, isn't he?"

Gleason dropped into the closest chair and wiped a hand across his face.

"So am I, but pissed at the way this whole thing was handled. There's nothing to do but admit we made most of this worse by ineffective response time and poor judgment."

Powers sat down in the chair beside him.

"That and the fact that the director chewed the hide off our asses," he said.

Gleason rolled his eyes.

"Yeah, there's that, too," he said, realizing this visit might be more difficult than he had assumed.

Nick pushed the door inward just enough to see if Quinn was still asleep and saw her sitting on the side of the bed, quietly staring out the window. Her expression was pensive and a little sad. He wondered what she was thinking about, but unfortunately, this was not the time to ask. He knocked softly on the door and then pushed it ajar.

"Okay if I come in?" he asked, as she turned toward he door.

"Of course," she said and patted the side of the bed.

He sat down beside her and gave her a brief hug.

"Are you ready for company?"

She frowned.

"Who?"

"The same Feds who came to the hospital," Nick said.

"What do they want now?" she asked.

"To tie you down as a witness, but I'll let them explain the details."

"I thought they'd blown off what I said."

He shrugged.

"Obviously something's come up. Are you ready now, or do you want me to tell them you'll be there shortly?"

"No, I'm ready now. The sooner I get it over with, the better I'll be."

"I already told them they only have five minutes. We have pizza waiting."

Her eyes widened in delight.

"Yum!"

He leaned in and brushed a kiss across her forehead.

"What was that for?" she asked.

"For my selfish pleasure," he said.

She shook her head, but was secretly pleased. Cradling her arm, she stood, then straightened the tail of her shirt and finger-combed her hair.

"Let's go do this," she said, taking comfort in the warmth of his hand against her back as they left the room.

Both of the agents stood when Quinn walked in.

"Miss O'Meara. Thank you for taking the time to speak with us," Gleason began.

Quinn looked back at Nick.

"I didn't know I had an option."

He grinned.

Gleason was just remembering that the last time he'd seen her she'd ordered both of them out of her room.

"So sit," she said shortly and eased herself down on the sofa, then pulled Nick down beside her.

"I know you didn't come to inquire about my health, so what do you want?" Quinn asked.

"I'm sorry we got off on the wrong foot the other day," Gleason said.

"Cut to the chase, please. I don't mean to be rude, but you showed up out of the blue, and I'm not a fan of cold pizza."

"Point taken," Gleason said. "You mentioned the car that followed you into Vegas from the murder site had a shaky headlight and a windshield that appeared to be missing?"

"Yes."

"A vehicle matching that description turned up in an impound yard. We discovered it belonged to Anton Baba and had Dev Bosky's fingerprints all over it."

"Who's Dev Bosky?" she asked.

"The man who tried to kill you in the hospital, which means he was also the one who shot you in the back," Nick said.

Her eyes widened. She was beginning to connect the dots.

"So the fact that I can testify to one of Baba's hired guns being at the scene of the murder has made me valuable enough that you now give a shit if someone tries to murder me again."

Gleason sighed.

"Yes, ma'am, we give a shit. So will you agree to testify if the need arises?"

Quinn glanced at Nick, but he wasn't trying to inject his opinion, for which she was grateful. This was her life, her decision. It just made her happy to know he was beside her.

"Where is Star Davis? What about her testimony?" she asked.

"We don't know where she is," Gleason said.

Nick frowned.

"Do you think Baba got to her again?"

"We don't know," Gleason said. "We don't know where he is, either."

"You mean he skipped out on you?" Nick asked.

"It appears so," Gleason said.

Quinn shook her head in disbelief.

"So far, my faith in the justice system is right where it was when I was seventeen. However, I don't need or want to hear any more. I'll testify."

Gleason decided to leave on a positive note.

"Thank you. We'll be in touch."

"I'd like a card, please," Nick said. "We might need to get in touch with you."

"Of course," Gleason said. "Here's mine."

"And mine," Lou said, handing over one of his cards,

as well. Nick put both of them in his pocket and walked them to the front door.

"Will she be staying here with you?" Gleason asked.

"Yes," Nick said.

They looked back at Quinn.

"Thank you, again, Miss O'Meara. Rest and heal. You'll hear from us soon."

She nodded.

And then they were gone.

Nick closed the door and turned to say something to Quinn, but she was no longer in the room. He headed for the kitchen and caught her with the pizza box open, picking a pepperoni slice off the pie.

"Caught you," he said.

She grinned and pulled one off for him.

"Open wide," she said and popped it in his mouth.

"I'll get the plates," Nick said. "What do you want to drink? Sweet tea or a soda?"

"Sweet tea, please," she said and tore off a couple of sheets from the roll of paper towels near the sink. "Napkins," she added and took them to the table.

"Uncle Tonio picked up your meds from the pharmacy for me. They're on the sideboard behind you. You need the antibiotic now and again tonight, and you can have a pain pill now and then once every six hours."

She shook out the dosages onto the table, then took them with the sweet tea he brought her while he took the lids off of the salads.

"You okay with Italian dressing?"

"Yes, it's my favorite with pizza," she said.

He grinned.

"Mine, too. That settles it, then. We like pizza and the same salad dressing. We were definitely made for each other."

Quinn laughed.

"You are such a nut."

Nick slid a couple of slices of pizza onto her plate and handed her a fork for her salad, then leaned over her shoulder, so close she could feel the warmth of his breath against her cheek.

Her heart was pounding. She didn't know what he was about to do, but it excited her to think about the possibilities.

"Do you want to heat it up?" he asked.

Her ears began to roar.

"Heat what up?" she asked.

He dangled little packets of red pepper flakes in front of her face.

"Your pizza…with pepper flakes. What else did you think I meant?"

She turned and glared.

Now his heart was pounding. Her lips were only inches from his mouth. He watched her pupils dilate and her nostrils flare.

"Quinn?"

"Cheese," she said.

He blinked.

"What?"

"Parmesan. For the pizza."

Now the corners of her lips were twitching. She was playing with him, and it was no more than he deserved.

"You are a glorious redheaded witch, aren't you?" he whispered.

He watched her green eyes blink—once in innocence, then in instant lust, which, thank God, she chose to ignore or he would have taken her there on the table with the pizza box for a pillow.

"Not stirring up any potions today. Take a seat."

He sat. For once he had no comeback for her and took a bite of pizza instead.

"I love pizza," Quinn said.

"Me too," Nick said. "What toppings do you like best?"

"Everything."

He laughed.

"Man, you are easy to please."

Quinn pulled a string of hot cheese off the side of her plate and ate it like a piece of spaghetti.

"I'm easy to please with food, but I'm damn picky about everything and everyone else. Pass me another packet of Parmesan cheese, please."

He shoved all of it within her reach, still thinking about what she'd said.

"You don't have to answer this if you don't want to, but…have you ever been in love?"

She shrugged. "What does that mean? Did I ever have a relationship with a man I wanted to marry? No. Have I had a relationship with a man who treated me good, in and out of bed…yes."

Her answer took him aback. Now he was thinking about making love to her—again. It wasn't the first time he'd thought about it, but it was the first time he'd thought about her with other men and realized he didn't like it.

"So what happened to that guy? The one who treated you well?" Nick asked.

"He wanted to marry me, but I said no."

"Why?"

"Because I didn't love him," Quinn said, finishing off her first piece of pizza. "So to answer your question," she added, reaching for a second slice, "no. I guess I haven't been in love."

There was something in the tone of her voice that made Nick stop asking her questions. He'd been a cop long enough to realize she didn't want to talk about herself anymore.

"I didn't mean to pry."

Quinn looked up.

"No, it's okay. It's just that people never ask me about myself. I always take that as they don't care enough to ask."

"I care."

She grinned.

"I can see that."

"You can ask me anything you want…assuming you care enough to ask," Nick said.

"Really? Anything?"

Nick nodded.

She took a bite of pizza and chewed, considering what she might want to know. She thought of Juana and Tonio, and the way Nick talked about his cousins.

"There's one thing I've always wanted to know, and you're the perfect person to ask."

Nick leaned forward, curious as to what it might be. "Ask away," he said.

"What is it like to belong somewhere?"

Sideswiped. His vision blurred. He looked down at the pizza in his hand and dropped it back onto his plate. His throat was tightening so fast he wouldn't have been able to get it down. He stood up, circled the table and took her in his arms.

Quinn wasn't expecting that reaction, but the moment his arms encircled her something happened. She'd lived her whole life with uncertainty, afraid to be happy for fear it would be taken away. After losing her Nicks, she'd refused to make any new friends…until now. For the first time in her entire life she felt safe. And then she heard Nick's voice in her ear.

"You break my heart."

And just like that, she was back on her own. That wasn't love. It was pity. She wanted to cry. Instead, she twisted out of his embrace.

"Don't feel sorry for me. I don't need that from you," she said and walked out of the kitchen without looking back.

Nick was taken aback. He started to go after her, but he wasn't sure how that explanation would go. How could he explain the regret and guilt he felt? Just because life took them in two different directions didn't mean anyone was at fault. The tragedy was that one of them thrived and the other had suffered. But sometimes life gave people a second chance. He wanted this to be theirs. What she wanted was still the unknown.

Eleven

Quinn was hurt and pissed at herself for thinking there could be some kind of special spark between them. He'd said it himself. She broke his heart. He felt sorry for her. She should have known better. Children didn't keep the same friends or the same heroes forever. It was blatantly obvious their lifestyles were vastly different, and the best thing she could do for herself was step back and let that brief dream of happy-ever-after die.

But as the day wore on, it was obvious Nick wasn't on the same page. He was being too nice. Ignoring her angry outburst as if it never happened. Was he just being a congenial host, or was there more? Used to keeping her feelings to herself, the whole thing was confusing to her, while on the flip side, Nick Saldano was completely comfortable with emotion and man enough not to give a shit what anyone thought about it. She wanted to be like him, but she didn't know how.

And, despite the headache Nick had yet to get rid of from the gunshot wound, he hadn't slowed down. She'd been watching him cleaning the pool for over an hour, admiring his lean muscular body and the warm cast to his olive complexion. The blue tank top he wore clung to his chest in the heat, as did the white swim trunks he was wearing. His wet hair gleamed coal black in the sunshine. He could have been a model. But he was a cop, trying to keep her safe.

The water looked so inviting, but she had the bandage on her shoulder, and he had already explained that keeping her out of sight was the safest thing for her until Anton Baba was arrested. She couldn't argue with that.

While she was daydreaming about his body, he had finished and was heading back inside. Embarrassed that he would catch her watching him, she jumped away from the window and headed for the kitchen counter and grabbed a glass from the cabinet.

But she missed the ultimate denouement, because as soon as Nick finished, he hung up the pool strainer, turned on the pump and then dived headfirst into the pool.

The cool water was a welcome blast against the heat of his skin, and he swam a couple of lengths of the pool for the heck of it before heading indoors, dripping water with every step.

Quinn was putting ice in a glass when he walked in.

"Hey, honey, would you make me one of whatever you're having? Oh, and… I forgot a towel, so if you don't want to be flashed, close your eyes until I get through the kitchen. I'm coming out of these wet clothes so I don't drip all through the house."

She froze, then immediately shut her eyes. The door

to the freezer was still open because she could feel the cold air on her face, which was just as well because her cheeks were getting hot as she imagined what was going on behind her.

Then she heard his footsteps on the kitchen tile, and as he passed behind her he flicked the backs of her legs with the wet tank top and then laughed out loud when it popped.

She yelped and turned around before she realized what she was doing, catching the brief sight of a tight bare butt and long legs before he disappeared. He was still laughing.

She sighed.

Wow.

Now what was it she'd been doing? Oh yes, making something cold to drink. After that little show, she needed something stiffer, but pain pills denied her anything stronger than a cold soda.

She tossed a few ice cubes in a second glass and filled both of them with Pepsi, then put their glasses on the table and was digging through the pantry for a snack when Nick came back and saw her poking about.

"Cookies at your ten o'clock," he said.

She found them and carried the whole container to the table.

"I hope you don't mind that I made myself at home," she said as she took out a couple of oatmeal and raisin cookies.

"I don't mind a bit," Nick said.

There was something in the tone of his voice that

made her look up, and then she didn't know what to do
about what she saw on his face.

It was like watching a lit fuse and wondering how
much longer it would burn before something detonated

And then there was a knock at the door.

Nick grimaced.

"Damn it to hell," he muttered.

Her heart was pounding. She didn't know whether to
be relieved or feel regret that the moment was passing.

Curious, she followed a distance behind and watched
Nick open the door. She couldn't hear what was being
said, but it was obviously someone he knew because the
first thing they did was punch each other on the arm.

Quinn stifled a laugh. Men had the strangest ways
of showing their affection for each other. And then the
man came in, saw her standing in the doorway to the
kitchen and grinned.

"So, Nick, introduce me to your girl," he said.

Nick looked over his shoulder, smiling at Quinn as
she moved toward them, hand extended.

"I'm Quinn O'Meara."

He shook her hand and smiled sincerely. "Santino
Chavez, Nick's cousin. It's very nice to meet you, Miss
O'Meara. I've never met a real heroine before." He
pointed at her shoulder. "Are you going to be okay?"

She was a little startled by the heroine tag, but let
it slide.

"Yes, I'll be fine, and just call me Quinn, okay?"

Nick thumped Santino on the shoulder again and
pointed at the laptop he was carrying.

"So, cousin...did you bring that laptop over here for a reason or just taking it for the ride?"

"Oh. Right. There's a virus on it that I can't get off. Would you fix it for me?"

"If you'd stay off those porn sites this wouldn't keep happening," Nick muttered.

"I do not look at dirty pictures and you know it!" Santino snapped.

"Only because Lara would break your neck if you did," Nick said, laughing. "Let's go to the kitchen table and I'll see what I can do."

"I'll get out of your way," Quinn said.

"You will never be in my way," Nick said softly.

Quinn's heart skipped, and when he held out his hand, she took it and followed them into the kitchen.

Santino saw the cookies and drinks on the table and clapped his hands.

"I'll make myself a drink and join you, but I'm going for chips and dip," he said and headed for the pantry.

Nick rolled his eyes.

"This is what he does. He screws up his laptop, brings it over here for me to fix and makes a party out of it for himself."

Quinn knew Nick wasn't really angry. In fact, he looked happy. She needed to clear the air between them while Santino was distracted, so she leaned a little closer.

"I'm sorry I flipped out earlier," she whispered.

Nick looked at her then. His voice was soft, keeping the conversation between them.

"About that. What did I say that upset you?" he asked.

She shrugged. "It was nothing. I'm blaming it on the pain meds—they make me an emotional wreck."

"Don't lie to me," Nick said. He wasn't upset, but she could tell he needed more from her than a weak brush-off.

Quinn shoved a shaky hand through her hair, blinking rapidly to keep away the tears.

"I just… I don't want you to pity me," she whispered, then looked away.

"Look at me," he said.

She sighed and then turned her head toward him.

"You don't want my pity, but what *do* you want from me?" he asked.

"Hey, Nick! You don't have any ranch dip."

Nick frowned as Quinn quickly looked away. Santino's timing sucked.

"Because I don't like ranch dip and this is my house," Nick said. "There's French onion dip on the top shelf."

He ran a finger down the side of Quinn's face.

"I will ask you that question again, when we don't have anyone to interrupt us, so you better be thinking of an answer."

Unaware of the ongoing conversation between them, Santino set a bag of potato chips in the middle of the table and popped the top off a carton of French onion dip, then went back for his drink.

"He's really turning this into a party?" Quinn asked.

"Every time," Nick said. "So, let's see what crap he's picked up this go-round."

Quinn watched Nick's fingers flying over the keyboard, clicking on one program, then another, and another, his gaze narrowed and fixed on the screen.

Santino set his drink as far away from the laptop as he could get and then smiled at Quinn.

"I spilled a whole beer on the laptop I had before this one," he said. "Fried it royally. I'm addicted to YouTube. There's some awesome stuff on there if you know where to look."

"If you stuck to YouTube, you'd be safe, but you don't. That's why you get viruses," Nick muttered. "You're clicking on every weird link known to man."

Santino shrugged and went for a chip, dragged it through the dip and popped it in his mouth.

Quinn was happy just listening and seeing another facet of what Nick was all about. Besides being a cop and having this wonderful, loving family, he appeared to be really tech smart. She couldn't help but think of what he'd accomplished in his life, while all she'd been doing was living from hand to mouth, day by day.

However, Santino's arrival brought her out of the doldrums. He was funny and adorable, and his presence took the tension away from the two of them being alone.

It took Nick a little over two hours to locate and scrub the virus from the laptop.

"Finally," Nick said, as he logged off the computer and shoved it across the table. "It's clean again, so don't click on any more sites that have anything to do with women with big boobs."

Quinn laughed out loud at the look on Santino's face.

"Are you serious? I was not looking at such sites," Santino said.

Nick grinned.

"No, I'm not serious about that. The virus was actually attached to an innocent site, and it wasn't a malicious one."

Santino shrugged.

"Anything that messes me up with the worldwide web is malicious to me, and thank you very much."

"You're welcome," Nick said, as he got up from the table and stretched, then gave Quinn a hand up and a quick hug before seeing Santino out.

Quinn was cleaning up the party mess when Nick came back. He loaded the dirty dishes into the dishwasher after she carried them from the table to the counter.

"Your cousin is funny," Quinn said, wiping off the table.

"He thinks so," Nick said.

She paused on the far side of the table, watching the play of muscles beneath Nick's T-shirt as he worked. She couldn't get over the way fate had played into their lives. She would not have recognized him if she'd passed him on a street, and yet here they were, under the same roof again. Even if this was only temporary, she would be forever grateful that life had put them together again.

Dinner was Chinese delivery.

The whole time they were eating, Quinn kept expecting him to bring up their earlier conversation, but he didn't. She was beginning to think that he'd forgoten it, and by the time they got to the fortune cookies she had completely relaxed.

"Here's your cookie," Nick said, as he dug them from the bottom of the sack. "You have to read it aloud. It's a rule."

She broke it open and put a piece of the cookie in her mouth, chewing as she unfolded her fortune. As she read, a flush was rising up her neck that she knew from experience would be clearly visible.

Then she took a deep breath, laid it facedown on the table and put the rest of her cookie in her mouth.

"You didn't read it aloud," Nick said.

"You go first," she said.

He grinned.

"Chicken."

He watched her eyebrows arch and her nostrils flare as she wadded it up and dropped it in front of him.

"Then you read it," she snapped.

He was still grinning when he picked it up and smoothed it out, but then the smile died on his face. He looked up, then reached across the table and took her hand.

"Yes."

Quinn felt the skin tightening across her face. She didn't know whether she should laugh or cry as she looked down at the words on the tiny scrap of paper.

A second chance at love awaits. Say yes.

Her heart was pounding. He'd said yes.

"Read yours," she said.

He let go of her hand and opened and read his, then looked up.

"I think we might be onto something here," he said and pushed the paper toward her.

Again, she looked down and saw the words.

Trust your heart. Your luck is changing.

Her voice was shaking.

"I don't believe in luck."

"Neither do I," Nick said. "But I believe in fate." He paused. "Now, that's enough of that. Do you want to go to the pool for a while? I know you can't get your bandage wet, but you can stay in the shallow end, and it's dark enough outside that I think it's safe."

The abrupt change of conversation was unexpected, but not unwelcome. It had gotten too serious, too fast.

"Sure."

"Do you have a swimsuit?" he asked.

She nodded.

"Then you go ahead and change. I'm going to clean up here first, but wait for me. Don't go outside alone."

"Okay," she said.

He started carrying the take-out containers to the trash as Quinn stood. When he wasn't looking, she picked up the fortunes and took them with her as she left.

When Nick came back to wipe off the table he realized they were gone and smiled. Maybe, just maybe, that wall she'd been hiding behind was finally coming down.

Quinn laid the fortunes in the drawer and pulled out her one and only swimsuit. It had seen better days, but so had she. She tossed it on the bed and began to undress.

The first thing to come off was the sling, and letting the muscles bear all of her weight was a little painful as she laid it on the bed. Her mind was spinning…her thoughts in free fall as she kicked off her shoes.

This time last year she'd been in Denver working at a bar. The year before that it was Miami, working in a greenhouse. She couldn't even remember the year before that, but looking back, it was painfully obvious she'd been wandering without an agenda. She'd never thought about it before all this. Before she'd nearly died—before she'd fainted in Nick Saldano's arms.

That bullet in the back had been her wake-up call. Every little-girl dream she'd ever had came back in a rush. Even the princess she'd wanted to be… She'd lost that dream when she lost her knight in shining armor so many years ago. Finding him again in this way seemed too improbable to believe, and yet here they were.

Her clothes came off far easier than they went on, and she reached for the bottom half of her suit. With a little tugging, she got it on, wincing again from the pull of sore muscles in her shoulder. But when it came to the top, no matter how hard she tried, she couldn't fasten it, so she put it on, then sat down on the side of the bed to wait for help.

It didn't take Nick long to come out of his clothes, but since he'd cleaned the pool earlier in his white swim trunks, the only other one he had was his Speedo. He put it on without thought and headed across the hall to get Quinn.

He knocked once.

"Are you decent?" he yelled.

"More or less," she answered.

He pushed the door inward and strode toward the bed.

Quinn stood and then stifled a gasp, too tongue-tied to speak. Nick was completely naked but for the tiny black Speedo stuck tight to his narrow hips.

He was admiring the alabaster beauty of all that bare skin when he noticed she was holding the bra part of her swimsuit against her with both hands.

She lifted her chin, refusing to be intimidated.

"I can't fasten it."

He leaned forward, reached around her back with both hands and grabbed both ends of the swimsuit top, then hooked them together in one smooth motion.

"That was fast," she muttered.

"You should see how quick I can unhook one," he drawled. "Are you ready?"

She nodded.

"Then let's go," he said and led the way as he strode out of the room toward the kitchen. He turned off the lights inside before they exited his house so that they wouldn't be silhouetted against the light, then paused outside for a moment, letting his eyesight adjust. Once he was satisfied all was well, he took her by the hand and led her out.

The moment Quinn walked out into the dark, she took a slow, deep breath. It was the smell of freedom.

Spending so much of her life outdoors and riding from state to state on her Harley, she didn't realize how much she'd missed it until she was no longer surrounded by walls.

"Okay?" Nick asked.

She looked up at him then. The kindness in the tone of his voice and the concern on his face touched her.

"I'm fine," she said.

"The shallow end is four feet. You can walk out to deeper water from there until it is up past your waist. I'll try not to splash water on your bandage, and we should be good to go."

Again, she let him lead her to the shallow end of the pool, then down the steps into the water.

Surprised, Quinn's voice lightened.

"Ooh, it feels like silk against my skin."

"Your skin is beautiful. You're beautiful," Nick said.

Quinn sighed as she moved a little deeper into the pool. When the water was just below her breasts, she stopped.

"I think this is far enough," she said.

"Agreed. Do you want to stay out here in the middle of the pool or move closer to the edge?"

"The edge, so I'll have something to lean against."

So he walked her to the side of the pool, and as soon as she was safe, he dipped his hand in the pool and made the sign of the cross on her face, first touching her forehead, then her chin, then a touch to each cheek before ending with a touch on her nose.

"My queen! You are now officially baptized in the waters of Saldano. The magic is strongest here in the dark, m'lady. It is my honor to be hosting such a royal beauty."

Quinn grinned.

"You always were fun to play with when we were kids."

"I'm still fun to play with," he said, then brushed a quick kiss across her lips before she could object and swam off into the pool before he got them both in trouble.

Quinn shuddered with longing as she watched him swim away. The warm ebb and flow of water against her mostly bare body was a sensual caress. She leaned back, resting her elbows against the side of the pool, and looked up.

Streetlights and the security lights of Nick's neighbors took away the density of the night. The stars above were scattered across heaven like diamonds, and the pool lights below the water gave the pool a strange, otherworldly glow. The air was still warm, and the slight splash of water as Nick swam to the other end of the pool made her wish she could get in and race him.

Water splashed. She looked up. Nick had turned around and was already swimming back in the other direction. He continued to lap the pool for several minutes. Once, he got out at the deep end of the pool and went toward the pump. She watched him squat down to adjust some kind of setting and then dive back into the pool, cutting the water with very little sound or splash. He lapped the pool one more time, and when he started back again, she realized he was coming toward her.

When he stopped in front of her and stood, they were

nearly at eye level. Then he leaned forward, grabbing on to the rim of the pool and encircling her with his arms.

Even though their lips were only inches apart, Quinn lifted her chin to meet his gaze.

"Sweet, fiery, unpredictable redhead that you are… I don't fully understand what I did to piss you off, but I will clarify one thing for you right now. I have all kinds of emotions regarding you and your presence in my home and not a damn one of them involves pity. It feels like my whole life has been about waiting for this moment…waiting for you."

Then he leaned in and brushed a kiss across her lips.

"And so, Your Majesty…there you have it. I laid my heart on the line. You know what I want from you. So what do *you* want from me?"

Quinn was blindsided, scared and ready to risk every kind of heartbreak. She didn't hesitate.

"I want you. No matter what tomorrow brings, I want you now."

"Your wish is my command," he said, then took her by the hand and led her out of the pool.

Quinn's heart was pounding, but she'd never been so sure of anything in her life as she was of making love with this man. Risk nothing, gain nothing.

Risk your heart, gain the world.

He stripped in the dark outside the sliding glass doors, leaving the scrap of a suit in a puddle beneath his feet, then stripped her, as well.

"You're shaking," he said softly. "Are you cold?"

"Not cold, just ready."

The words were a punch in the gut. Now he couldn't get her inside fast enough.

The air-conditioning was a shock against their skin as they stepped inside. He locked the sliding doors and set the alarm, then picked her up as if she weighed nothing and carried her through the house.

He set her on her feet beside his bed and then pulled back the covers.

"We'll get the sheets wet," she said.

"Yes, we will," Nick said.

She eased down onto the bed, but when she reached for him she winced in pain.

"Don't! Let me," he said and crawled into bed beside her. He rested on one elbow to gaze at the beauty beside him.

"Truly a queen," he whispered and rubbed the edge of his thumb along the sensuous curve of her lower lip.

She cupped the back of his head and pulled him closer. He watched her eyes closing and heard her breathing quicken as he rose up to straddle her body. Bracing himself above her, he stole the first kiss as she was taking a breath, and swallowed the moan that came up her throat. He moved down from there, to the hollow at the base of her throat, then her breasts, circling first one hard pink tip with his tongue and then the other. By the time he got down to her belly she was moaning. As he began to push his knee between her legs, she moved instinctively to let him in.

She was whispering something over and over as he settled within the valley between her thighs. When he realized she was saying "hurry," he thrust his hard aching erection into her waiting warmth as deep as he could go.

She arched up beneath him with a groan and met the first few thrusts with timed precision. Before he knew it, she was coming so hard and fast that the tremors inside her body rolled around him in a quick, wet heat.

Her climax rocked him so hard he feared for a few moments that he would lose it, but finally gained control. Even as the aftershocks pulsed through her in waves, he was still moving inside her in slow, deep strokes.

Quinn didn't want to open her eyes for fear she'd see herself floating above her body, convinced no one could have experienced that kind of rush and lived through it.

It took her a few moments to realize that not only was she still alive, but Nick was still inside her, still hard as a rock and still stroking, determined to take her back to her point of ignition all over again.

She'd never had this feeling with another man. Nothing had ever felt this good or this right. She wrapped her legs around his waist and pulled him deeper, holding him tighter until she felt that coil of muscles deep in her body beginning to tighten all over again. She fell into his rhythm, riding the ripples of that feeling. She was hanging on the edge of a second climax when he began to go faster—deeper. Then he broke rhythm between one stroke and the next and let out a deep groan of release as the climax rolled through him.

It was the warmth of his seed spilling deep inside her that sent her over the edge. She cried out as wave after wave of the climax shot through her.

Nick collapsed and rolled so that she was stretched full out on top of him.

No one moved.

Sleep caught them in the afterglow and exhaustion pulled them under.

Twelve

Hours later, Nick woke to find Quinn asleep on the pillow beside him. He glanced at the clock, then fingered the healing wound on his head. It would be dawn within the hour, so he slipped out of bed to get a pain pill. He'd been taking less and less of them each day, but hadn't been able to shake the headache. It wasn't always intense, but it was always there.

After taking the pain med, he turned off the house alarm and went out on the patio to pick up their wet swimsuits, locked and reset the alarm and then tossed the suits in the washer in the utility room. He stopped off in the kitchen and started the coffeemaker before going back to bed.

Last night with Quinn had been an awakening. He'd had sex with women, but after being with her it was apparent to him that he'd never made love. Now she was in his blood, and the timing of what was happening in their lives was crazy. At first, he thought the immediate attraction they'd had for each other was based on

the bond they'd had as children. One might have ar
gued it was a knee-jerk reaction to sexual attraction
but no more. He couldn't explain it, but he didn't wan
to lose it—or her.

He slipped back into bed, rolled over onto his side
and pulled her close. The even rise and fall of her breasts
against his arm lulled him right back to sleep, and the
next time he woke up Quinn was watching his face.

He smiled slowly, taking in the pure green of her eyes
and that tumble of red curly hair spread across his pillow. Then he reached for her, brushing his thumb across
her lip as he cupped the back of her head and kissed her.

Her lips were as soft and yielding to him as they had
been last night. He rose up on one elbow, taking in the
glorious sight before him.

"Good morning, sweetheart. You are a most wonderful, magnificent and loving woman, and this is exactly the way I want to wake up for the rest of my life."

Quinn arched an eyebrow.

"I was wondering what the morning after was going
to be like with you, and now I know. It rocks almost as
good as you do," she said.

Nick rubbed a thumb along the lower curve of her
lip, thinking about how much he wanted to start last
night over again, but timing was off.

"This conversation could take us both to a whole
other thing…but I'm thinking I need to move so you
can get up?"

"Unfortunately, yes," she said.

He got up and then helped pull her to her feet.

She patted his butt and blew him a kiss, then walked into the bathroom and closed the door.

All he could do was grin.

A few minutes later she came out with her hair wound up on top of her head and minus the bandage on her shoulder. Nick had left the room, so she put on a pair of shorts and her sports bra and headed barefoot into the hall, carrying her shirt with her.

Nick was pouring himself a cup of coffee when she entered the kitchen. She could hear the washing machine running and smelled bread toasting in the toaster.

"Hey, Nick?"

He was smiling as he turned, but it faltered when he saw her.

"You took off the bandage."

"I need you to look at my back. I think there might be some infection. It feels weird."

He hurried toward her as she turned around, and then his stomach rolled.

"You're right. It does look infected. We need to get you back to the doctor."

"Damn it."

"I'm sorry, honey."

She shrugged.

"Will you help me get this T-shirt over my head?"

"Absolutely," Nick said and eased the shirt over her sore shoulder first before pulling it over her head. "I'm so sorry," he said and hugged her.

Quinn sighed. The hug was worth the aggravation of an infection, for sure.

He kissed the top of her head and then turned her toward the table.

"You sit down and I'll bring toast and coffee. Do you want a bowl of cereal to go with it?"

"No, toast and jelly sounds good to me, but I can help," she said.

"I've got this," Nick said, and so she sat down at the table while he went to get breakfast.

He was waiting for toast to pop up when he started thinking about how to handle this unexpected problem.

"I'll call your surgeon after we eat and see how he wants to handle this. I'm not parading you through the lobby of any hospital or having you sit in a waiting room in his office with a dozen other people. Not with Baba in the wind."

"No one really knows me here," Quinn said.

Nick hated to say it, but she needed to know.

"If Anton Baba knows your name, everyone will know you."

She felt the blood draining from her face as the implications of what he said began to sink in.

"But he doesn't have people looking for me like he did Star...does he?"

"A couple of days ago I would have said no. But after that visit from the Feds, they qualify you as a viable witness, and with his connections, Baba will know that, too."

"This is such a nightmare," Quinn said.

Nick grabbed the toast, slipped it on a plate and carried it to the table and sat down beside her.

"We'll get through it," Nick said.

Quinn was moved by what he'd said. She'd never had a "we" in her life before. She glanced up at Nick when he wasn't looking, trying to gauge his mood, but couldn't.

"You don't even know if I can cook," she said, as she reached for a piece of toast and smeared it with jelly.

Nick grinned at her.

"I know how."

"I have no job skills beyond serving food or drinks," she said and took a big bite.

His grin widened.

"Are you trying to warn me, or talk me out of what we're doing here?" he asked.

She shrugged and then swallowed.

"Just being fair, I guess."

He stirred some cream into his coffee.

"So...can you cook?" he asked.

Quinn burst out laughing.

"You are outrageous."

He wiggled his eyebrows at her.

"That's what all my women say."

This silly banter was easing her anxiety, which was exactly what Nick intended.

"Yes, I can cook. I'm a regular Martha Stewart."

"As long as you don't start making your own wrapping paper, we should be fine," he said, licking jelly off his thumb and stuffing the last bite of toast into his mouth.

She laughed.

His job here was done.

* * *

Four hours later Nick pulled into the back of the building where Quinn's surgeon's office was housed and made a quick call. A couple of minutes later the door to the service entrance opened. When he saw a lady in blue scrubs standing in the doorway, he and Quinn got out and rushed inside.

"Hi, I'm Rachel," she said.

Nick flashed his badge.

"Detective Saldano, and thank you so much for this," Nick said.

Rachel smiled at Quinn, giving her a curious look, but saying nothing as she began to lead them through a maze of hallways until they got to a back exit in the doctor's office.

"Right in here," she said and led them into the exam room across the hall. "I have her chart in his office. Dr. Munoz will be with you shortly. Miss O'Meara, you'll need to take off your shirt and put this gown on. Do you need any help?"

"No, ma'am," Quinn said.

"Then I'll give you a few minutes to change before I come in to get your vitals."

"Thank you," Quinn said.

And then the nurse was gone.

Nick quickly helped her out of her shirt and sports bra, put the hospital gown on her, then helped her up to the exam table.

"Okay, honey?" he asked, as he brushed some un-ruly strands of hair back into place. As he did, he felt her forehead. It was hot—too hot. "I think you have a fever now," he said.

Her shoulders slumped.

"I don't feel good."

"Damn it. I let you get in the pool and then took you to bed as if nothing was wrong with you. This is all my fault. I'm so sorry."

Quinn grabbed his hand and lifted it to her cheek.

"It's no one's fault but the sorry bastard who shot me, and thanks to you, he won't be shooting anyone else. Please don't say you're sorry about last night. It was the best night of my life," she said.

Nick pulled her close.

"Me too, Quinn. People are going to say we're crazy, that this is all happening too fast, but it feels right to me."

She shook her head.

"I don't care what anyone says. We both learned early in our lives to take joy when we found it, and for me those times were few and far between. Finding you again feels like an apology from the Universe for separating us the first time."

"That's beautiful, sweetheart. An apology from the Universe. I like that."

"I think I want to lie down now," she said.

Nick was frowning as he eased her down on the exam table. To relieve the inflamed shoulder, she turned onto her side, stretched out and closed her eyes.

She was getting worse—fast.

Rachel came back, took Quinn's vitals and also

brought a lightweight blanket to cover her up before she left again.

He waited impatiently another five minutes and then was headed for the door to find out where everybody went when the doctor walked in with Rachel on his heels.

"Hello, Detective. And here's my missing patient," Munoz said, giving Nick a look.

Nick wasn't going to apologize.

"It became necessary to move her as quickly as possible. I didn't think you would appreciate another shooting in your hospital," Nick said.

Munoz's eyes widened.

"Uh, no, certainly not. So what's happening here?" he said.

Quinn had been dozing and was waking as she heard men's voices. She heard the doctor's question and struggled to sit up.

"I've got you. Let me help," Nick said and eased her into an upright position on the exam table.

"Hello, Dr. Munoz," Quinn said.

The surgeon smiled.

"Hello, Quinn. Can you tell me what's wrong?"

She pointed at her back.

"I think it's infected."

"Are you taking your antibiotics along with the pain meds?"

"Yes, sir. Regularly."

"Then let's take a look," he said and tapped Nick's arm. "Can you turn her a little so I can get a better view?"

Nick and Rachel helped Quinn turn sideways, and then he stepped to the side as the doctor began his exam.

Dr. Munoz's face was hard to read, but Nick could tell he wasn't pleased. The wound opening had been little more than a jagged hole. The exit wound was not much worse. But now it was inflamed around the wound entrance and hot to the touch. He prodded and poked, looked at the entrance and exit areas, and decided the entrance was the crux of the problem.

"I'm sorry, Quinn, but we're going to have to open this up."

"Then do it," she said.

"Either put her to sleep or deaden the hell out of it," Nick muttered.

The doctor blinked. The anger in the detective's voice surprised him.

"Of course. Which would you prefer, Quinn?"

"Deaden it. I don't like not being in control of what's happening to me."

"But I'm here," Nick said.

She sighed.

"I know, but I don't want to be put to sleep, okay?"

"Of course, honey. It's totally your call."

Dr. Munoz nodded.

"He's right. It is your call, but I'm still going to give you something to relax," he said and ordered Rachel to start an IV.

Quinn sighed. This wasn't good news, but pretty much what she'd expected.

Nick got on the far side of the exam table so he'd

be out of the way, but at the same time he had a clea
view of her face.

The moment Nick walked into her line of vision she
reached for his hand.

"I'm so sorry," he said.

"Thank you, Nick. So am I."

Rachel approached, wiped down the area with antiseptic swabs and started an IV and drip line with a
med to level her anxiety. Then she began numbing the
red area around the wound.

"Big stick, honey."

Quinn didn't flinch.

Rachel injected the second needle, then the third, and
Quinn had done nothing but close her eyes.

"Can you feel anything?" Rachel asked, after she
had disposed of the needles.

"Feels like I'm floating," Quinn said.

Rachel eyed Dr. Munoz.

"I'd say the anxiety meds are working."

Dr. Munoz nodded and began to remove the two
stitches he'd used to close the wound. The moment they
were clipped, pressure was released and infection began
coming out.

"Rachel, flush this, please," he said, pointing to the
now open wound.

Rachel did as he ordered and continued to flush the
area until it was clean from infection.

"Quinn, are you still okay?" Nick asked.

She gave him a thumbs-up and winked.

He grinned. She was feeling no pain, which was
great, but the tension grew as Dr. Munoz continued

to probe the wound with no luck finding the source of the infection. Munoz stopped long enough for Rachel to wipe the sweat off his brow and then went back at it.

"Well, what have we here?" Munoz said, as he pulled out a two-inch length of thread from the wound.

"What is that?" Nick asked.

The doctor laid it on his tray.

"Quinn, what were you wearing when you were shot?"

"One of my designer dresses," she said and then giggled.

Nick chuckled.

"She was wearing a leather jacket and a blue shirt beneath it."

"Knit or fabric?" he asked.

"Fabric," Nick said, remembering his first sight of her, the baby and the blood. "Blue fabric."

"That's what we pulled out. A thread from the woven fabric. It was debris we missed during the first surgery. Bullet-driven debris inside the wound."

"So she should be feeling better soon, then?" Nick asked.

"Yes. We'll flush it out once more, then close her up. She'll have an injection of antibiotic before she leaves and then up the meds she's already taking. She should soon be on the mend."

"Great news," Nick said.

Munoz pointed at Nick's head.

"How's that feeling?"

"If I could shake the headache, I'd say great."

"Fairly normal when you have a bullet wound to the

head. Another millimeter to the left and we would have been digging a bullet out of your brain."

"I'm not complaining," Nick said.

Rachel ended their conversation.

"Dr. Munoz, ready to flush and close," she said.

They flushed the wound one last time and closed it back up. When he was finished, he ordered a double dose of antibiotic in her IV and stripped off his latex gloves.

"That does it," he said, as he patted Quinn's foot. "How do you feel?"

Quinn jumped as if he'd hit her foot with a ball bat.

"I didn't do it!" she cried.

Munoz looked at Nick and frowned.

"Hard life in foster care," Nick said.

"Sorry to hear that," Munoz said and repeated his question. "Quinn! How do you feel?"

Quinn opened her eyes and glared.

"What? How do I feel? Like some asshole shot me in the back again," she mumbled and then reached for Nick. "Hey, good-lookin'."

The doctor laughed out loud.

Nick grinned.

"How much antianxiety medicine did you give her?"

"Obviously enough," Dr. Munoz said. "At any rate, she should be on the road to healing once more. Of course, call if you have another issue, but those stitches will dissolve. When you feel it's safe, I'd like to take a look at her in a couple of weeks before I completely release her."

"You got it," Nick said. "Thank you again for seeing her like this. Send the bill to my mailing address and—"

"No charge for this. It shouldn't have happened. Rachel will see you out," he said and left.

Nick glanced down at Quinn. Her eyes were closed, but she still held on to his hand.

Rachel came back with a wheelchair.

"Can you wake her up enough to get in the chair?" she asked.

Nick just scooped her up in his arms.

She woke up in midair.

"I'm flying," she said.

"No, Queenie, you're not flying. You're just high. I'm going to put you down in this wheelchair. Can you sit up?"

"Of course I can sit up. I'm not a baby."

The moment he put her down in the wheelchair, her eyes closed and her chin dropped.

"So much for that thought," Nick said. "I'll keep her upright. You lead the way," he said, and so they followed Rachel back through the maze of halls all the way back to that exit.

She held the door open as he paused, looking all around the delivery entrance before he wheeled her out to his car.

Hit by the fresh air and sunshine, Quinn roused again as Nick was unlocking the car.

"Where are we?" she said.

"Going home now, honey. I need you to get in the car, okay?"

"Sure thing," she said and would have gone face-first onto the pavement if he hadn't caught her.

By now Nick was laughing.

"Come on, baby…into the front seat with you. I'll recline the seat and you can sleep all the way home."

"I'm not sleepy," she said and then fell asleep on his shoulder as he was buckling her in.

Nick pushed the wheelchair back to Rachel.

"Many thanks for all your trouble."

"Happy to help," she said. "Stay safe."

"Yes, ma'am," Nick said and jogged back to the car. He started the engine and turned the air-conditioning on blast.

Quinn roused.

"Is it going to snow?"

He burst out laughing.

"Honey, you are without doubt the cutest drunk I've ever seen."

"Don't drink," she muttered.

"I'm beginning to believe you," he said and patted her arm. "Just relax. We're going home."

She tried to sit up but kept sliding sideways and grabbed on to his arm to steady herself.

"I don't know home. Have I ever been there?"

The question hurt his heart.

"You're already there," he said softly. "You just don't know it yet."

He put the car in gear, drove back up an alley to get to the street, then disappeared in traffic, unaware they'd been made.

Paco Cruz used to run with the big boys. He'd worked for Anton Baba until his addiction to drugs got him arrested. He did five years, and came out minus one eye and crippled after a fight with his cell mate.

Baba was sympathetic to his plight but had no need for a hard-ass with a bad limp and one eye, so that was the end of Paco's return. He went to work for his uncle's cleaning company, but had kept a foot in the business by becoming one of his old boss's better snitches. He made it his business to stay abreast of all that was happening with Baba and was surprised when he learned there were two women who could actually bring him and his dynasty down. The last he'd heard, Baba's woman had gotten completely away from him, and the witness who could link him to the death of two Feds had disappeared off of Baba's radar.

Like Baba, things were not looking up for Paco anymore, and he'd gone to work today with an attitude. He'd been cleaning window blinds at the law office of Daniels, Daniels and Wicker when he saw movement at the back door of the professional building across the way.

He recognized the nurse. Her name was Rachel and he thought she was hot. He recognized the man in the doorway—a cop named Saldano, who had once arrested him. And, from what he'd heard, he was the cop who'd taken down Dev Bosky. He hadn't liked Bosky much, but liked cops less. And then he saw the redhead in the wheelchair and all of a sudden his heart skipped a beat.

Dev was after the witness.

Cop was guarding witness.

Cop killed Dev.

Witness disappears from hospital.

Now cop comes out of doctor's office with a woman in a wheelchair.

What were the odds that this woman was the missing witness? Damn good odds to bet on, that's what.

Paco started to grin. He knew Baba was "out of town," which translated to "in hiding."

He stepped back from the window as the cop drove away and quickly made a call to the personal number Baba had given him. The phone rang and rang and then went to voice mail.

"Mr. Baba, this is Paco. I have some information about a certain missing witness you were looking for. I just saw a redhead coming out of the back of a doctor's office with a cop named Saldano—the same cop who took Dev out. I don't know where they're keeping her, but it appears she's still in Vegas under protective custody. I thought you would want to know." Then he disconnected.

Quinn was an enigma.

Nick already knew she was closemouthed about her past and only shared bits and pieces of it when pushed to her limit, but the meds Dr. Munoz gave her also lowered her defenses.

From the time it had taken him to drive five city blocks, he'd heard her go from a little-girl voice saying prayers for God to rescue her, to an adult, angry voice telling some man named Rob that if he messed with her bike again, she was going to break his neck. When he stopped for a red light, the lack of motion roused her. She rose up, asked if this was where she got off to find the free health clinic, then lay back down without worrying about an answer. When she started crying, the sound of her sobs were so heartbreaking he couldn't focus. He had always wanted to be someone's knight in shining armor and had imagined over the years what kind of woman his damsel would be, but never would he have imagined a woman like Quinn O'Meara. She triggered every protective instinct he had, and the one night they'd spent making love had filled up the empty place in his heart. He knew she was broken, but he was damn good at fixing things. She was also funny, and brave, and she was a thief, because she'd already stolen his heart.

He shook her twice, trying to get her to wake up because the tears were killing him. When he spotted his favorite frozen custard shop, he turned off the street and into the drive-through lane for a much-needed pick-me-up.

Quinn woke up when the car stopped, felt the tears on her cheeks and frowned.

"Am I sad?" she asked.

"Just having a bad dream, baby," he said softly. "We're getting frozen custard. Do you want it plain in a cone, or in a cup with hot fudge sauce?"

"Plain so I don't get fat!" she mumbled.

"A little hot fudge won't make you fat. You're perfect."

"Okay. Yes to fudge!" She giggled and then struggled to sit up. "What happened to my bones?"

He smiled at her.

"Nothing happened to your bones."

She whacked him on the arm.

"Yes! Something did too happen to my bones. They won't hold me up." She started laughing. "I have hones bones. They won't hold me up. Get it? Hold up? You're a cop. You should get that."

Nick leaned across the seat and kissed her square on the lips.

Quinn put her fingers on her mouth and then sighed.

"You turn me on. You are a very good lover and an even better man. I'm going to be a good girl, and you will love me forever and never throw me away," she muttered and then started to cry again. "They always throw me away," she whispered.

There were tears on Nick's face as he moved up in line.

"I will never throw you away, and you're getting hot fudge on your frozen custard."

She sighed.

"You love me, don't you, Nicks?"

"Yes."

"I love you, too," she said. "This much." And she stretched out her arms.

"Thank you, Lord," Nick said and pulled up to the call box, gave his order, then pulled up to the next window to pay.

Within minutes, they had their treats, and he'd pulled over into the parking lot of a strip mall so they could eat.

Quinn took her first bite and then moaned.

"This is so good. Thank you, Nicks. You are the best man ever."

"Keep that in mind after that medicine wears off," he said.

"Yes, I will. It's easy to remember that I love you and hot fudge sundaes."

He chuckled.

"I don't know how I ever lived a day of my life before you showed back up."

"I don't either," she said and scooped up a big bite of the hot fudge. "Look! If you eat this much chocolate at one time, your tongue will be happy."

Nick laughed aloud.

"I don't have to eat a thing right now to know I'm happy all over."

She grinned.

"It's because of me, right?"

"Yes, it's because of you. Just keep eating before it melts."

She nodded, then winked.

"No worries, Officer. I got this."

Nick looked at her then—red curls all over the place and her green eyes so full of light he felt blinded. He was so far gone, it was pitiful.

Thirteen

Henderson, Nevada

It was nearing dinnertime, and Justin Davis had gone to the supermarket for more food. They'd gone from one guest to three in less than twenty-four hours.

Donna was racing around trying to get a room ready for Justin's parents and feed everyone as well, but her main concern was Star's back. As a nurse, she knew it needed tending, and that Star needed prescriptions for antibiotics and pain meds. Aware that secrecy was of utmost importance, she called Dr. Andrew Charles, the doctor she worked for, and without going into too many details, she got him to make a house call.

She was watching for him, and when she saw him pull into their driveway, she met him at the door.

"Thank you so much for coming, Dr. Charles."

Andrew knew Donna's husband was a member of the state police, and felt confident that whatever was going on was important.

"Happy to be of service in such a serious case," he said. "Where's the patient?"

"In the bedroom with her parents. They're still in shock that she's even alive after all this time. Follow me."

Star was lying on her belly, drifting in and out of sleep, only half listening to her parents' conversation. But when she heard the knock at her door, she opened her eyes. She saw Donna walk in accompanied by a stranger, and quickly rolled over and sat up as Donna introduced him.

"Everyone, this is my boss, Dr. Andrew Charles. He has kindly agreed to take a look at Star's back and prescribe some meds for her. Dr. Charles, these are my in-laws, John and Connie Davis, and this is Starla Davis, my sister-in-law."

"So nice to meet you," Connie said. "We appreciate you doing this for our daughter."

"Certainly," Andrew said and then focused his attention on the tiny blonde sitting in the middle of the bed. "So, Miss Davis, I need to see what we're dealing with here, so you'll need to remove your shirt. If you're uncomfortable with so many people here we can—"

"No matter," Star said. She turned her back to the room and pulled her T-shirt up and over her head.

Andrew frowned.

"How did you incur these injuries?"

So once again, Star explained the wreck and being thrown out of the sunroof. To her relief, he didn't ask her why she left the hospital in her condition, and she began to relax.

He put on a pair of latex gloves and then examined her injuries inch by inch, paying close attention to the areas that had staples and the ones that had been left open to heal on their own.

"Donna, if you'll please open my bag, we'll begin."

Star had prepared herself for more pain, but to her relief it didn't happen. She knew he was putting some kind of medicine on her because she felt an occasional sting, but it was minimal.

Finally, Andrew stepped back.

"It all looks good. You're healing well, but I'm going to leave prescriptions for antibiotics and for pain. Are you allergic to anything?"

"No, sir," Star said.

He peeled off the latex gloves, got out his prescription pad and wrote two prescriptions.

"The antibiotic has one refill. The pain pills do not," he said and handed them to Donna. "The staples still have to be removed. I want to give them at least another five days to heal, and then Donna can take them out. She's fully capable, okay?"

Donna nodded.

"Yes, that won't be a problem, and thank you so much, Dr. Charles."

"Happy to have been of service," he said. "I'll be on my way, and just so you know, as far as I'm concerned, this visit never happened."

Justin returned less than a half hour after the doctor had left and began helping put up groceries as Donna started prepping the meal.

"You missed Dr. Charles," Donna said.

"What did he say about Starla's back?"

"That it's healing well. He left two prescriptions to be filled."

Justin glanced at the clock.

"I think I'd better get those filled before it gets any later. I'll get Mom to come help you with dinner."

"No need," Donna said. "Let them visit. They can't get enough of being with Starla, and I can only imagine how they feel."

"You are a jewel," Justin said. "Thank you for taking this chaos in stride."

"Honey! They're family."

Justin sighed. "Yes, they are. So where are the prescriptions?"

"Over there on the sideboard."

"I won't be long," he said. He kissed her on the cheek and headed back out the door.

Donna went back to work.

Down the hall, Star's parents were hovering, and she was exhausted. She fell asleep as they were talking about which spare bedroom in their house would best serve as a nursery.

Connie glanced over at her daughter and saw she'd fallen asleep. She covered Star with a lightweight blanket, and then she and John left the room to let her rest.

Star was dreaming that she was in one room and Sammy was in another. She could hear him crying, asking for his mama over and over, but there was no doorknob on her door and she couldn't get it open to get to him. She was beating on the door and screaming his name, and the last time she screamed, it was a real one that not only woke her up, but brought everyone running.

Justin burst into the room with his gun in hand, looking around the room for signs of an intruder, but Star was alone, sitting up in the bed, sobbing.

Connie ran to her and took her in her arms.

"Starla, darling! What's wrong?"

"I could hear Sammy crying for me, and I couldn't get to him. I'm sorry I frightened everyone."

Connie patted her cheek.

"Go wash your face and come to the kitchen. We're making dinner and having a very good time, but we'd have a better time if you were with us."

Star wiped away tears.

"Yes, all right," she said. "You all go on… I'll be there shortly."

As soon as they were gone she washed up and joined them, but the dream had only affirmed her intention to get her baby back immediately. She went barefoot to the kitchen, made herself a glass of iced tea, snagged a handful of almonds from the dish on the sideboard and noticed the meds Justin had brought for her.

"Donna, is it okay if I take these now?"

"Yes. Just read the directions and follow accordingly," she said.

Star shook out one pain pill and one antibiotic and downed them with a swallow of tea, then put the almonds on the table by her glass and popped one in her mouth. The slightly salty taste helped settle her stomach, and the comfort of being surrounded by her family was something she'd never thought would happen again. Slowly, the happy sound of laughter and their voices calmed the anxious feeling in her belly. They loved her without care for how degrading her life had been, and were ready to embrace her son the same way. Tomorrow she was going to have Justin put her in contact with Special Agent Gleason of the FBI and tell him she wanted her son returned to her now.

Dinner and dishes came and went. Her parents were reluctant to leave Star on her own in the bedroom, afraid she would have another nightmare, or somehow disappear again, but she insisted she was fine. Later in the evening, when they finally went to their room, Star went looking for Justin as he was locking up and setting the security alarm.

"Justin, I need a favor," she said.

"Sure. What do you need, sis?"

"Get the phone number for Special Agent Gleason of the FBI. He's the one who set up my rescue from Anton, and he's the one who took Sammy from the emergency room after the wreck. I want my son back."

"If Gleason finds where you are, the wrong people could also find out."

Star's shoulders slumped.

"I feel like I'm only half alive," she said. "Sammy is going to forget who I am."

"No, he won't, honey. I hate to say this and hurt you more, but right now, if Sammy is with you, he will be an even larger target."

"I hate this," she said and started crying.

"Let's do this," Justin said. "Let's still call this Gleason and tell him you're willing to testify *if* the Feds file charges against Baba now with what they already have. If they tell you they still want to gather some more information, then tell them you're no longer willing to testify and that you want your son delivered to you now or you're gone."

"Can I do that? Can I get away from the FBI?"

"They'll always know where you are, but they can't force you to testify."

"What if they won't let me have Sammy?"

Justin frowned.

"They can't refuse. You are not a criminal, and your brother just happens to be in law enforcement, too, which means I won't let them bully you."

"I just love you," Star said and threw her arms around Justin's neck and hugged him.

He ruffled his hand through her hair.

"I love you, too, honey. You're not alone anymore, so no more tears. I'll walk you to your bedroom, and we'll stop by the kitchen to get your meds. It's time to take them again."

They got the meds, and then he left her in her bedroom with a promise.

"Remember, Donna and I are right across the hall. You're safe here. So sleep well, and we'll tackle the dragon in the morning, okay?"

"Okay," she said and didn't make a move until she watched him leave.

Only then did she go to the bathroom to get ready for bed.

She was tired—so tired of fighting to survive. She

just wanted her baby and a car, and she'd be gone from this place so fast their heads would spin.

It was just after 8:00 a.m., and Gleason was on his way to a meeting when his cell phone signaled a call. He glanced at caller ID, and when it came up out of area he almost didn't answer it, then changed his mind.

"This is Gleason."

"This is Star Davis. We need to talk."

Gleason froze.

"Oh, my God! Star! We thought Baba had you. Where are you?"

"Well, Baba doesn't have me, and you don't need to know where I am because bad people follow you wherever you go, and I'm done with bad people. Understand?"

"Yes, yes. I am on my way back to my office, so I can talk more freely."

"How's my son?" she asked.

Gleason was hurrying so fast he was getting breathless. He was sadly out of shape.

"I'm sure he's fine," Gleason said.

"What do you mean, you're sure? Don't you know? Do you people not keep tabs on his care and condition?"

"Yes, of course… Well, not me personally but…"

"That does it!" Star shrieked. "I wasn't going to go this route, but I am now. I want my son back in my arms today."

"What are you going to—"

"Today!" she screamed. "I have authorities *I trust* who will gladly assist me in this. I will not show my

face to you or any of your people ever again, but I wil
show up in court the day I'm needed to testify and that's
all the fucking assurance you are ever going to get from
me. I have been used for the last time!"

Gleason groaned inwardly. They couldn't and wouldn't
withhold a child from a parent just to coerce testimony.
And he had to admit, they had only themselves to blame
for how she felt.

"I'll contact the people right now and wait for your
call."

"It won't be me you'll be speaking to. It will be a
member of law enforcement and whoever he deems capable of caring for a child during transport. If I find
out you have had him followed, I will take Sammy and
disappear off the face of this earth. And you and your
so-called case can go straight to hell. Do we understand
each other?"

"Yes, ma'am," Gleason said.

She disconnected in his ear.

He sighed.

The upside was Anton Baba did not have her.

The downside was neither did they.

True to her word, Gleason got a call a couple of hours
later from Star Davis's go-between.

"This is Officer Davis of the Nevada State Police.
I'm calling on behalf of Miss Davis, no relation, to set
up a pickup site for the return of her child, who is in
your custody. I will have caretakers with me to aid in
transport back to his mother."

Gleason began to argue.

"How do I know if you are—"

"Your responsibility toward the child is obviously
condhand, which does not assure Ms. Davis in any
ay that you have any interest in her son's well-being.
at's how you know I'm the real deal. It's exactly what
e said to you. Now, you will have the child brought
a designated GPS location at 4:00 p.m. today. The
ild will be transported in a single car to that loca-
on without accompanying guards or helicopters. Do
u have a pen?"

"Yes," Gleason said.

"The GPS location is…"

Gleason took it down, read it back to him to con-
rm, and then before he could say anything else, the
ne went dead.

"Well, hell. The way she's acting, you'd think we
ere the bad guys," he muttered.

He pulled up the number to the foster home where
e kid was being kept, and as soon as they answered,
e explained that he and his partner would be coming
ter Sammy within the hour and to have him ready,
en disconnected and called his partner, Lou, only to
nd out Lou was in the ER with food poisoning. He
lled his boss, who told him to take a female agent
ith him instead.

"Yes, sir, but I need an agent with experience with
ids. Just because she's a woman doesn't mean she
n keep a two-year-old happy for a long car ride with
rangers."

"Yes, of course," the director said. "I'll have someone who's baby-capable join you. What time are you leaving?"

"Within the next thirty minutes from our office," Gleason said.

"I'll have someone meet you there."

"Thank you, sir," Gleason said. He figured the kid might be hungry on the long drive, so he went to the break room to get some snacks from the vending machine. About to select a bag of chips, he realized a kid that little might not have the teeth to eat some of this stuff, so he pocketed his change again and made a quick run down to the cafeteria.

He came back with a couple of bananas, little lunch cups of applesauce, a handful of vanilla wafers in a small sealed container, a packet of wet wipes and some plastic spoons. Then he settled in to wait for the other agent to arrive, absently wondering as he waited who it would be.

Ten minutes later a short, stocky man came hurrying into his office with a big smile on his face. His suit was rumpled, his tie was askew, and as he came closer, Gleason could see food spots on his tie and another one on his lapel.

What the hell?

"Agent Penny reporting for duty," he said and flashed his badge.

"What department are you from?" Gleason asked, knowing immediately that this guy had not seen any action—at least not recently.

"Payroll," Penny replied.

"Payroll? The director sent someone from Payroll to accompany me? Did he say why?"

"He thought I was a good fit for the job."

"Really?" Gleason said. "Have you ever worked in the field?"

"No, sir," Penny said.

Gleason frowned.

"Are you qualified on the gun range?"

"Nearly," Penny said.

Gleason stared. How did one nearly qualify?

"Then what skill do you possess that he thought would be perfect for this?"

"My wife and I have eight children, one of which I delivered...not by choice, just by consequence."

Gleason sighed. He had asked for this.

"All right, then," Gleason said. "Let's get started."

"I need to get some stuff out of my car before we leave. It's in the parking garage."

"Like what?" Gleason asked.

"Disposable diapers, some wet wipes and a lovey."

Gleason's eyebrows arched high enough to take flight.

"What the hell is a lovey?"

"A toy to sleep with. I keep a new one or two in the car for emergencies."

"Emergencies?" Gleason echoed.

"Yes, like being forty miles from home before one of the kids discovers they've left their own lovey behind by mistake. You cannot imagine the hell of driving eighty miles round trip to go back for Leroy."

Gleason sighed. He should have let it go, but by now he had to know.

"Who is Leroy?"

Penny smiled. "A stuffed giraffe with a broken neck and one ear. He's Lucy's favorite lovey. Lucy is my youngest."

And that's when Gleason got it. The director knew exactly what he was doing. Gleason was the one slow on the uptake.

"Then let's get going," he said. "We have to get the kid and then drive a good distance to reach the drop-off site."

"Absolutely," Penny said.

Star was beside herself with anxiety. She was so homesick for her baby she couldn't talk about him without bursting into tears.

Once her family learned about Star's ultimatum, they went into overdrive. Her parents went to town with a list Star had given them of things they would need for a toddler. Basic clothing, a couple of lightweight blankets, one pair of little tennis shoes in his size, even a baby toothbrush and toothpaste, toys and diapers. Her parents were over the moon getting to buy stuff for their first grandchild and hurried to fill the list. They didn't have as much time to dawdle over the adorable baby things, though, because they would be going along with Justin to bring Sammy back, posing as foster parents helping with transport.

Justin already had the rest of the week off and was immediately ready. When he made the call to Gleason, his heart was pounding. There should not be any danger to this at all. The location he'd chosen was in the middle of nowhere, and with nothing for anyone to hide behind. It was as straightforward as he could make it.

Star kept thanking all of them over and over. It had been so long since she'd had anyone on her side that she'd forgotten what it felt like to know people had her back. Hopefully his arrival wouldn't cause Justin and Donna an even bigger hardship, and they wouldn't be there long. Her parents were already planning to take her home, though she kept explaining the danger that might put them in and the need for her presence at home to be under wraps. No journalists at the door wanting to interview the missing girl. No neighbors in and out wanting to see the baby.

And then her father stopped her.

"Starla. It's going to be all right. The house on our right is for sale, and the old woman who lives on the left has a caretaker and never leaves her house. Honestly, there aren't any people left in our immediate area who knew you or even know we had a child go missing. I think it will be fine, okay?"

"Okay."

Donna was at work, and so when they all left, Star was in the house by herself. She locked all the doors, got out the pistol she'd stolen from Luis and settled down to wait. It was going to be the longest three hours of her life.

Gleason had never been so happy for Penny's presence, because the little boy was unhappy with both of them. The only thing that had calmed him was the food he'd brought and Penny's lovey, a stuffed chicken named Henny. Despite the kid's constant shrieking, Penny seemed to be enjoying himself.

"You are a fine little man, yes, you are," Penny cooed and casually draped the little blanket around Sammy's shoulders.

Sammy's eyelids were droopy, and Penny was hoping the child would soon fall asleep. The blanket might speed up the process.

Sure enough, Sammy's head began to nod. His shrieks morphed into prattle as he rubbed his lovey against his face.

Agent Penny smiled. His oldest son, Reese, used to do that when he fought sleep. Slowly, the chatter tapered off, and when silence finally fell, Gleason gave Penny a thumbs-up.

Penny smiled at him in the rearview mirror and then leaned back against the seat and closed his eyes. But no sooner had they shut than he opened them again and sat up a little straighter, reminding himself that he was on a case, not a family car trip.

He got a couple of wet wipes and quietly went about cleaning up the vanilla wafer crumbs from the child's seat and from Gleason's upholstery, then wiped his hands and put everything in a sack he was using for trash.

"How much farther do we have to go?" Penny asked softly.

"About fifteen minutes or so."

Penny took a three-sixty view of the land in which they were driving.

"There's nothing here… Miles and miles of nothing but desert with mountains on the horizon," he said and then settled back against the seat.

Gleason agreed. Now that they were in the area, he understood the thinking behind this meeting place. There was nowhere to hide and no sneaking up on anyone. Pretty smart move on the part of the state cop.

He glanced up in the rearview mirror to the sleeping toddler. Now that he was quiet, Gleason had to admit he was pretty cute. All that dark curly hair and a really sweet face. He looked like his mother, except his hair was dark. He wondered what it was going to be like to grow up with a father who was the head of an organized crime ring.

And then he looked back at the highway and glanced at his GPS. They were almost there.

Justin had been parked at the location for almost thirty minutes now and had come early on purpose, not wanting any surprises. His parents had been talking nonstop about this, but the closer it got to the time, the quieter they became. He hoped he had impressed the need for cool detachment from both of them. They were supposed to be a set of foster parents who had volunteered for this duty, and nothing more.

He glanced up in the rearview mirror and saw tears on his mother's cheeks.

"Mom?"

Connie quickly wiped them away.

"I'm sorry. I just keep thinking about what Starla has gone through, and I just can't understand why things like this happen to good people."

"Bad things happen because of bad people waiting to take advantage of innocent people."

"It's just so horrendous, it's hard to wrap my head around that world she was in, and the things she must have had to do to—"

"Stop it!" John said. "Just stop it right now! That shit doesn't matter. It's never to be talked about unless she brings it up. Understand?"

Connie was crying again.

"I know. I just—"

"Damn it, Connie! We thought she was dead! I'm sorry for everything bad she went through, but I am so grateful that she found a way to live through it. We have our family back, plus a bonus grandson. How freaking awesome is that?"

Justin frowned.

"Mom, wipe your face and get it together. They could be here at any time now."

Connie grabbed a handful of tissues and wiped her eyes and blew her nose, then took a brush to her hair.

John leaned over and kissed her.

She smiled.

Justin sighed. Disaster averted.

Another minute passed, and then he saw a vehicle topping a rise in the road and grabbed his binoculars.

"Someone's coming," he said.

"Is it them?" Connie cried.

"I don't know yet," Justin said and kept watching.

As the car approached, Justin could guess by its make that it was the Feds. And when that car began slowing down, he knew he was right.

"Yes, it's them. Just sit. When I need you, I'll motion for you to get out. And remember what I said."

"We know, son. We won't let you down," John said.

"We're all here for Starla. Remember that," Justin said, and then he opened the door and got out.

Fourteen

Gleason saw the car about a half mile before they reached the site. Watching it through the heat waves dancing up from the pavement was like seeing it through a veil. The car was not a state police car, which bothered him at first, and then he realized the cop might not be doing this on government time.

"Is that them?" Penny asked, as Gleason started slowing down.

"I would assume so since there's not another vehicle in sight and they're in the exact GPS location they said they would be."

Penny started gathering up the baby's things. He gently rubbed the little boy's knee, and when Gleason came to a full stop, Penny unlocked his seat belt.

"Wait here until I make sure everything is on the up-and-up," Gleason said.

"Yes, sir," Penny said.

The fact that they were no longer moving had already roused the toddler, and when Gleason got out, the

lick of the door woke him up the rest of the way. He
sat up, looking all around, and then stuck his thumb in
his mouth and started sucking as the desert heat rolled
through the interior of the car.

"You are such a good boy," Penny said and ruffled
the dark curls.

Sammy pointed at the lovey.

"Henny," he said.

Penny beamed.

"Yes, your Henny," he said and tucked it in the little boy's arm as Gleason approached the man getting
out of the car.

"I'm Agent Gleason," he said and flashed his badge.

Justin showed his, as well.

"Officer Davis, Nevada Highway Patrol," he said.
"Where's the baby?"

"In the car," Gleason said and then motioned at
Penny.

Justin was antsy. He watched the other man get out
and circle the car to get to the baby. At that point he motioned to his parents. They came out of the car a little
too fast, but did maintain their personas.

Justin's heart was pounding as he watched the man
come toward them with the toddler in his arms. This
moment would be forever etched in his heart. That
sweet little dark-haired boy was his nephew.

When his parents stopped beside him, he addressed
them impersonally for Gleason's sake.

"One of you take the child, the other one get his
things."

"Yes, sir," John said.

And as much as they'd worried about Connie, when it came down to it, she was the one who sold it.

"Has he been fed?" she asked, as Agent Penny handed the toddler and his stuffed toy to her husband.

"Some cookies and fruit on the way here," Penny said and handed her the sack with what was left over.

"Is he in diapers still, or pull-ups?"

"Diapers," Penny said. "Extra-large."

Connie nodded. Then as much as she wanted to throw her arms around the child, instead she reached out and felt his forehead.

"He has no fever. Has he been well or is there anything we'll need to know about his recent health history?"

Penny shrugged and looked at Gleason.

Gleason sighed. Once more they were coming up short.

"We assume his health has been maintained or else we would have been notified," Gleason said.

Connie frowned, then waved John away, careful to call him a name other than his own.

"It's hot, Peter. Get the child inside the car. I'll be right behind you."

She turned away from a hot gust of wind as Penny handed her the rest of the toddler's things, including the blanket.

"Anything else we need to know?" she asked.

"The lovey's name is Henny," he said.

She smiled primly.

"A perfect name. Simple. Easy enough for him to learn to say. Good job, sir," she said and nodded at her son and headed back to the car with a calm and steady stride.

"That's that, then," Justin said and turned to walk away.

"Wait!" Gleason said. "How can we get in touch with Star when we need her?"

"I'm not privy to any of that information, sir, but I'll pass that question on to her when I deliver the child. She will probably be in touch with you. You both go back to your car and leave now," he said.

Gleason frowned.

"Why do we—"

"Sir. I have strict orders to make sure we are not followed. I remind you. Star's threat to disappear is not a hoax. Piss that woman off again and she's gone."

Gleason pivoted and strode back to the car. His stride was long, and Justin could tell by the way he was walking that he was mad, but as his mother was so fond of saying, they could get happy in the same pants they got mad in.

He stood in the heat with the sun beaming hot against the back of his neck until the car was out of sight, and then made a run for his own car.

Connie was changing Sammy's diaper as Justin got in.

"Mom, take off everything he has on, even the shoes, and give them to me," he said.

"But why?" she asked.

"I'd bet a month's wages there's a bug in them somewhere."

"The hell you say," John muttered.

Sammy laughed when they began taking off his clothes. Connie grinned.

"I've never seen a little child who didn't like to be naked."

She handed the pieces of clothing to Justin as she took them off, and he began inspecting them seam by seam, hem by hem, and found the first bug in the hem of the little shirt he'd had on. The second bug beneath the inner sole of his shoe.

"Dad, run your fingers through his hair carefully, feeling to see if there's something stuck to his head that would be hidden within all those curls."

John did as he was told, his hands shaking in disbelief that this was even necessary.

"What would it feel like?" John asked.

"Maybe like a little mole," Justin said.

"I don't know. I can't tell," John said.

"Give him to me," Connie said. "I used to comb the kids' hair for lice when they were in elementary school. There was always someone coming to school and spreading it around," she muttered.

She pulled a comb from her purse and began gently combing through the curls in one quadrant after another until she'd covered the entire head.

"No. Nothing here."

"Then it was all in the clothing," Justin said and tossed it out the window.

"What about this toy?" Connie asked.

Justin took the stuffed chicken.

"Did you bring another toy with you?" he asked.

"Yes, we brought several," Connie said.

"Then this is going out the window, too," Justin said. "You did bring other clothes, right?"

"Just a little T-shirt and diapers. Everything else is back at the house."

"So get him dressed in that and hurry," Justin said. "I want out of here as fast as possible, and I need him safely in the car seat first."

Connie had him changed and buckled in his car seat in less than three minutes.

Justin was impressed.

"Buckle up, everybody." He put the car in gear, then sped away, heading north to Henderson as fast as he dared to go.

Agents Gleason and Penny pulled over less than a mile away from the drop site.

"What's wrong?" Penny asked, as Gleason reached for his laptop in the back seat.

"Just checking to see if the tracking devices are active."

Penny's eyes widened.

"Oh, wow… You mean we bugged the kid?"

"Of course. How else will we know where Star Davis is at?"

He booted up the laptop, then clicked on the tracking program. Almost instantly a map of the area appeared with a blinking cursor on the GPS site they'd just left.

"There it is," Gleason said. "It's working fine, and see, they're still there. Probably getting the kid settled in."

"Or they may have had to change him," Penny said.

"Right," Gleason said, and they sat, staring at the map and waiting for the cursor to begin moving.

They waited for over five minutes before Gleason started to frown.

"This has been a long damn time," he muttered.

Another ten minutes passed and the cursor didn't move.

"I don't get it," Gleason said.

He handed the laptop to Penny and turned around and headed back.

"Why do you think they haven't moved?" Penny asked.

Gleason's eyes narrowed, but he didn't speak, and when they topped a rise in the highway less than a quarter of a mile from the site, Gleason sighed.

"Son of a bitch."

"What?" Penny asked.

Gleason drove up on the site, saw the clothes scattered about the area. When Penny saw the stuffed toy he'd given the boy lying in the sand, he frowned.

"This toy wasn't bugged," he said.

"They didn't know that," Gleason said.

They both got out and gathered up the things, then got back into their car.

"Cop was smarter than I gave him credit," Gleason said. "He obviously found the bugs and that's why they dumped the toy, too."

Penny brushed it off, then laid it in the seat beside them.

"I'm taking it home. My kids will like it. Damn shame. Sammy liked it, too."

Gleason was thoughtful as he returned to the highway and headed back to Las Vegas. Now they were going to have to trust Star Davis to keep her word, which meant they had to keep theirs, too, or the deal was off. Next thing on their agenda: filing official charges against Anton Baba.

Justin kept an eye on the rearview mirror as he drove. They were five miles down the road before they met their first car. He knew the highways in this state as good as anyone, and this old highway was rarely used except for the people who lived out this way. It had been a good place for the drop-off and a good road to keep an eye on the possibility of pursuit. When he was certain there was no one behind them, he glanced at his parents in the rearview mirror instead.

It was obvious his mother was in love.

"Just look at him, John! He's beautiful. Absolutely beautiful. Get one of those toys we brought. He's nearly through with his vanilla wafer."

John dug through the shopping bag and pulled out a storybook. It was a small board book with a half-dozen pages—easy turning for little fingers. And it was about Winnie the Pooh.

"How's this?" he asked.

"Perfect," Connie said. "Let me get the cookie cleaned off his fingers and then we'll read it."

While Connie was wiping him down, John pointed at Sammy's belly.

"Who's that?" he asked.

Sammy looked up at John.

"Sammy," he said, patting his belly.

"Welcome to the family, little man," John said softly and then settled in for the ride.

Star was sick to her stomach with nerves. Every time she looked at the clock it seemed to be on the same time, and the longer her family was gone the more worried she became. When the house phone finally rang, she ran to answer.

"Hello?"

"We have him," Justin said. "We should be home within the hour."

"Oh, my God!" Star said and sank to her knees. "Is he okay? Is he crying? What do Mother and Dad think about him?"

Justin chuckled.

"He's pretty damn perfect…a regular little rock star, sis. No, he's not crying and has already charmed us all."

"Thank God. Did the Feds give you a hard time?"

"Not really. I told them you'd stay in touch and warned them not to try and follow. Oh… I checked what he was wearing and found two different tracking bugs. We tossed the clothes, so he's coming home clean. Are you okay?"

"I'm okay. I'll be even better when I see my boy."

"I can only imagine," Justin said. "See you soon."

"Yes, see you," Star said and then ran to her bedroom and hid the gun back in the shoe box at the top of the closet.

She was leaving the room when she caught a glimpse of herself in the mirror and stopped. She looked so difrent with her hair practically gone—what if her baby dn't recognize her?

But then as fast as she panicked, she let it go. There as no way to assume how Sammy would react, but she as still Mama. He would figure it all out on his own.

She ran straight to the kitchen and checked what od was on hand that she knew Sammy would eat. here was plenty. By the time they got here it would e dinnertime.

Oh, my God, oh, my God, her baby was coming me.

Sammy's patience was gone.

"Want down," he shrieked, and he was trying to un- ckle the restraint keeping him in the baby seat and as throwing toys on the floor and vanilla wafers at e back of Justin's head.

"Not yet, darling," Connie said. "Almost home. We're most home. We're going to see Mama, okay? I can't lieve we didn't ask if he still took a bottle. Is there still me water left in one of the bottles?"

"A little," John said and took off the lid and handed to her.

"Sammy, want a drink?" Connie said.

"Yes, a grink," Sammy said and opened his mouth ke a little bird.

Connie held it to his lips and slowly poured, giv- g him time to swallow between breaths. Some water ent down his chin and the front of his shirt, and some f it went in his mouth, but it was enough. As soon as she screwed the lid back on the bottle, Sammy let out another shriek.

"Mama!" he cried and tried even harder to get out.

"Connie, I would say it was not a good move mentioning his mother," John said.

"Well, you try something," she muttered.

"As you can tell by the applesauce on the front of my shirt, I have already been dismissed."

Justin glanced up in the rearview mirror.

"I'm sorry, guys. It's not much farther," he said.

John wrapped the blanket around Sammy's neck.

"Here you go, buddy."

Sammy grabbed one end of the blanket, stuck his thumb in his mouth and started rubbing the fuzz back and forth across his nose. Within seconds, his eyes were rolling back in his head, and silence reigned.

Connie gave her husband a thumbs-up and leaned back against the seat in exhaustion. Then she looked at her husband and stuck her thumb in her mouth, too, which made John grin. They were both exhausted.

"Poor little man," John said. "He's been with strangers ever since the night of that wreck. I can't imagine what must be going on in his head."

"We're less than five minutes from home," Justin said.

Connie began gathering up what Sammy had tossed, and John pulled out a handful of wet wipes and began wiping down the seats.

When Justin finally turned down his street and they saw his home, all three of them gave a big sigh of relief, and when Justin parked the car and killed the engine, Sammy woke back up again.

Justin saw the front door open and wished he'd had the foresight to tell Starla not to come outside, but then he realized she was standing back in the shadows… She could see out, but people couldn't see much of her.

Good girl, he thought, and got out.

Sammy's attitude shifted straight to happy when John lifted him out of the baby seat and handed him to Connie.

Connie gave him a quick kiss on the side of his cheek.

"You are such a good boy," she said.

Justin helped them out, grabbed all the gear and quickly ushered his parents inside out of the heat.

Connie was anxious on her daughter's behalf, hoping this reunion would be all she needed it to be, but she needn't have worried. The moment they crossed the threshold, Sammy saw Star and squealed.

"Mama!"

Star burst into tears as she took him out of her mother's arms while Sammy kept patting her face, and then pulling at her hair, and saying "all gone" over and over.

"Yes! Mama cut her hair! Now it's short like yours. I missed you so much, my little man. Mama is so glad to see you."

Sammy went from the bad mood he'd had earlier to clinging to Star so tightly it was hard for her to breathe. And that's when she knew her absence had frightened him. He didn't have the words to ask where she had been, but he had missed her.

Everyone was smiling and just a little teary-eyed a
the sweet reunion.

"I feel like we just pulled off a heist or something,"
Connie said.

Justin grinned.

"You were awesome, Mom. You and Dad were perfect. You should have seen them, Starla. Mom was al
business and working her foster parent persona like a
pro. She even called Dad Peter, so if anyone started trying to trace them as foster parents, they wouldn't have
proper names to start with."

Star turned to her family with her baby clutched tight
against her breasts.

"I will never be able to thank you enough for this
When the car we were in started rolling, I wasn't sure
we would even live through what was happening, then
knowing he was alive and not being able to hold him
was awful. Now I have my baby back, and I'm back
with my family. For the first time in seven years I feel
whole."

"Mama cry?" Sammy said and poked a finger in the
tears on her face.

"I'm okay, Sammy. They're just happy tears," she
said.

Sammy tucked his face against her neck and pulled
the blanket up to his face.

"I think it's time to get some dinner started," Connie
said. "Starla, you go get reacquainted with your boy.
We've got this."

"I want to go home," Star said.

"Absolutely," John said. "We've already talked about

how we can set up the spare bedroom for a nursery, and it's right next door to your old room."

"I want to leave tomorrow," Star said.

Justin frowned.

"I don't know if we'll be able to get plane tickets that soon."

"We can't fly," Star said. "I don't have any ID, and if I did, it would leave a trail for Anton to follow."

John nodded, surprised they hadn't considered those problems. "You're right. Don't worry," he said. "We'll rent a big roomy car and drive home."

"Anything you want, darling. Anything you want," Connie said.

"I want to go as far away from this place as I can safely get. I want to go home," she said.

Tears were still running down her cheeks as she carried Sammy back to her room and closed the door.

Back in Vegas, Anton Baba's absence was beginning to be felt. There was a small explosion and fire in the kitchen of one of his bordellos outside of the city, while in another part of the state the manager of another bordello was desperately trying to contact him about two deaths in the house, both of which were under investigation. One had been a suicide and the other was an overdose.

The day manager in Baba's Lucky Joe's Casino was in an all-out war of words with the night manager over punishment for one of the dealers who'd been caught skimming.

And then out of the blue, a stranger showed up at the

bordello near Reno where the fire had taken place. The janitor saw him drive up in a gold Lexus, and when he parked in Anton's special parking place he called out to the receptionist.

"Hey, Lola, some dude in a gold Lexus just parked in Mr. Baba's parking place. He's coming inside."

"Thank you, Barry. Now get that trash wagon out of here before he walks in the door."

"Yeah, okay," Barry said and pushed the big bin down a hall and out of sight.

Lola was watching the door when the man walked in. Average height. Nothing remarkable about him—until he came closer and Lola had to stifle a shudder. While everything about him appeared perfectly normal, there was something terrifying about his eyes. Something distant, something hard, something…cold as ice.

"Good morning. My name is Mr. Stewart. You are…?" he said.

"Good morning, Mr. Stewart. I'm Lola, the day manager of this establishment."

He was carefully eyeing the setup and the decor as he moved to the counter.

"I'm making the rounds today and introducing myself. I'll be handling all of Anton's holdings now that he's out of the country."

Lola frowned.

"He's out of the country? He didn't say anything to us."

"He didn't have much time to wind things up. The Feds— Well, let's just say Mr. Baba is otherwise occupied at the moment and his holdings will need to be tended to. We're old business partners, so I'm doing this favor for him in his absence."

Lola frowned.

"The Feds? We didn't know about any federal investigation."

Stewart ignored her.

"Is the fire damage being repaired?"

"Yes, sir, they worked on it some today and then ran into a snag and will be back tomorrow with different wiring."

"Good, good. Now, if you'll show me to his office, I'll take a quick lay of the land. I'd like to check out the girls, as well, so please have them in the lobby within the hour. I need to speak with all of them at once, and then I'll have to be on my way. I still have to stop in at our other locations."

She showed him to the office, then quickly called all of the girls and ordered them to the lobby, dressed and smiling.

Stewart smirked, thinking about Baba hiding out down in Mexico, unaware that his empire was being taken over by new owners. After a quick check of the books, he went back to the lobby and did a quick run-through of the hookers on site.

"Just so you ladies are aware, I'll be taking over in Mr. Baba's absence. I don't know what your rules were before, but I'll tell you now that I expect superb grooming habits and high-end lingerie. I will have a doctor in weekly to do drug tests and blood tests for communicable diseases. No one gets a free pass. One strike and you'll be on the first transport out to Asia. You don't really want that to happen, because that's where old hookers go to die, so do yourself a favor and make sure you're up to snuff."

The fear on their faces was obvious, but he was unconcerned. He moved among the women, getting a closer look at their skin, the circles under their eyes and the carefully hidden needle marks. He even recognized a couple of them from older shipments and nodded at them in turn.

"Becky…right? And you, your name is Elizabeth… no, Elspeth…right?"

They nodded and then looked down, unable to meet his gaze.

"Well, now, this is a fine group, Lola. See that you keep them this way," he said. Then he turned and left as abruptly as he'd arrived.

Lola scowled as the girls all started talking at once.

"Get on with you," she snapped. "I have some phone calls to make."

Back in her office, she tried for two hours to get in touch with Anton before giving up and leaving him a message.

The manager of the other whorehouse got the same visit from Mr. Stewart, but was glad to see him arrive. He was exactly what they needed to get the cops off their backs regarding the deaths of two girls in one week. He took control of the situation and soon had death certificates clearing them of any wrongdoing.

On the third day, Mr. Stewart showed up at Lucky Joe's Casino with the same story for the manager as

'd told the others. Stewart soon had access to Anton
aba's office.

Everywhere he went, he left questions and confusion
hind. No one was sure if they could trust this stoic
ranger who'd just barged in and snapped up control.
it the frantic phone calls to their trusted boss went un-
swered, and so for now they all resigned themselves
accepting the new leadership.

Fifteen

Since his arrival in Mexico, Anton had been deep-sea fishing, frequenting a different bar each evening and entertaining a different woman at his estate each night. He was oblivious as to what was going on within his empire because he'd misplaced his phone the first night—a mistake that now seemed to him an unplanned blessing. It was almost as if the troubles of home didn't matter anymore. If he didn't know about them, they couldn't hurt him.

On his third night away, he'd brought home a young woman from the village and was already making plans to coerce her into the business when he went back home. He had lots of customers wanting Spanish-speaking hookers, and this one was stunning. Even though he usually depended upon Mr. Stewart to populate his bordellos, it never hurt to pick and choose a woman himself now and then, so he chose Estella.

Anton spent the entire night in what some would call an all-out orgy involving Estella and two other women.

Anton was exhausted when it was over, but thoroughly sated.

The next morning, he rose from bed and made a call to his kitchen staff to ready his breakfast as the women were getting ready to leave. One of them was down on her hands and knees looking beneath the bed for a missing shoe. When she stood a few minutes later, she'd not only found her shoe, but Anton's missing phone, as well.

"Senor…is this yours?" she asked.

Anton looked up from his coffee and the paper he'd been reading on his laptop with surprise.

"Yes! Where on earth did you find that?"

"Beneath the bed, Senor."

"Thank you," Anton said, and he tipped her an extra hundred dollars for the discovery.

As soon as they were gone he got the phone cord out to recharge, plugged it in and went down to breakfast. It was midmorning when he remembered the phone and ran up to his suite to retrieve it.

He read the first message in horror and then saw repeated messages from all of his holdings in Nevada, as well as a message from his lawyer that there was a federal warrant out for his arrest.

"Damn it all to hell," he muttered and then went down the list of people he needed to contact. This was exactly why he hadn't missed his cell phone.

The law firm was the first on his list.

"Prosper, Prosper and Gooch," the receptionist said.

"This is Anton Baba returning Conrad's call."

"Yes, sir, one moment," she said and put the call through.

"This is Conrad."

"Conrad, this is Anton."

"Where the hell have you been? I've been trying to contact you for days! Are you in Vegas?"

"No. I'm not even in the States."

"Well, then. We need to discuss this situation."

"I'm coming home," Anton said wearily. "I'll come by the office when I get back in the city."

"The Feds will have you in jail the moment you cross back into US territory."

"Not if they don't recognize me," he said.

"Okay, it's your call. But if you wind up behind bars, call me and we'll see about getting you arraigned quickly and out on bail."

"This arrest warrant is going to go away," Anton said.

"Are there witnesses?"

"Not for long," he snapped.

"I don't want to know, but stay in touch," Conrad said.

"Yes, of course," Anton said.

Then he began returning the many missed phone calls.

It didn't take long for the bordello managers to figure out Baba had an enemy who was trying to take over his holdings.

"Just don't let on that you've spoken to me," Baba said when he'd learned about what Stewart had been up to. "I'll see to him, personally."

One by one, the managers agreed.

When he called Lucky Joe's to put them on guard

he soon found out Stewart was using the casino penthouse for a residence, and swore the manager to secrecy.

It was midafternoon by the time he called his pilot, Paul Franklin. The phone rang three times before Franklin picked up.

"Hello? Paul speaking."

"Paul, this is Anton. Listen, has anyone contacted you about using the jet?"

"No, sir. Should I be expecting them?"

"No. Just making sure where I stand. I have someone who's trying to take over my holdings."

"Oh no!" Paul said.

"Exactly," Anton said. "So I need you to come get me."

"Yes, sir. What day and time?" he asked.

"Tomorrow morning around 10:00 a.m. Vegas time."

"Yes, sir. I'll file flight plans tonight."

"I don't want anyone to know you're coming after me," he said.

"Not a problem, Mr. Baba. I can work around that. Don't worry."

"Perfect," Anton said. "I'll see you in the morning."

"Yes, sir."

"Oh…and don't bother bringing Linda. The fewer people who know I'm coming, the better."

"No problem," Paul said.

Anton disconnected.

Now all he needed was to call Paco Cruz and find out if he truly did find one of the witnesses.

He tried to contact him by phone but got voice mail,

and he wasn't about to leave a message. He'd just have
to try later.

Right now his focus needed to be on getting back
into the States undetected, and he'd long ago prepared for such a contingency. He'd not had a haircut
in weeks, nor had he shaved since his arrival, and now
the salt-and-pepper beard he was growing was going
to prove useful.

Quinn didn't remember anything about the ride home
from the doctor's office and had no idea how much she'd
revealed about herself.

What she did notice over the next two days was that
Nick seemed rattled by the fact that the infection popped
up the morning after their first time making love, and
that he'd been treating her like she might break ever
since. She'd dropped hints that she wanted him to take
her back to bed, but eventually he came right out and
told her he wasn't putting her in that danger again until
she was well.

In her opinion, it wasn't all his decision, and she
certainly wasn't on the same page. She wanted that
closeness and the mind-blowing sex that came with it
back again.

She wanted him.

And it was hard not to want him when he was around
all the time. He'd been working on some cases from
home recently, so he could be around to take care of her.
When he wasn't doing that, he spent time with Quinn,
and by now they had learned a number of small details
about each other. He knew her favorite color was yel-

ow. She liked ginger ale and eating cheese sandwiches with potato chips between the bread and cheese, and she liked yoga.

She knew his favorite color was red. He liked Budweiser beer and hot dogs with homemade chili, and he was really good at dancing the two-step.

And every evening after the sun went down, Quinn went with him out to the pool, sat on the side with her feet dangling in the water and watched him swim his laps.

What they didn't know was that someone else was watching them, too. Someone named Paco Cruz. It had taken him two days to find out where Nick Saldano lived, but when he'd come to check out the address and found the redhead there, he was already counting the money Anton would be giving him for that info.

He watched them through a crack in the privacy fence just long enough to determine they seemed to have a personal relationship as well, and then slipped away.

Unaware Quinn's safety had been compromised, Nick continued to swim, trying to wear himself out so he'd be able to sleep, when all he wanted was to take her to bed and make love until the sun came up.

Eventually, he got tired and swam up to where she was sitting.

"It's about time you came to rescue me," Quinn said and put both hands on his wet chest and pulled him close.

"I didn't know you were in danger," he said as he waded between her legs.

"I'm not yet, but I was hoping you might feel reckless." She locked her hands around his waist.

"You have no idea what's going through my mind," he said, then slid his hands beneath her hair and kissed her until she was trembling.

"Are you cold, baby?" he asked.

But before she could answer, Nick heard his front doorbell ring.

"That's weird," he said, as he climbed out and grabbed a towel, tying it around his waist as he took her by the hand and went inside. "Wait here," he said.

She stood in the darkened hallway as the doorbell rang again. Nick turned on the exterior light and looked through the peephole, then opened the door to see one of his neighbors standing on the doorstep.

"Hey, Rick, what's going on?" Nick said.

"Hey—listen. This may sound strange, and it might not mean anything, but you need to know there was a guy on the back side of your security fence watching you while you were in the pool just now."

The skin crawled on the back of Nick's neck.

"Did you get a good look at him?"

"So-so. He was so busy looking at you, he didn't even know I was in my backyard. He was Latino, I'm sure of that. Midthirties, I'd guess. He ran with a limp and drove off in an old car."

"I don't suppose you got the license plate?" Nick asked.

Rick grinned. "As a matter of fact…" He handed Nick a piece of paper with the tag number on it.

Nick grinned.

"This is great, Rick! Thank you."

"Hey…you give the whole neighborhood a sense of safety because we have a cop living among us. I'm happy to give back. Have a nice night."

"You, too," Nick said and closed the door. As he turned around, Quinn walked into the room.

All the joy that had been on her face was gone.

"They found me, didn't they?"

"I don't know, but I'm going to run this plate and then we should know more. Come to the office with me while I call this in."

And just like that, Quinn was afraid all over again. She'd sold herself on this false sense of security because it was Nick protecting her, but she could no longer kid herself. She needed to be making a backup plan. Nick might not always be around.

Nick circled the desk to get to his computer, logged on, then made a quick call on his landline to his department.

"Homicide, Daniels speaking."

"Hey, Daniels, it's me, Nick."

"Saldano…how goes it, buddy? Still got an extra hole in your head?"

"It's healing," Nick said. "Doctor won't release me for duty yet, but I'm okay. Listen, I need a favor. One of my neighbors just caught some guy doing a Peeping Tom routine in my backyard tonight while I was in the pool. He got a tag number. I need you to run it for me."

"You got it," Daniels said. "Give me the number."

Nick read it off.

"Okay…got it. Just give me a few seconds to run the plate," Daniels said.

Nick winked at Quinn as he waited, but she wasn't even pretending everything was okay.

"Okay…here we go," Daniels said. "Are you ready?"

"Yes," Nick said and grabbed a pen and a notepad.

"The plate belongs to a perp named Paco Cruz. He's got quite a rap sheet. Done time in a federal prison… Whoa…here we go."

"What is it?" Nick asked.

"Used to work for Anton Baba."

Nick's heart sank.

"Used to?"

"Last known employment is a cleaning service, but nothing linked to Baba."

"Do you have an address for him?"

"Yes. Are you ready?"

"Give it to me," Nick said and then wrote down the address. "Thanks a lot, man. I owe you."

"Just get well soon. We miss you. Murphy's not near as much fun as you are," Daniels said.

Nick heard him laugh and knew Murphy had probably thrown something at him.

"Thanks again," Nick said and disconnected. Then he typed in the address on his computer to get a location and printed off a map of the area.

When he turned around to talk to Quinn, she was no longer in the office. He got up and went looking.

She was standing in the middle of her bedroom looking as lost as she had the first day he'd brought her home.

Nick walked up behind her, slid an arm around her waist and kissed her behind her ear.

"Well, is he connected to Anton Baba?" she asked.

Nick sighed.

"Yes."

"I need to leave," she said. "Staying in Vegas is suicide. I should have left days ago."

Nick's heart skipped a beat.

"No, no, you can't leave," he said and turned her around to face him. "He would just follow you until he found you somewhere else, only then I couldn't protect you."

"We're both nursing bullet wounds," she said. "Who's to say we'd be so lucky as to survive a second round of gunshots?"

Nick was trying not to panic as he took her in his arms.

"Please, Quinn. I'll keep you safe. I promise. I don't want to lose you. Ever."

Quinn's composure shattered. He'd finally said what she'd been longing to hear, but now there was no joy in hearing it. She started crying.

"I don't want to lose you either, but you already got shot once because of me."

"Hell, no," Nick said. "That's my job. It could have been anybody, and I still would have jumped in front of that bullet. That's something you'll have to come to terms with no matter what. My job is to protect people. And I'm always going to have someone pissed off at me, but I'm not going to live my life in hiding. If some-

one else had shot me—someone completely unrelate
to Baba—would you leave me?"

"No."

"Then this is the same thing to me. Just part of m
job. I hate that in this case it's also a threat for you, bu
if you left me, it wouldn't change the danger I face ever
day. And on top of that, I'd be so lonely without you
Damn it, Queenie…is this where you suddenly decid
you can't love a cop?"

She leaned forward, her forehead against his ches
and her fingers in the belt loops of his jeans.

"Just shut up. I can't think when you're making sense.

Relieved, Nick put his arms around her and pulle
her close.

"We'll figure this out together. Okay?"

"Okay."

"And no leaving me."

"No leaving."

"Promise?"

She looked up.

"I promise I will never leave you…so if you happe
to come home some day and find me missing, you bet
ter come looking for me, because I left under duress."

"I will. Quinn, I'm sorry this is happening, baby, bu
we both knew Baba would not give up easily. He has
lot to lose if he goes to prison."

Her shoulders slumped and she sighed, but then sh
seemed to gain some resolve, looking up with a sultr
grin and a gleam in her eye.

"Well, I don't give up easily, either. Now tell me, d
you think I'm still too delicate to take to bed?"

He laughed out loud.

"Probably not."

"Then lock the doors, set the alarm and follow me. And don't waste time. I might start without you."

She poked him in the chest with her finger and then left him standing in the hall as she walked away.

Nick took off through the house, locking up and setting the house alarm, and then headed for his bedroom on a run.

The room was dark but the night-light from his bathroom was on, and it was clearly enough light for him to see that Quinn was in the middle of his bed, her long red hair splayed out across two pillows, and naked as the day she was born. With only swim trunks to shed, he was naked and beside her in seconds.

"Thanks for waiting," he said.

"Time's up," she said and parted her legs.

He moved between them, and without so much as a pretense at foreplay, he slid inside her. She locked her legs around his waist as he began to move.

Nick was hard and Quinn was hot, and making love didn't get any better than this. They rode the blood rush all the way to a hard and fast climax, then settled into a slow-motion repeat of the same.

Sometime after four in the morning they fell asleep, only to wake again at dawn, making love one more time before facing the ugly truth of a new day.

Paco Cruz got drunk, then he got himself arrested. All of his belongings, including his phone with Anton Baba's phone number, were in a big manila envelope with his name on it, and if he got bonded out he got his shit back. If they sent him to jail for something else, he didn't. He was so pissed off at himself he couldn't think what to do. He had this important info that could be worth hundreds of dollars in his pocket, and he had no way to let Baba know.

It had taken John and Connie Davis a little over two days to drive from Henderson, Nevada, to Nashville, Tennessee, with their precious cargo aboard. Starla and Sammy had been good travelers, but they'd stopped far more often for the baby to run and play than they ever would have for themselves.

Now they were less than five miles from the city limits of Nashville. Starla had traded seats with her mother a couple of hours ago so that she'd get a break and Connie could play with her grandson some more. Though she was beginning to recognize some of the landmarks, she was also shocked at how much had changed in the seven years she'd been gone.

"There are new apartments and condos everywhere," she said.

John nodded.

"I told you our old neighborhood had changed, too. Lots of people still chasing dreams here in Nashville, and lots of new businesses built up, as well."

"I'll find a job when this mess with Anton is over, and I'll get an apartment for Sammy and me."

"You don't have to do that," John said. "You've been gone so long, we are in no rush to be rid of you."

"But I want to," Starla said. "I haven't had a life of

my own, and I need some independence to grow a different kind of guts. It would be far too easy to let you and Mother take care of us."

"Well, we'll talk about it after all the danger has passed," he said.

"Talk about what?" Connie asked from the back seat.

"Oh, nothing…just plans for the future," Starla said.

"Do you see where we are now?" John asked.

"The mall! We're almost home," Starla said and then teared up. "I didn't think I'd ever be here again."

Less than ten minutes later, John turned down a tree-lined street and watched Starla scoot to the edge of the seat. When he turned up the driveway and parked beneath the portico, Starla began to shake.

"Wait until I get the door unlocked," John said.

She nodded, then looked over her shoulder. Her mother and her son were looking at her.

"Hey, little boy," Starla said. "We're home!"

Sammy liked the tone of her voice and laughed, then crawled over the seat and into her lap.

When John motioned for them to get out, Starla was the one who carried Sammy into the house. She walked from room to room in total shock. It was as if she'd only been gone a few hours, just back from a quick trip to the store. Everything was exactly the same. Even the furniture.

"It's just like I remembered it," Starla said, as she turned to her parents.

"We left it this way on purpose," Connie said. "Just in case we ever found you. Just in case you came home."

Still holding Sammy, she walked into their arms and

had one last cry for the years she'd lost. Then she made a silent promise to herself and to Sammy: from this day forward, it was all about the future.

Anton was standing at the airstrip waiting for his jet to arrive, but Franklin was not going to recognize him.

He was wearing his gardener's clothing, huaraches on his feet, and he'd dyed his shock of white hair black as coal, though he'd left his full beard its natural salt-and-pepper color. He had a worn-out sombrero on his head for shade, and his money belt with ID, credit cards and cash was around his waist and well hidden by the loose cotton shirt hanging over his baggy pants. He had an old bag with a few small belongings hanging over his shoulder—it was all he needed to go home and finish what he'd started.

When the jet finally flew into view and landed on the strip, he hurried toward it and met the pilot coming down the gangplank.

When Anton started up the steps, Paul stopped.

"I'm sorry, senor, but this is a private plane."

Anton paused and looked up.

"So, I did pass muster, didn't I?"

Paul's expression ran the gamut of emotions.

"Mr. Baba? Is that you?"

"Yes, it's me, Paul. Are you ready to go, or do you need to refuel?"

"Refueling here would be wise," he said.

Anton waved him back into the plane and then ran up the steps and into the cabin. Paul pulled up the steps

nd then taxied toward the hangar, killed the engine
nd got out to refuel.

Anton was making himself comfortable inside the
lane, pouring his own drink and gathering up some
nacks to eat on the way back.

By the time Paul reentered, Anton was on his iPad
hecking messages. If the Feds had his email hacked,
vhich he assumed they would, they'd think he was in
aint-Tropez, because that's where he'd had his com-
uter tech route the signals.

It wasn't until he'd checked his phone a while later
hat he realized he had a text from Paco Cruz. Why the
ell that hadn't shown up at his estate was beyond him.

He read it with interest. It appeared Paco had actu-
lly seen Quinn O'Meara, the woman from the desert
vho'd found his son. Baba wasn't sure what the Feds
ad on him, but if they'd finally filed charges and had a
varrant out for his arrest, he had to assume the evidence
vas substantial and likely backed by witnesses willing
o testify. Getting rid of the two women who held the
ower to incriminate him should level the playing field,
o this information couldn't have come at a better time.

He wanted to call Paco back, but decided to wait until
e got to Vegas and got a burner phone—no need to add
nore heat to the fire. So he took a sip of his drink and
ettled down to eat while he waited for takeoff.

Sixteen

Paul Franklin came back inside the plane and pulled the steps up behind him.

Anton was waiting for him.

"When we get back to Nevada, just fly straight to the hangar. I'm taking the old truck into Vegas. I trust it still runs."

"Yes, sir. Runs fine, just looks rough."

"That's what I need," Anton said.

"Yes, sir," Paul said. "Take a seat, sir, and buckle up for takeoff."

Anton returned to the table, logged out of the iPad, refilled his drink and then buckled up near the window, watching as the jet began to taxi and then finally lifted off. He got one last glimpse of the estate as the jet circled the area and couldn't help but wonder if this would be the last time he'd see it. There was no way to tell how this trip was going to play out, but he was a realist. If this all blew up in his face, he'd rather die on the run than in prison.

* * *

After finally getting out of bed and into their showers, Quinn and Nick began their day. They'd woken up to a text from his aunt Juana inviting them to dinner tonight, and Quinn was excited and at the same time a little nervous. Once he was dressed, Nick sent a text back saying they would be there. By the time he reached the kitchen, Quinn was already making pancakes. He gave her a thumbs-up on the invitation and then began setting the table. When he finished, he came back to the stove and put a hand at her waist as he looked over her shoulder, admiring the cakes coming off the grill.

She was too close and too sexy to ignore, and he buried his face in the curls pulled back at the nape of her neck and thought to himself that she smelled like sunshine and flowers.

"Those look amazing, honey," Nick said.

"Thank you. I told you I could cook," she said, managing a smile even though she was still rattled about the Peeping Tom from last night.

Nick could hear the tension in her voice and was angry that, once again, she was frightened for her life. He intended to spend the day finding Paco Cruz and learning what he had done with his information. He had no intention of letting Quinn out of his sight, so unless she was willing to stay with his aunt and uncle today, she was coming with him.

They had just sat down at the table to eat when the doorbell rang. Quinn frowned, but Nick rolled his eyes.

"How much do you want to bet it's Santino again?"

"Really?"

"Yes, really. Get all of the pancakes you want on your plate now before I go to the door, because he'll eat what's left on the platter."

Quinn laughed and took one more to put on her plate while Nick took a whole stack and then left the kitchen.

Quinn heard him open the door, heard voices, and then two sets of footsteps coming back into the kitchen. Only it wasn't Santino after all.

"Honey, this is Billy Daniels. He's Las Vegas Homicide like me. Daniels, I know you remember Quinn."

"Yes, ma'am, only you look a whole lot better than the first time we met."

Quinn eyed the fortysomething man, thinking he looked like a bodybuilder squeezed into a suit one size too small, but he seemed friendly and Nick liked him.

"So you must have been present at my ever-so-graceful face-plant on the floor of Homicide," she said.

"You didn't face-plant. I caught you," Nick said.

"And I caught the baby. Lord, Lord, I can't say I've ever been as surprised as I was to see him beneath that jacket," Daniels said.

Quinn saw him eyeing the pancakes.

"We have extra pancakes, if you're hungry," she said.

"Don't mind if I do," he said and took off his jacket.

Quinn saw his bulging biceps and thought, *Bingo. Bodybuilder for sure.* She grabbed an extra plate and some utensils while Nick poured Daniels a cup of coffee.

Billy Daniels wasn't bashful, and before long they were eating and talking as if they had been friends for years.

"These sure are good pancakes," Daniels said.

"Quinn made them. She's a regular Martha Stewart," Nick said.

"But I don't make my own wrapping paper," she added, and then they burst into laughter, leaving Billy at a loss as to what exactly was funny.

"Sorry," Nick said. "She was just calling me on something I said a few days ago."

Daniels shrugged and grinned.

"At any rate, you're a good cook, ma'am."

"Thank you," Quinn said.

Nick shoved his plate aside and then refilled their coffee cups.

"I know you didn't come here for breakfast, so what's going on?" he asked.

Daniels wiped his mouth and patted his tight belly as he leaned back in the chair.

"So, when I got to the office this morning, I heard more about Paco Cruz. Guess who got jailed on drunk and disorderly and put in Clark County Detention early this morning?"

Nick's eyes widened.

"Are you serious?"

"Yep. And he's not even scheduled for arraignment yet, so if you wanted to interview him, now's your chance."

"Yes, yes, yes," Nick said and then pointed at Quinn. "Honey, we're going to pay our Peeping Tom a visit this morning. You go get ready, and I'll stack the dirty dishes in the sink. We'll clean up after we get back."

Her green eyes flashed with poorly disguised anger.

"I don't suppose we'll be able to put our hands on the bastard?"

Nick grinned.

"No, ma'am, and you're going to wait elsewhere while I talk to him. It's best he isn't distracted by your presence, okay?"

"Whatever," she said and left to go change clothes.

Nick was stacking plates and carrying them to the sink when Daniels laughed.

"She's a real shrinking violet, isn't she?"

Nick thought of the life she'd had to fight through to still be here.

"She is a warrior and lucky to be here."

Daniels's smile disappeared.

"Hard life?"

Nick nodded, then turned off the coffeemaker and grabbed his car keys and phone as Daniels headed for the door.

"Thanks for the heads-up," Nick said.

"No problem. I was on my way to interview a possible witness anyway. We got two new homicides last night."

"Hopefully I'll get a release soon and can get back to work," Nick said.

"Heal first. You were one lucky dude that was just a graze."

"Noted and agreed," Nick said. "Maybe I'll see you later. Be careful."

"I'm not going alone. I'm picking Murphy up on the way."

"Good," Nick said, then stood at the door until Dan-

iels drove away before running back through the house
to find Quinn.

"Need any help?" he asked, as he walked into her
bedroom and saw her standing in front of a full-length
mirror with a frown on her face.

"Yes. I still can't fasten a bra."

He kissed the crease between her eyebrows and
reached behind her and hooked the bra without looking.

"The fact that you are so handy with women's underwear should piss me off, but you're too cute to fight
with," Quinn said.

Nick grinned.

"Which shirt?" he asked.

She pointed at a short-sleeve pullover and raised her
arms.

He pulled it down over her head, then gently over
her wounded shoulder.

"Need help with anything else?" he asked.

"No, I think I've got this," she said, then stepped
into backless sandals and slipped her cell phone in her
hip pocket.

She ducked in the bathroom and swiped her lips with
a pink gloss and glanced at herself in the mirror. Red
curls, green eyes and the same straight nose and stub-
born chin. She would do.

"You look awfully pretty for such a badass," Nick
said.

She grinned as he leaned in for a quick kiss and
then headed to the garage. When they opened the door,
Quinn glanced at her Harley in the corner against a
wall. This had been the longest time she'd gone with-

out riding, and it felt weird. But this whole experience was weird. She got into the car and was buckled up and wearing sunglasses by the time Nick backed out into the sunshine and drove away.

"Where is the detention center located?" Quinn asked.

"On South Casino Drive. It's not far."

"It feels good to be out of the house," she said.

"I'm sorry you have to feel so cooped up right now, but I think it's best."

"I'm sure you're right. It was just a selfish comment on my part. I'm used to being outdoors and on the move."

He frowned.

"Are you saying you're going to feel confined staying in one place?"

She immediately reached for him, making certain he understood what she meant.

"Lord, no! My dream since childhood has been to put down roots somewhere and have a home," she said.

"Okay, then. I was starting to wonder if I was going to have to kidnap you and put you in the basement to keep from losing you," he said.

"You don't have a basement," she said.

He grinned.

"Well, there's that, but you know what I meant."

"You're trying to make me believe you love me or something," she said.

"Or something? You still doubt?"

She grinned.

"You have a most wicked smile," Nick said. "Should I be worried?"

"Of course you should be worried. You've gone and tied yourself to a redhead. We're notoriously dangerous, or something else equally scary. Take your pick."

"I pick you," Nick said and reached for her hand.

Quinn surprised him by clasping it tight.

"I am beginning to adore you to distraction," she said.

"Adoration accepted," Nick said.

Every day spent with her, he felt himself growing happier, more fulfilled.

How have I been living without this woman? How did I even exist?

The thought of Anton Baba wanting to harm her made him crazy. They had to find that man and get him behind bars.

Within a few minutes Nick reached the detention center. He parked and headed indoors with Quinn beside him. He signed in, requesting to speak to Paco Cruz regarding a case, and was taken back to an interrogation room. He had settled Quinn in a viewing room where she could hear and see what was said and done, and then Nick waited for Paco to be brought to the room.

A few minutes passed, and then the door opened and the man was brought in shackled and handcuffed and seated opposite Nick. A guard stood inside the room a few feet away.

Nick could tell Paco was nervous. It must have been uncomfortable to be cuffed and sitting in front of the detective you'd been spying on the night before.

"Saldano," Paco said, feigning a brave face. "What are you doing here?"

"Trying to find out why you were trespassing on my property last night. That doesn't really sound like your usual work. But then, you aren't quite the man you were last time we met. What knocked you off the tough-guy list and down to Peeping Tom?"

Paco was stunned. "How did you—" But the moment he said it, he groaned. He'd almost admitted to being in his backyard. The cop was right. He'd definitely lost his edge.

Nick slapped his hand on the table.

"I know shit because I'm a cop. So, Anton Baba still has you doing his dirty work, I see."

"I don't work for him no more," Paco said.

"Oh, no? But you snitch for him, right? Where is he? Why did he send you to my home?"

"I said I didn't talk to Baba," Paco said.

"I can get a search warrant for your phone…the one we have here on site, and I can listen to messages and see the name and number of everyone you've called. We can do it that way, stretch it out long and slow and keep you chained up in the meantime, or you could tell me now and make it easier on yourself."

Paco dropped his head, staring at the cuffs around his wrists.

"So? I'm waiting," Nick said. "Start talking, or you're going to wind up behind bars for aiding and abetting a man charged with the murder of two federal agents and God only knows what else they're going to nail him with."

Paco panicked. What the hell? This was not the kind of shit he meant to get involved in.

"I don't know nothing about no federal agents. But… yeah, I did call him the other day. Only he never called me back!"

"I'm supposed to believe that?"

Paco shrugged.

"So go check the phone and find out for yourself," he muttered.

Nick tried another angle.

"Why did you call him in the first place?"

"I heard he was looking for two women. I don't know what for, but I saw one of them a few days back and thought I could make a little extra dough. But I didn't know where she was staying, so I went looking."

"Why did you come to my place?" Nick asked.

"I heard you took out Dev Bosky at Centennial Hill Hospital while you were guarding the redhead Baba wanted gone. Then I saw you with the redhead when I was at work. Maybe it was coincidence, but I figured there was a chance she was staying with you. A good-lookin' woman like that? I thought maybe you wanted to help her out…off duty." Paco smirked at him with a knowing glint in his eyes.

Nick felt sick. He thought he'd been so careful, but even then with all the care he'd taken to get Quinn to a doctor and back, it hadn't been enough. They'd still been seen.

"So what did you see?" Nick snapped, hoping this punk had been looking at the wrong time and hadn't caught a glimpse of Quinn while they were outside.

Paco shrugged.

Nick slapped the table again.

"What the fuck did you see?"

"I saw her at your place, okay? But I didn't tell anyone, so relax! I…" He paused, looking embarrassed. "I decided to celebrate a bit before I talked to anyone, but it got outta control and…here I am."

Nick sat there staring at him, trying to figure out how he could make all this work and still keep Quinn safe. And then it hit him.

"Okay, asshole. You want a way out of this? Here's what's going to happen. I'm going to get your phone, and you're going to send Baba a text telling him that you found one of the women he's looking for, and you're going to give him an address. Not mine, but one I'm going to give you, understand?"

"You want me to be the one to help bring Baba in? Jesus! He'll kill me if I fuck him over," Paco whined.

"And *I'm* going to kill you if anything happens to the woman," Nick added. "Your choice."

Paco glared at him.

"You're a cop. You can't threaten me like that."

Nick leaned forward until his voice was just a whisper.

"You misunderstood. I wasn't threatening you. That was a promise."

Paco shuddered.

"What's in this for me?"

"Well, for one thing, I won't kill you," Nick said.

Paco cursed.

Nick waited a beat, then added, "And maybe I can try to forget you were caught snooping around my house."

Paco glared at him.

Nick got up and headed for the door.

"Wait! Wait!" Paco said. "I'll do it."

Nick pointed at him.

"Don't move. I'll be back."

Nick left.

The guard took a stance between Paco and the door.

Paco looked at him and then looked away. It was hell cooperating with the cops.

Nick had to call the sheriff and let him know what was happening and get the okay to access Paco's phone. Then he made a phone call to Gleason, as well.

Gleason answered on the second ring.

"This is Gleason. What's up, Saldano?"

Nick quickly filled him in, explaining that the Peeping Tom was actually one of Anton Baba's snitches who had come looking for Quinn. And since she was now a federal witness, anyone threatening her was a federal problem.

"I'll go interview him this afternoon," Gleason said.

"He won't be there," Nick said. "He got picked up on a drunk and disorderly, and once he's arraigned this morning he'll be gone."

"And we don't have anything to hold him on? He hasn't made a threat or tried to harm O'Meara, has he?"

"If you don't find a way to keep him here, don't blame me if Quinn decides to leave you high and dry. She won't feel safe if he goes free and is able to get in touch with Baba."

"I thought you two were in a relationship? Can't you convince her to testify?" Gleason asked.

"If people are trying to kill her and no one other than me is willing to help, what would you expect her to do?"

Gleason sighed. "Okay. We have a safe house here in the city. You give Paco that address, and if Baba shows up there, he's ours. Let Miss O'Meara know we'll do what we can do to get this guy behind bars so she can feel safe again—safe enough to testify."

"Thanks," Nick said, taking down the address Gleason gave him.

Then he went to get Paco's phone out of evidence. They would have to get a search warrant and turn it over to the Feds and hope there was a record of calls or texts to Baba. If there wasn't, then they had nothing on Paco Cruz but a simple Peeping Tom report. It was crucial that Cruz cooperate willingly, so Nick took the phone back to interrogation.

As he walked in, he glanced up at a mirror on the wall opposite the table where Paco was waiting, aware that Quinn was behind it, watching and listening.

"What took you so long?" Paco muttered.

Nick put the phone down on the table between them, then gave him a piece of paper with an address on it.

"Send your boss a text telling him the girl he's looking for is at this address," Nick said.

All of a sudden Paco got defensive. "What happens to me if I don't?" he snapped.

Damn it, Nick thought. He had left him sitting alone

too long. He'd had too much time to think about repercussions. Nick picked up the phone again and headed
for the door without so much as a word. He wouldn't
be able to offer Paco anything he wanted to hear, so
his best bet now was to make him fear the unspoken.

This was not what Paco had expected. An argument,
sure. Maybe some kind of deal for participating willingly. But the cop was just going to walk out and leave
him again, so Paco panicked.

"Wait! Hey, wait!" he yelled.

Nick paused, then turned around.

"I'll do it!" Paco said. "I'll send the text. Just tell
me what to say."

Nick walked back and laid the phone in Paco's hands.

"This is what you type—'I found the redhead you're
looking for. She's at this address.' Then send this address to him," he said, laying down a piece of paper
with the safe-house location scrawled in pen.

"And that's all?" Paco said.

"Yes. That's all," Nick said, then watched Paco open
the phone and pull up the right number in Contacts.
Nick stood behind him to watch, making certain he
typed only what he'd been told to say. The moment Paco
hit Send, Nick took the phone and then signaled for the
guard that he was finished and to lock Paco back up.

"Wait! When am I going to get out of here?" Paco
yelled as Nick headed for the door.

"I don't have any idea," Nick said. "When you sent
the text to a man wanted by the Feds, you immediately
became part of their case."

Paco stared.

"But you're the one who came to me. You're the one who was making all these threats to my life and then bringing me the phone to send your message. Why is this happening? Why am I now involved in a federal case because of your request?"

Nick walked back to the table and leaned down until he and Paco were eye to eye and so close he could smell the hangover on his breath.

"Because you messed with what's mine," Nick said. "Whatever happens to you with the Feds is unimportant to me. But if I ever see your face again, or if you ever mess with me or mine, I will make you sorry. Understood?"

Paco was shaking. A cop could easily look the other way for one of their own. It had just occurred to him how easy it would be for this man to kill him and get away with it.

Nick stood up and left the room. He had come close to crossing a line with this punk, and it had never occurred to him to pull back. Protecting Quinn was what mattered, and now he was going to get her and take her home. They had a sink full of dirty dishes and a family dinner to go to tonight. A life to live. He was done with bottom-feeders for today.

He paused in the hallway and called Gleason back.

"All right, Gleason. My Peeping Tom sent a text to Baba pointing him to your safe house. Now you make sure you file charges on him for abetting a man with a warrant out for his arrest."

"Yes, yes, I'll get someone on that," he said.

Nick hung up, then kept winding his way through

he hallways until he got to the observation room and
vent inside.

Quinn had gone through the gamut of emotions
watching Nick work his magic on Paco Cruz. She was
afraid that, once Cruz was released, he would be back
or some kind of retribution. And then Nick did some-
hing that forever sealed the deal with her. She'd asked
him once what it felt like to belong to family and now
she knew. The moment she heard the words "don't mess
with what's mine" come out of his mouth, she lost composure completely.

Today was the beginning of the rest of her life.

This time, when she watched Nick walk out of interrogation, she knew he was coming back to her. She
turned her back to the two-way mirror to watch the
door. One minute passed into another and then another,
and then she heard footsteps and saw the door beginning to open. When she saw Nick, she walked directly
into his arms.

Nick could tell by her silence that what she'd witnessed had rattled her. Maybe one day she'd trust him
enough to admit she was frightened, but for now it was
enough that she loved him.

"He's more bluff than business," Nick said as he
wrapped his arms around her. "You'll be okay. You'll
see. And the address he gave Anton Baba is to a federal
safe house. They'll be waiting for him when he shows."

Quinn heard, but was afraid to believe it could be
this easy.

"Don't you believe me?" he asked, sensing her tension.

She lifted her chin and looked at him then. It was time for her to trust someone besides herself.

"Yes, I believe you," she said.

He cupped her face with both hands and then kissed her, gently at first and then deeper until they were both a little shaky when he stepped back.

"Come with me, baby. I have to take the phone back to evidence and then we're out of here."

Quinn didn't hesitate. She took his hand and together they walked away.

Anton was in the galley returning his dirty dishes and tossing out what was left of the food he didn't eat when the pilot's voice came over the intercom.

"We're ten minutes away from landing at the hangar, sir. Please take a seat and buckle up."

Anton wiped his hands, made a quick trip to the bathroom and then checked his disguise one last time before he returned to his seat.

Even though his white hair had been dyed black, he looked older this way. Maybe it was the salt-and-pepper beard and the condition of his clothing. He looked like a peon, and driving that old truck would add another layer to his disguise.

He went back to the main cabin and checked to make sure everything he needed was in his bag, then dropped his cell phone into the pocket of his jacket and buckled up.

There were many details to take care of, and they had to be dealt with in a timely fashion. He was in this mess because the people he'd sent had not done their jobs properly. So he'd already decided that the things that mattered most he would deal with himself.

When the plane began to descend, his gut knotted. Except for killing Ian for leaving Sammy behind at the wreck, it had been years since he'd had to get his hands dirty. Maybe it was a good thing to revisit from time to time. He didn't want it ever to be said that Anton Baba had lost his edge.

The landing was perfect.

Paul emerged, lowered the stairs and then went to carry Anton's things down.

But Anton stopped him.

"No, no, I've got this," he said. "What I need you to do is go get the truck. If it needs gas, fill it up. I have a couple of calls to make while I'm waiting."

"Yes, sir," Paul said and took the stairs down two at a time and hurried toward the hangar.

Anton took out his phone to check for messages and saw he had one from Paco Cruz. He opened it, read the message and then smiled.

"Good man. Good man," he muttered. "If she's a smart girl, she's hiding from me, so she won't be going anywhere anytime soon. I'll leave her on ice for the time being."

He checked for other messages, but there were none, which he viewed as positive. He thought of his place here in Vegas. Elegant. Luxurious. Servants to do his bidding. Women waiting in his bed whenever he asked. And directly in the sights of federal agents. Like it or not, he was going to have to huddle with the masses. Just like old times back in Istanbul when he was a boy.

Fuck them all.

He'd be back on top again soon enough.

Then he heard the sound of an engine and looked out Paul was bringing the old truck to the plane.

"Damn. It looks worse than I remembered," he mumbled and then shouldered his bag and started down the steps to the tarmac.

Paul got out and held the door open for Anton.

"Will there be anything else I can do for you, sir?"

"No, but thank you for your service, Paul. It is always appreciated."

"It's my pleasure, sir," Paul said, then watched Baba toss his old bag into the seat and get in. "Safe travels Mr. Baba."

"It's Petrova now. Manny Petrova. Remember that in case I need another ride."

"Will do, Manny," Paul said and gave him a thumbs-up.

Anton put the old truck into gear and drove out of the private airstrip and headed toward the city.

Seventeen

Anton hadn't seen Vegas from the front seat of any vehicle in years, and it had been even longer since he'd been behind the wheel. But driving was like sex—once you knew how it worked, you never forgot.

He purposefully took backstreets to get to his casino, marveling at the shops he'd never noticed. Little shops, small businesses, a local gym, a hair salon. These businesses and the people in them had been there all along, living their small, insignificant lives while he was pulling in millions by the month. They would never have come on to his radar now but for what was happening. When you live big, you have a very long way to fall, and at the moment he was as far down as he ever cared to go. Even now he wasn't certain he could pull himself out of the shit he was in, but if he couldn't, he was sure as hell taking people down with him when he fell.

He saw the bright lights of Lucky Joe's long before he reached the building itself, and the closer he got, the bigger the knot in his belly became. But by the time he reached the casino he was cold and steady-handed, ready to take back what was his. His old truck garnered little notice as he drove around back to the delivery entrances and parked against the building a good distance from the door.

He put his bag behind the truck seat so it wouldn't attract some petty thief to bust a window to get to it. Then he grabbed the toolbox from the floor in the front seat, took a pair of cheap, black plastic eyeglasses from his pocket and put them on. They were the final addition to his disguise.

He got out, locked the truck, then pulled the old sombrero down tight on his head. As he headed toward the back entrance, he made sure to keep his shoulders stooped and his walk a shuffle. When he reached the entrance he opened the door and walked in, expecting to be stopped by a guard asking for an ID and what business he had on the premises. But there was no one there.

Frowning, he finally saw his guard down a darkened hall with his back to the door, humping a waitress for all he was worth. The woman was moaning, and he could see that the guard was on the verge of climax, even as he watched. They were too far gone to even notice him, and he didn't want witnesses to what he was about to do, so he knew they would agree—timing was everything.

He slipped up the back stairs to the second floor and headed down a hall past a bank of meeting rooms, then took a sharp right at the ice machines. There was a small, insignificant-looking door near a blind corner that opened only by a key code. There were no security cameras in this hall because he'd designed it this way,

but he still made sure he was alone before he punched
in the code.

Immediately, the door slid into a pocket in the wall
revealing a small, private elevator. When he stepped
into the car, the door slid closed behind him. He had a
card key for the penthouse, and once he swiped it, the elevator started moving upward. He put on a pair of latex
gloves as he rode, and when the car came to a silent
stop, it opened up into the far end of a walk-in closet.

Anton grabbed his toolbox and stepped out as the
door closed behind him. He put the toolbox down by
the door, took a large hunting knife from his boot and
quietly made his way out of the master bedroom, paus-
ing every few steps to listen for sounds that would alert
him to Stewart's presence.

Just when he thought the place was empty, he heard
a toilet flush.

*Hope you're done, Mr. Stewart, because real shit is
about to fly.*

He knew the layout like the back of his hand and was
ready for anything. Just thinking how this sorry sucker
had walked in and taken over what he'd built drove his
bloodlust higher. He shifted the knife from one hand
to the other and waited to see which way Stewart went.

He heard the bathroom door open. Stewart exited
wearing dark purple lounge pants and a white billow-
ing shirt hanging loose over his belly. He was blowing
his nose and clearing his throat as he walked by.

Anton followed a ways behind. When Stewart suddenly stopped, so did Anton, holding his breath as he

waited for Stewart to disregard the sound he heard and let go of suspicion.

He watched as Stewart shrugged it off and went into the living room, poured himself a double shot of bourbon, took a sip and then sank down into an easy chair and reached for the TV remote.

Anton had thought long and hard about how he would do this. Was he going to let Stewart live long enough to confront him, to make him answer for what he'd done? Did it matter enough that Stewart knew he'd been caught? And at that moment, Anton decided the answer was no. Swift and efficient, that's what this needed to be. Enough mess had already been made, and there was no time to risk any mistakes.

Stewart had the sound on the TV turned up loud, which masked Anton's steps as he walked into the living room. Just as Stewart let out a big burst of laughter at the show he was watching, Anton plunged the hunting knife into the top of his skull.

The glass of bourbon hit the floor and shattered as Stewart's body began to jerk and seize.

Anton circled the chair for a last look at the traitorous son of a bitch and realized from the wide-open mouth and the tip of the knife clearly visible in the back of his throat that Stewart had literally died laughing.

"Joke's on you, you sorry bastard," Anton said and then headed for the media room to destroy the footage captured on the security camera.

He not only sabotaged the cameras, but removed the discs and backups and took them with him.

Now that the deed was done, he was anxious to

leave. He made a quick run through the rooms back to the master bedroom, then into the walk-in closet. He grabbed his toolbox, keyed in the code, and then while he was riding down in the elevator he put the security discs into a plastic bag, took a hammer out of the toolbox and beat everything in the bag until nothing was left but shards. Then he wrapped the bag and the latex gloves in a handful of paper towels and put it all in his toolbox.

When he exited again on the second floor, he shuffled out into the hallway, retraced his steps to the stairwell exit and went down the same way he'd come up.

The guard was on duty now and seemed surprised to see the worker come down the back stairs, but as Anton passed him, the guard chose to ignore him.

Anton nodded politely to the guard anyway and exited the building with his shoulders in a slump, his feet shuffling. He walked out into the sunshine, got into his truck and drove away.

In less than an hour, he'd found himself a nondescript motel, whipping out a driver's license with his picture and the name Manny Petrova beneath it. He signed the register without a hitch, paying for two nights in cash, then took his bag and toolbox inside the room. Once there, he flushed the contents of the plastic bag down the toilet, then went back into the room.

"One down, two to go," he said and crawled into bed and closed his eyes.

Quinn wanted to look nice for dinner at the Chavez house, but didn't have much in the way of clothes that fit the event. She finally opted for her best pair of jeans and a simple yellow top. After she had figured out her clothes, she went looking for Nick and found him in the garage filling up the tank in her Harley and checking the oil.

"What are you doing?" she asked.

"Checking it out for you."

"Are you running me off?" she asked.

Without warning, he swept her into his arms and pushed her back against a wall.

She saw a glint of hunger in his eyes just before he centered his mouth on her lips and kissed her breathless.

He let her go as abruptly as he'd grabbed her.

"I'll take that as a no," Quinn mumbled.

He shook his head.

"You are a smart woman who persists in asking the dumbest questions. I thought maybe you needed show-and-tell."

She shrugged.

"I almost forgot why I came looking for you. I have a favor to ask."

Nick stroked the side of her cheek with the back of his hand.

"What do you need, baby?"

"I want to wash my hair."

"Okay. You have plenty of time. Wash away."

She sighed.

"I can't...uh... I don't want... It's not possible to wash my hair in the shower."

The realization of what she was saying swept through

him in one horrifying memory of her falling to pieces during the hospital fire alarm.

"Oh, hell, Quinn, I'm sorry. I forgot. How can I help you?"

"So, I have two options, both of which involve your participation because of my shoulder."

Nick put his arms around her and pulled her close to him, then rocked her where they stood.

"I will do anything to make that easier for you. What's your plan?"

"You wash my hair at the kitchen sink so I can keep a towel over my face, or you get in the shower with me and wash it there. I can cope if I have my back to the water…if it's not coming down at me, or in my face, but I have been taking baths not showers since my back got infected."

"Which would you rather do?" Nick asked.

"You wash it at the kitchen sink."

"Then that's what we'll do. You go get whatever you need and I'll be in the kitchen waiting."

Quinn hugged him.

"Thank you, Nick. You're the best."

He kissed her again, but this time slow and softly, brushing his mouth across her lips in a featherlight touch.

"We're partners here, right? So that means we do the hard stuff together. Go get your towels and shampoo."

"I'll be right back," she said and hurried out of the garage and into the house with Nick following behind her.

It didn't take long for them to get set up. Quinn cov-

ered her face with a towel and then leaned over the
kitchen sink while Nick proceeded to shampoo her hair
Just before he went to rinse, he stopped.

"Honey, are you doing okay?"

She just nodded, her face still covered with the towel

"Right now I'm going to rinse it, then put the conditioner on it and rinse it again, and we're through."

She took a breath and readjusted the towel.

"I'm ready," she mumbled.

Nick turned the water back on and worked as quick
as he could, but her hair was long and curly and getting
all of the soap and conditioner out was time-consuming
By the time he was finished, he noticed her shoulders
were shaking.

"All done," he said and wrapped a dry towel around
her hair.

She stood up and put the wet towel aside that she'd
been holding over her face. That's when Nick saw she'd
been crying.

"Quinn…baby…why didn't you say something? Why
didn't you tell me to stop?" he asked, as he took her into
his arms with wet hair dripping all over both of them.

"I couldn't stop the tears, but I didn't get scared. I
knew it was you," she said.

Nick was sick with knowledge that he'd been the
cause of her tears.

"This is never happening again," he muttered as he
helped towel-dry her hair. "You're going to find a hair
salon and never put yourself through this misery another time."

"I will," she said and then stopped him with a kiss

"I'll finish it from here. You are forever my knight in shining armor. I just wanted to look pretty for you at dinner."

Again, the naïveté of her need, and what she was willing to go through just so he would be proud of her, made him sad. She was warrior-strong in some ways, and in others, so fragile she broke his heart.

Oblivious of what Nick was thinking, she gathered up the wet towels and took them all to the utility room and put them on top of the washer, then hurried back to her bedroom to wet-comb her hair before it became an unmanageable mess.

Nick was still rattled, and he hadn't told her the truth about why he was checking the Harley. He needed to know that if she was ever here alone and needed to get away that she had the means. Until Anton Baba was behind bars, he wasn't going to rest easy.

A couple of hours later they were dressed and on their way to Juana and Tonio's house.

"Santino and his wife will be there, too, right?" Quinn asked.

"Yes. Her name is Lara, remember?"

Quinn nodded, but she was too quiet.

Nick sighed. There were only so many ways he could show her she was loved. The acceptance would have to come from her, so he started talking about the family.

"I think I told you already, but in case I didn't, Juana and Tonio have two children. Melina is younger than Santino but they're both older than me. She and her husband, Aidan, live in Bakersfield, California. He works at a body shop repainting cars. She teaches school."

"So there are no babies in the family?" she asked.

Nick threaded his fingers through hers.

"No. No grandbabies for them yet, although we all get less-than-subtle reminders now and then."

Quinn thought about little Nicks running around, and her heart fluttered. She glanced at him.

"How do you feel about babies?" he asked.

"You mean do I want children one day? The answer is yes. But I didn't want to have any without setting up a place to call home first," she said.

Nick gave her another glance, but she was staring out the window with a sad look on her face, and he didn't want to ask her what she was thinking about.

He slowed down for a stop sign, and then as soon as he stopped, he lifted her hands to his lips and kissed them.

"When you were little, you had a baby doll you called Mary. Mary went everywhere with you. Even when our foster mother told you to leave her at home, you still took her. Do you remember that?"

Quinn nodded.

"Why wouldn't you leave her at home?" Nick asked.

"Because she was my baby, and I promised I would never leave her behind like my mama left me."

Nick was silent for a couple of blocks and then next time he had to stop for a red light, he got up the courage to ask.

"Did you ever know your mother, or why she left you?"

Quinn shrugged.

"Not until I was older."

Nick stayed quiet, waiting to see if she would elaborate on her own.

"When I was in high school, one of the case workers let it slip that my mother was dead. She thought I knew the story, since it was the reason I'd ended up in care. I pretended I did know so she would keep talking, but she clammed up pretty soon afterward."

"Did she say what happened? If you had any family anywhere? Stuff like that?"

She shrugged. "All I know is she committed suicide. The man she loved dumped her. She killed herself out of grief. I was two."

Nick shook his head.

"That's horrible."

"I guess," she said and looked out a side window as he began slowing down.

"So you had no other family?" Nick asked.

"I guess not. None that ever came looking for me, anyway," Quinn said bitterly.

Nick realized he'd ventured too close to a touchy subject.

"I'm sorry. I didn't mean to get so personal."

"No worries. If we're going to make this work, you have to know what makes me tick," Quinn said.

"And what hurts you," Nick added. "I have to know what hurts you so I'll know how to protect you."

"I appreciate knowing you will always be my backup, but I'm not a baby. I know how to take care of myself," she said.

Nick smiled.

"Duly noted, and here we are," he said, as he pulled

up into the driveway of a gray stucco house with white trim around the windows and white shutters. The landscape was typical Vegas, tiny gravel, sand and cactus—one of those water-saving touches that mattered when people built a city in the middle of a desert.

"Santino is already here," Nick said. "That black Camaro is his."

Quinn was getting nervous butterflies again but managed to hide her anxiousness.

As Nick helped her out of the car, he was more than a little mesmerized by the bright yellow shirt she was wearing and the way the setting sun highlighted the long red curls framing her face.

"It's going to be a beautiful night, but not as beautiful as you," Nick said and kissed her. "Mmm, your hair smells like oranges and lemons."

She grinned.

"I have a great hairstylist. If you want, I can give you his number."

Nick laughed as they went up the steps and knocked at the door. Uncle Tonio welcomed them inside with a grin and a hug.

Quinn was just getting her first glimpse of the house Nick had grown up in when the room erupted with noise. Juana came out of the kitchen, Santino and his wife, Lara, behind her, and everyone began hugging and kissing and talking at once. She vaguely remembered being introduced to Lara in the midst of it all.

Later, as they were getting ready to sit down to dinner, Nick leaned down and whispered against her ear.

"So, how do you like my family?"

"They're wonderful," Quinn said.

Nick put his arm around her waist.

"You asked me once what it felt like to belong to a family. Well, this is it," he said.

Quinn leaned against him for a moment, yielding to the pull of their physical attraction.

"It's wonderful, isn't it?" she said.

He smiled.

"Yes, baby, it's pretty wonderful."

Paco Cruz was pissed.

He'd been picked up for nothing more than drunk and disorderly. He should have already been arraigned and bonded out. But he was still in jail, and all they would tell him was that he'd been turned over to the FBI.

So he'd demanded a lawyer and been told one was coming, but still none had shown up, and he was about to spend his second night in jail. Furious, he demanded his phone call, claiming he hadn't asked for one last night when they jailed him, and if they were keeping him again without arraignment, then that phone call was his right.

Surprisingly, they let him have it, and now he was about to enact his own little version of payback for that asshole cop's stunt. But he didn't call a bondsman or a lawyer. He called his brother.

The phone rang three times, and just as Paco was starting to panic, his brother picked up.

"Hello?"

"Jesus, it's me. Get a pen and paper and hurry. I don't have much time."

"Paco? Where are you, bro?" Jesus asked.

"Jail—being held by the Feds. Don't ask. Just do this for me. Please."

Jesus didn't argue.

"I'm ready. Tell me what you need."

"I need you to call a number and this is what you say. Tell them you're my brother, then say *'Paco's last message was from the cops—it's a trap. She's not there. The woman you want is at this address.'*" Paco carefully recited Saldano's address, the place he knew the redhead was really holed up. Then he gave him Baba's phone number.

"Madre de Dios," Jesus said. "Brother, what have you gotten yourself into?"

"It doesn't matter. But I'm being fucked over by the cops *and* the Feds, and I don't want Baba to think I ratted him out."

Jesus gasped.

"This number belongs to Baba?"

"Yes. You need to give him that address—it's the house of a cop named Saldano—and tell him to ignore the other text. Don't mess this up, Jesus."

"Yeah, okay. I wrote it all down. I promise," Jesus said.

"My time is up. Gotta go," Paco said. Then he hung up and smiled to himself. He might still be fucked, but at least now so was Saldano.

Anton was dreaming he was in the pool playing with Sammy. Star was reclining on a chaise watching them, and he was about to toss Sammy up in the air when the dream shattered around him. It took him a few moments to go from the dream to the realization that what he was hearing was his phone.

He rolled over, fumbling for the phone on the bed behind him, and finally answered with a muffled hello.

"Mr. Baba, my name is Jesus Cruz. I'm Paco Cruz's brother. He gave me a very important message for you."

Anton sat up. Paco had just broken protocol by giving someone else his number.

"And why the hell wouldn't he give me the message himself?" Anton said.

"He's in jail, sir. Paco called me in a panic and gave your number to me. He said to tell you that the text you received earlier was from the cops…and the Feds, I think. Paco said to tell you it was a trap. He said the lady you're looking for is someplace else—"

"Where is she?" Anton snapped, and he heard Jesus swallow nervously before reciting a new address.

"Apparently it's a house that belongs to a cop named Saldano?"

Anton stifled a gasp. He knew Saldano was responsible for Dev Bosky's death. He threw off his covers and hurried to the nearby desk.

"Give me the cop's address again," Anton said, writing quickly on the motel notepad as Jesus read it off.

"If this is a trap, you will be sorry," Anton said, then heard the tears and panic in the caller's voice.

"No, sir, no, sir, I swear on the name of the Holy Mother that I am Paco's brother and this is the message he asked me to give you."

"And he's in jail?" Anton asked.

"Yes. He didn't say why and that's all I know. H
used his one phone call to warn you."

"Is this all?" Anton asked.

"Yes, sir, this is all," Jesus said, and as he was lis
tening, the line went dead.

He was shaking when he hung up. He didn't want t
be on the wrong side of Anton Baba. People died wh
crossed this man.

Eighteen

Before the evening with the Chavez family was over, they had all fallen in love with Quinn, mostly because they could see how much Nick cared for her. If Nick loved her, then they did, too. And in a family of people with olive skin and black hair, Quinn O'Meara's pale skin and red hair was unique.

Lara was the first to comment and told her how beautiful it was. Quinn thanked her.

Santino made a joke about fiery redheads, but Quinn didn't bite. She just laughed at the joke along with everyone else and let it go.

Then Juana asked Quinn what she remembered most about Nick from when they were little.

"Ah, come on, Aunt Juana, give her a break. She was really little. I doubt she remembers all that much," Nick said.

"I don't mind. I remember enough," Quinn said.

"Okay, then, don't say I didn't warn you," Nick said, wondering what she might say.

Without thinking, Quinn laid her hand on his arm.

"I remember lots of things…how he wouldn't let the bigger kids pick on me, how he taught me to tie my shoes. Oh…and he gave me my nickname, Queenie."

Juana's eyes welled, sympathetic to a little girl with no family and all the things she'd had to learn on her own.

A shiver ran up Nick's spine. Such small things had been a big deal to a little girl, and he'd never known it.

"That is so sweet," Lara said and then poked Nick to tease him. "Why did you call her Queenie?"

"I'll tell you," Quinn said. "I got it in my head one Halloween that I wanted to be a princess. I was really little, but the foster family didn't spend money on costumes for us, and of course I was sad. So Nick made a crown for me out of cardboard and tinfoil and said I could be a queen, that they were better than princesses."

Nick grinned.

"And you wore that crown so much I started calling you Queenie, and that was the only name I called you after that."

Lara's teasing manner shifted. The story was too touching to tease about.

"Oh, Nick, that was such a special thing to do for her."

Nick shrugged it off.

"Yes, that's me, Saint Nick himself."

Quinn grinned. One of the things she was learning to love most about Nick was his sense of humor.

And then Juana asked Nick the same question.

"So, Nicholas, what is your strongest memory of her when you were in that foster family together?"

Nick's smile disappeared as he grasped Quinn's hand and held it.

"When I thought she was going to die."

Quinn gasped.

"When was this? I don't remember that."

And suddenly everyone at the table was silent. Everyone was waiting for Nick's story, especially Quinn.

Nick was absently running a finger over the knuckles of her right hand. His eyes narrowed slightly, as if he was seeing, as well as telling, the story.

"You came home from school sick one day, and by evening your fever was so high you were burning up and talking out of your head. I told our foster parents you were sick, and they said it was just the flu and you'd feel better tomorrow."

Quinn's heart was racing. She remembered what he was talking about now, but she'd never known how it had affected him.

"Was she better the next morning?" Juana asked.

"No. She got worse. I was afraid to go to school, but they made me, and when I came home that evening, they thought she was sleeping, but she was unconscious. I raised hell, and when they realized her condition, they took her to the hospital. She was in there three days, and I thought she was dying and they wouldn't take me to see her. All of us kids were worried about her."

Tears were welling in Lara's eyes.

"This is so awful. I never realized that foster families were so careless with the children in their care."

"Not all of them are. There are wonderful families out there—great homes. Just not the one we were in..." Nick glanced at Quinn, but she wouldn't look at him, and he knew she was remembering the man who killed and then revived her.

"So, what happened then?" Juana asked.

"Yes, what happened then?" Quinn asked. "I only remember being sick. I didn't know you'd saved my life."

Nick tried to make light of it and tweaked her nose.

"Well, as you can imagine, by then I didn't trust our foster parents, so when you came home from the hospital, I waited until everyone went to sleep at night, and then I took my pillow and blanket and slept on the floor by your bed every night for a week. I wanted to make sure you didn't die...like my parents."

"Oh, my God," Juana cried and got up from the table and hugged the both of them. "I am sorry. I am so sorry we didn't take you with us then. I didn't know there was such a bond between you two. Nick asked about you, but I didn't know. I didn't understand."

Quinn felt those arms around her neck and Juana's tears on her face and felt so overwhelmed she couldn't bring herself to speak.

It was Nick who took the tears out of the conversation.

"Well, if you had, we would have grown up brother and sister, and right now I'm really glad we're not kin," he drawled, then leaned in and kissed her full on the mouth to make the point.

It was the perfect way to end what had become a tragic story.

"Too many sad stories!" Tonio announced. "I am ready for dessert now!"

"Dessert! After that wonderful dinner? What did you make?" Nick asked.

"Dinner wasn't anything...enchiladas, some beans and rice. And you know what dessert I make when you are coming to dinner!"

Nick patted Quinn's leg.

"You're going to love this. It's my favorite."

"What is it?" she asked.

And everyone at the table yelled...

"Tres leches cake."

Quinn grinned.

"It's my favorite cake, too."

Nick threw up his hands.

"See? Meant to be. I'm in this for the long haul now, for sure."

"Then maybe Juana will show me how to make it one day," Quinn said.

"Yes, yes, she will show you," Tonio said. "But for now, can we please just eat it?"

Juana went to the kitchen to get the cake. The dessert dishes were already on the sideboard behind the dining table, and Nick got up and set them on the table as Santino and Lara cleared the dinner plates.

"I can help," Quinn said.

"You are a guest this time," Tonio said. "Next time, you wash the dishes."

Quinn grinned.

"It's a deal."

The next two hours passed in more laughter, and it was nearing midnight before everyone finally left.

Nick drove away from his aunt and uncle's home, out of the quiet neighborhood and then later down the strip beneath flashing neon lights, until he turned into his neighborhood.

All the way there, he kept thinking—the last piece of the puzzle in his life had just fallen into place. The woman asleep in the seat beside him was not only his forever love, but—if he got his way—she would be his partner, the mother of his children, the woman he wanted to grow old with. Tonight, life just got perfect.

The next morning Nick woke up to an empty bed and the scent of fresh coffee brewing. He stretched lazily, thinking of the way they'd made love last night, and dreading the day he had to go back to work and leave her on her own all day. He guessed she would be job hunting when she was able, though, and let that worry go.

He began to think of all the ways he could safeguard her welfare even when he wasn't around until this mess with Baba was over. After a quick shower and shave, he headed for the kitchen in a pair of bike shorts and a tank top. He needed to clean the pool and check the chlorine level, but not until after breakfast.

When he walked into the kitchen barefoot and saw Quinn at the counter in a pair of cutoff jean shorts and a T-shirt, making toast in her bare feet, he grinned.

"Two peas in a pod," he said.

"What?" Quinn asked as she turned, and then she

saw what he was wearing and got the joke. "Oh, this is priceless."

"Good morning, my love," he said softly and planted a quick kiss on her lips. "Sorry I slept in."

"I attributed it to an overdose of tres leches cake and let you sleep."

He laughed and patted his belly.

"I'll work that off a little later in the pool. Now what can I do to help?"

"I was waiting for you before I made eggs. Do you want them scrambled or fried?"

"Scrambled sounds good," he said.

She got a bowl of eggs out of the refrigerator and set them on the counter, then turned on the skillet, added butter and began cracking eggs into another bowl to scramble while she waited for the pan to get hot.

Nick got out the butter and jam and poured himself a cup of coffee while Quinn dumped the beaten eggs into the hot skillet and started to stir. He pulled down two plates and laid them near the stove, but as he watched her work, his thoughts returned to how he'd keep her safe.

"Hey, Quinn. Do you have a cell phone?"

"Yes. Everyone has a cell phone," she said.

"I've never seen you use it."

"It's out on the Harley. I really only carry it for convenience's sake because there's no one I know who would call me. There's not even anyone I know who has the number."

"Does it have a tracking app on it? You know...the

kind where, if you lose it and activate the app, it wil take you to the phone?"

"No. It's basically what some people call a burner phone. I don't use one often enough to warrant a contract with any phone company."

"Good grief," Nick said beneath his breath.

"I heard that," Quinn said.

"Sorry."

"No, you're not," she said. "And don't pretend you are."

"Not sorry," he called out.

"That's better," she said, finishing off the eggs and serving them onto the plates Nick had set out.

Nick arched an eyebrow. She was a smart-ass for sure, and that, plus the wild, crazy way they made love, pretty much sealed the deal for him. But he wasn't done with her yet.

"I have an extra phone with that app. If I asked you pretty please, would you carry that phone instead of your own?"

"Why?" she asked, frowning.

"Why not?" he fired back.

"Okay, but that's not an answer," she said and stood her ground.

He sighed. "Until Baba is arrested and imprisoned, I am not going to feel you are safe."

"What does a tracking app have to do with keeping me safe? If he finds me, he's not going to kidnap me. He's going to point a gun and pull the trigger."

Nick froze. It was obvious by the way it came out that she'd already thought about it—accepted it.

"Then what's your plan?" he asked.

"If I'm in this house alone, I'll get my gun."

"You have a gun?"

"Yes."

"I didn't know you had a gun." He wondered what other secrets he still might not know about her.

"I suppose now you want to see it," she said.

"Yes."

"Breakfast will get cold."

"I have a microwave," he muttered.

"Whatever," she said and turned off the stove and headed for the garage with Nick at her heels.

She ran her hands beneath the seat of her Harley, and all of a sudden the front of the seat rose up, revealing a hidden compartment beneath it. She pulled out a 9 mm Beretta.

"Ammo in there, too," she said and laid it in his hands.

"Get it," Nick said, while looking at the handgun. It was one of the lighter Beretta models.

She took out two full magazines of ammo and pushed the seat back down.

"I never knew the seats raised up like that," he said.

"It came like this when I bought it."

"I'll feel better knowing you have this gun in the house somewhere, okay?" Nick said. "It's not going to be much use to you hidden out here. I assume you know how to use it?"

"I'm as good with the gun as I am on the Harley, and I'll use your fancy phone with the tracking app, and we'll both be happy. How's that?" she asked.

"Works for me," he said. "Eggs now."

She grinned. He was going to be a fun guy to spend the rest of her life with.

They sat down to eat and, after a rough start to the day, enjoyed breakfast and the chitchat that came with it.

About an hour after they had eaten and cleaned up the kitchen, Nick's cell phone rang. Quinn was in his bathroom gathering up towels to take to the washer, but when she came back into his room he was still on the phone, listening intently to whoever was on the other line, but his expression told her that his conversation was about her.

When he cursed and wiped his hand over his face, as if in disbelief, her legs gave way. She staggered backward and sat down on the lid of the commode with the wet towels clutched against her chest and her gaze fixed on him. When the call ended, he dropped the phone back in his pocket and stood, looking down, almost as if he'd forgotten she was there.

"Nick?"

He jumped at the sound of her voice and then ran toward her.

"I'm sorry. Here, let me help," he said, reaching for towels.

She dropped them in a pile at her feet and grabbed his shirt with both hands.

"Fuck the towels. What was that call about?"

He blinked. So much for keeping her out of this one.

"It was Billy Daniels. You remember—"

"Yes, I remember Daniels. He ate my pancakes. Was he calling to ask for the recipe?"

The sarcasm in her voice was a shade sharper than the fear in her eyes.

"He was calling about a new case."

She took a deep breath.

"Don't make me get this out of you one question at a time. I need to know if that phone call had anything to do with me."

He didn't hesitate. "It's not clear yet, but it might."

She bent down and picked up the wet towels.

"I'm listening. You can talk while we walk."

And so he did.

"They found a dead man in the penthouse of Lucky Joe's Casino. He'd been murdered."

"That's Baba's place, right?" she asked and dumped the towels into the washer.

"Yes, but it wasn't Baba they found. It was a man who called himself Stewart. It seems he showed up at the casino a few days ago and basically stepped in to take control of Baba's empire. Either Baba appointed him in charge in his absence, or else…he knew Baba was gone and took advantage of the situation."

"Do they know who killed this guy?" she asked.

"No, all of the security cameras in the penthouse were destroyed, and the discs and backups are gone. And according to the guards on that floor, no one went in or out except Stewart."

"What do the cops think happened?" she asked.

Nick sighed.

"The way he was murdered…it was bizarre. This was

no random killing. Nothing was stolen, from what they can tell. Nothing's missing except the security discs."

"What do you mean the murder was bizarre?" Quinn asked.

"Someone stabbed a hunting knife into the top of the guy's head."

Nick saw a muscle jump at the side of her jaw, but she didn't say anything except "pass me the detergent," so he did.

Quinn felt like someone had just cut off her legs. She felt trapped and scared to death, and at the same time angry this was happening.

"Okay. Why don't you go get that cell phone and show me how to work it," she said.

Nick turned on one heel, moving through the house in long, angry strides. Like Quinn, he was pissed this was happening. Whether Baba had done this or sent someone to do the deed for him, it was all the same. What mattered was that Anton Baba was cleaning house, and Quinn was one of the people who could put him behind bars—which meant she was on his list.

He came back with the phone, sat down in the kitchen and showed her how to keep it turned on when she was gone.

"Okay, I've got it," she said and put it in her back pocket, then stood up.

"Where are you going?" he asked.

"To switch the laundry," she replied and walked out of the kitchen.

Nick was sick to his stomach with worry, and yet she could just carry on and finish the laundry? She ei-

her had nerves of steel or she was faking it better than
anyone he knew. He got up and followed, only to hear
her throwing up in the back bathroom. As much as he
wanted to stay and comfort her, instinct told him to
back off and let her deal with this her way.

Later that day, he got a phone call from Agent Gleason checking on Quinn, which pissed Nick off.

"We already know about the murder in the penthouse. Is this your way of checking to see if the killer
had already hit here, too?"

Gleason sighed. That thought had been in his head,
and he hated being so obvious, but he was still going
to defend himself.

"Of course not," he said.

"Do you know if Anton Baba is in Vegas?" Nick
asked.

"We have no reports and no sightings of him," Gleason said.

"You had to know after Paco Cruz sent that text for
you that it would be an invitation for Baba to come out
from wherever he was hiding."

"Of course," Gleason said. "We've had agents at the
borders ever since his disappearance."

"Do you even know if he ever left the state?" Nick
asked.

"We think he went down to his place in Mexico."

"And does anyone know if he's still there?" Nick
asked.

Gleason shifted nervously in his chair.

"The estate is empty, and a plane was seen taking
off from that location yesterday morning."

"Where is that plane now?"

"I don't know. But Baba has a plane, and it's in the hangar," Gleason said.

"Was it in the hangar yesterday morning?"

Gleason cleared his throat.

"I don't like being grilled as if I answer to you, Saldano. I don't have to tell you anything."

"Works both ways," Nick said and hung up.

Gleason was stunned that the cop had just hung up on him and immediately called back.

Nick answered, but didn't speak.

"We did not have anyone on stakeout at the airport," Gleason muttered.

"Great job you guys are doing. So, to answer your question, Quinn O'Meara is not okay. She's scared out of her mind, and right now I don't feel much better. Is Paco Cruz still behind bars?"

When Gleason began to stutter, Nick tensed. As it would happen, he'd been right to be concerned.

"Uh, about that," Gleason said. "We didn't get the paperwork filed in time. He bonded out before we could—"

Shock went through Nick so fast he had to sit down.

"You aren't serious?" he asked.

"Yes, I'm afraid—"

Nick was shouting now, having moved past being courteous to realizing he was dealing with idiots.

"Then don't expect anyone to show up at your damn safe house, because we both know Paco Cruz has already alerted his old boss as to what went down. There's no way Baba is walking into your safe-house trap now.

The only place he's heading is directly to my house, since that's where Paco first saw her. Thanks for nothing, Gleason. Don't call here again."

Nick hung up and went looking for Quinn, and found her asleep in the middle of her bed. He sat down on the side of the mattress, and when he did, she woke, saw the look on his face and sat up.

"What's wrong?"

"The Feds didn't get their paperwork done in time, so Paco Cruz was let out of jail. I was just on the phone with Gleason. They don't know where Paco is and you can bet he sent a follow-up message to Baba, filling him in on our little plan."

Quinn rolled off the bed and began putting on her shoes.

"Cruz will send Baba straight to this house. Where do we go?" she asked.

Nick was sick. He'd promised to keep her safe, and now he didn't know what to do to make that happen.

"I don't know, but we can't stay here. We'll pack a few things and figure it out as we go."

She threw her arms around his neck.

"It's not your fault. Stop looking like someone stomped on my toy and you're afraid to tell me it's broken. I'm a big girl. Just tell me what to do and I'll do it."

Grateful she wasn't angry with him, he began to focus.

"Pack for a few days on the road and don't forget your pain pills. I'm going to pack some stuff, too, and then we'll leave here for a while. I need to let my boss know what's happening."

"What about Gleason?" she asked.

"At this point, I don't think we can count on the FBI for anything," he said.

"Okay."

Nick gave her a quick kiss and then ran across the hall to pack. While he was there, his cell rang, and again it was Daniels.

"Hey, Nick. We're still working the homicide at Lucky Joe's penthouse, but there's been a development I think you'd be interested in. There was a guard who mentioned seeing a strange man come down the back stairs earlier."

"So, what's the big deal about that?" Nick asked.

"Well, it seemed odd because he said he never saw the guy go up. Only come down. So we pulled security footage for the delivery entrance, and we have a pretty good image of an older man—looks Latino. He was dressed in work clothes and carrying a toolbox, but no one reported the need for an outside repairman that day."

When Daniels paused, Nick pressed him further. "I know there's more, or you wouldn't be trying to warn me. What aren't you saying?"

"We ran the image through facial recognition and… it came through as a match for Anton Baba. He must've been in disguise."

"Shit. He's already back in Vegas."

"Yeah, and hiding in plain sight as a Mexican laborer. I think you two need to—"

"We're already packing. Gleason called about something else that led us to believe it wasn't safe to stay here."

"Okay, but if you need anything, let us know."

"I'm about to call the sheriff right now," Nick said. "Keep me updated."

"Will do," Daniels said and disconnected.

Nick sat down on the side of the bed, put in the call and quickly updated Sheriff Baldwin on the situation, then finished packing.

Anton was rattled by the roundabout message from Paco Cruz, but he was in a serious situation and didn't have the manpower or resources to send someone else to check it out.

He read the text he'd gotten from Paco and then thought about the phone call from Paco's brother and decided to trust his gut. Paco Cruz had never let him down, so he decided to trust his brother. He sat down at the end of the bed and turned on the television, wondering if Stewart's body had been discovered yet, and when he flipped to a local morning show it was evident that it had.

Reports stated that an as-yet unidentified man was murdered in the penthouse of Lucky Joe's Casino, owned by Anton Baba. Baba's whereabouts were unknown, according to the broadcaster, and there was a federal warrant for his arrest on unrelated charges.

Just hearing all of that on the morning news was warning enough that he had no time to waste.

He was likely their first suspect, though they'd have to prove he was in the state. They'd be looking at videotape from all over the city, so he hoped his disguise would hold for one more day.

The phone call from Jesus Cruz was not how he had envisioned this day beginning, but now that he was up, he needed to finish what he'd come to do.

He would drive by the address Jesus had given him to get a feel for the location and layout, but he had to be careful. A cop would not be a fool with regards to home security, and would obviously have weapons on the property, as well.

All he needed was the advantage, and two kill shots later, one of two federal witnesses against him would be dead. He didn't know where Star was, but he knew the Feds didn't either, and since he was a betting man, he was betting his life that she would rather go into hiding from him and the law than endanger Sammy again. In a way, it would be as if his own son was saving him from jail. He liked that thought.

Even though he'd paid for another night at this motel, instinct told him it was time to move. So as he dressed for the day, he was also packing, and when he left, he left his key on the bed and a three-dollar tip beneath it. Nothing too ostentatious or it wouldn't fit his disguise. A laborer would not be tipping with ten- or twenty-dollar bills.

He drove until he came across a strip of fast-food joints and went through the drive-through of one to get breakfast. A bacon, egg and cheese biscuit was not what he was used to for a meal, but it served the purpose. Two of those and a large coffee later he drove out of the parking lot and back onto the streets. Now he had to find the cop's house.

He pulled out his cell phone, clicked on to a map app and typed in the address. Within moments, the directions were on his phone, telling him where to go and when to turn.

Technologically, it was easy to get where you needed to go these days, but he didn't like doing all this for himself. A man accustomed to the finer things should not be forced to find his own way through life. There were people for that. He wanted his servants and that lifestyle back, but the only way to get it was to ensure his name stayed cleared. So for now he'd continue doing the grunt work, following the prompts on his phone until he spied Saldano's house.

Now it was time to get serious.

Nineteen

The garage doors were up.

The car was already being loaded.

Nick went inside for another bag, passing Quinn, who was on her way out with more luggage, just as an old truck drove past the house. Quinn paid no attention to it, but the driver was certainly looking at her.

Anton grinned.

It was the troublesome redhead—and she was all alone. This was a gift from the Universe today. Without giving himself time to think his actions through, he turned up into the driveway, intentionally blocking their car from leaving as he put the truck in Park with the engine still running.

Quinn tossed her bag into the trunk of Nick's car just as she heard the vehicle pulling up behind her. She turned and saw an older man getting out of an old beat-up truck. She didn't recognize him, but the expression on his face was unsettling, as was the way he'd blocked them in. Her gut told her she was in danger.

She moved on instinct, reaching behind her back for the Beretta in the waistband of her jeans. In the same moment, Quinn saw his arm come up, got a glimpse of the gun in his hand, but swung hers around and fired first, hitting the sombrero as it went flying off of his head. She dropped to the floor of the garage, lying flat as his shot went wild, hitting the back tire of Nick's car.

Quinn fired a second shot, and the man ducked behind the door of the truck for protection and began firing into the garage.

Quinn was on her belly against the wall when Nick came flying out of the house, shooting.

His first shot burned the side of the man's chest; the second got him in the shoulder. He leaped into the truck, yanked the gearshift into Reverse and stomped the accelerator. The squeal of tires and the scent of burning rubber filled the garage as the old man backed out of the drive, shifted gears and sped away.

Nick turned in a panic to check on Quinn, but she was already scrambling to her feet.

"I'm okay," she shouted, as Nick turned to give chase, running into the street quick enough to get off one shot before the truck turned a corner.

But just as Nick shot, a young teenager came around the corner on a bicycle, swerved to miss the speeding truck and skidded sideways as he fell.

There was a split second of panic when Nick thought the kid might have been hit, and he watched in fear as the boy rolled over and crawled up into a yard and hid behind a bushy shrub.

Nick ran toward him, praying with every step as he got to the yard, and yanked the kid out of the bushes.

"D-Man… Donny…are you okay?" he cried.

The boy was shaking, but was nodding yes.

Nick threw his arms around him.

"Thank God you're okay. Get your bike and go home. This neighborhood is about to become a crime scene."

The boy ran toward his bike, limping as he went, and pedaled away as fast as he could.

Nick turned to go back toward his house when he began hearing sirens, and to his horror, he saw Quinn coming out of the garage on her Harley.

"No, Quinn, no!" Nick shouted, waving his arms to stop her. But she swerved around him, shouting as she went.

"Track me on the app," she yelled and sped away.

"Lord have mercy," he said and started running back to his house.

It wasn't until he got into the garage that he saw his back tire had exploded. He heard the first patrol cars arriving on scene and ran back into the street to flag them down.

The first car slid to a stop as Nick flashed his badge.

"Detective Saldano, Homicide. I've got a woman in pursuit of a man who just tried to kill her. She's chasing him on a motorcycle."

"Get in!" the patrolman shouted, and Nick jumped into the car as the cop radioed to the cars behind him that they were going into pursuit.

Nick pulled the app up on his phone, and almost immediately, he had a map of the city and a swiftly moving blip.

"That way!" he said.

The cop took off again, running with lights and sirens, and less than a block away, two more patrol cars followed suit.

Anton was in so much pain he could hardly think. His side was burning, and the shot he'd taken in his shoulder had clearly broken something. He could no longer raise his arm.

He was driving the old truck as fast as it would go through neighborhood streets, barely missing pedestrians, running through stop signs, hitting the back end of a car going through an intersection, but he never once slowed down.

It had been years since he'd been this afraid, and it was not a memory he enjoyed thinking about. He'd killed an old woman for her car and money—a pitiful crime, one he was never proud of. That was nearly forty years ago and a continent away, but now he was running in fear again, only this time he was bleeding, and time was running out.

He knew the moment he got shot where he would have to go. To the TomCat Club—his first whorehouse and the place where he'd amassed his first fortune. Delilah would hide him and the truck, and his girls there were loyal. He would be safe and he could heal, but there were fifteen miles between him and the club, and he was bleeding like a son of a bitch.

"No cops, no cops, no cops," he kept saying, as if turning that into a mantra would make it real.

He saw the street up ahead that would take him out of Vegas toward the TomCat and tried to go faster, but the old truck was already smoking and shaking.

"No cops, no cops, no cops," he repeated and took the turn.

Quinn didn't think, she just reacted when she realized that son of a bitch was going to get away. It had to be Anton Baba. No one else wanted her dead, and when he shot at her, something in her snapped. She had been a victim too many times in her life, but no more. She ran for the Harley, jammed the helmet over her head and swung her leg over the bike.

Even though it hadn't been ridden in days, it started like a charm. She patted her pocket to make sure Nick's cell phone was still there, checked quickly to make sure it was on and then flew out of the garage after the truck.

Nick was running back toward the house—toward her. She knew he was going to try to stop her, but she didn't have time to explain.

"Follow me on the tracking app," she yelled and then accelerated through the streets trying to catch a glimpse of that truck.

It wasn't until she realized she was following a trail of wrecked cars and skid marks through intersections that she guessed she might be on the right path.

She saw the smoke coming from the tailpipe first and then noticed the truck up ahead and breathed a sigh of relief. It was him. She didn't know where he was going, but figured he was trying to get out of Vegas as quickly as possible. Her best bet was to try to catch up with him and shoot out his tires. That would stop him, and hopefully Nick and the cops would be right behind her.

She made a point to stay about a half block behind, waiting and waiting for police cars to appear so she could make her move, but it didn't happen.

Between trying to keep up with Baba and watching for cops, she'd ridden all the way out of the city before she realized how far they'd gone.

Nick! Nick, where are you?

The traffic was heavy on the road out of town, which helped to keep Baba in her sights with just enough cover to hopefully go unnoticed. She didn't want to catch him without backup, so she just kept up the chase, driving straight into the heat waves rising up above the highway.

When he suddenly veered off the highway onto a smaller road leading out into the desert, she had no choice but to follow or lose him. If she followed, he would see her then, for sure. She didn't know what he would do when he realized she was behind him, but she had her gun and a full clip of ammo. It was time to make a move. If she could get close enough before he noticed her, she'd end this race right now.

She leaned forward, lowering her body to counteract wind resistance, and accelerated even more. There was a knot in her belly and a hot sun burning down her back.

God help me.

* * *

The relief of exiting the highway onto the county road was huge. In less than ten minutes he'd be at TomCat's and sanctuary. He imagined the look of dismay on Delilah's face and knew she would take care of him.

He was light-headed from blood loss and pain, but he would get well and get out of the country. It no longer mattered as much about losing this empire. Empires were made to be lost and won. He built it up once. He could do it again somewhere else. This wasn't the end for him, he was certain.

Until he glanced in the side-view mirror and his heart nearly stopped.

"What the fuck?"

It was a biker—directly on his tail. There was always the chance that this guy was just some customer heading to the TomCat, but something about the way the bike moved suggested an urgency that worried Anton. He accelerated, but the truck was already at its maximum speed, so he just concentrated on driving it with one hand.

Another minute passed, and he glanced in the mirror again. The biker was closer—and now he could see long red hair beneath the helmet.

The redhead?

"No fucking way," he muttered, reaching for his gun before being overcome with a shooting pain—a violent reminder that his right arm was out of commission.

He glanced down and stifled a gasp at the sight of himself.

He was sitting in blood. Blood was everywhere.

The biker was coming closer and closer, and his panic was climbing with every second. He would not, by God, be brought down by some *woman*.

He heard a sound, something like a pop, and quickly realized she was shooting at him.

"No, no, no!" he shrieked as he heard another pop, then two more, and just like that, she'd flattened both his back tires.

One moment he was on the road and the next he was in the sand and frantically steering from side to side to keep from rolling.

He caught a glimpse of motion out the window beside him, saw the biker, red hair flying from under the helmet, and the gun in her hand was pointed straight at him. He hit the brakes. It was a mistake.

The truck rolled twice, coming to a stop upside down in the dirt.

The bike's tires squealed as she also hit the brakes, did a one-eighty on the blacktop and then killed the engine and dismounted, running toward his truck.

The glass in all the windows was gone, and he was struggling to move around inside the cab, hurt and disoriented and trying to find a way out.

"Give me your hand!" the woman shouted at him as she reached inside the front window.

He took the offer gladly, his desire to live stronger than his desire to kill her, and grabbed on to her wrist with one hand.

The woman grabbed on to him with both hands and began pulling him backward. The truck was beginning to smoke, he noticed with cold panic.

"Hurry!" he shrieked. "It's burning!"

He was in so much pain he could barely move, but she kept pulling and pulling until the upper half of his body was free.

Something inside the truck burst into flames.

"Don't let me burn!" Baba screamed in panic.

Despite her hatred for this man, she was not about to let him die. He deserved to spend the rest of his life in prison, not death, no matter how gruesome. She dug her heels in the sand and leaned backward, just as she began to hear sirens in the distance.

"Finally," she muttered and pulled harder.

The flames were higher now, and Baba was screaming nonstop. The woman was struggling with his weight when all of a sudden there were men beside her.

Someone grabbed her around the waist.

"Run!" Nick shouted, as he pulled her away from the fire.

Hearing his voice was the most beautiful sound, but it was the panic she heard that made her lengthen her stride.

Behind them, more cops had pulled Baba out and were dragging him through the desert as they ran from the crash.

When the truck exploded into flames, the force of the blast knocked all of them down. The cops were immediately back on their feet and pulling Baba a safer distance away.

Nick rose up on one elbow, looked down at the bloody smears on her face, the dirt on her clothes and the smell of smoke in her hair, then shook his head and covered her lips with a groan, kissing her over and over as if he would never get enough.

Quinn felt the fear in his touch and the desperation in his kiss as she put her arms around his neck.

After another minute, he finally pulled himself away, then stood up and lifted her to her feet.

"Bloody hell, Queenie. I have never been so scared in my life. You took ten years off my life just now. Promise me…don't ever do this again."

"I'm sorry I scared you, but I thought he was getting away. I didn't want to live the rest of my life looking over my shoulder. I'm so tired of being afraid."

Nick shook his head and then pulled her close in a shaky embrace.

"You rode that Harley like a bat out of hell. The team will be talking about that for years."

She shrugged and then turned around to look at the scene, making sure the bike was far enough away from the fire, and it was. Then she saw the body on the ground.

"Is he still alive?" she asked.

"I don't know but we can find out."

An ambulance was coming toward them in the distance.

"Here comes his ride," Nick said.

Quinn kept walking until she reached the spot where he lay stretched out upon the ground. He was moaning and mumbling, begging for help. Someone had applied some kind of field dressing to his side while another held a pressure bandage to his shoulder.

She stopped at his feet and then stood there for a moment, just staring at him. The ambulance was getting closer. They were going to do their best to save him, but she was wishing him dead.

His eyelids fluttered, then opened. And then he was staring straight at her face.

A rage swept through her as he moaned and then closed his eyes.

"Hey!" she shouted and kicked the bottom of his boot, startling everyone, including Anton himself.

His eyes came open.

"You!" he said.

"Yes, it's me!" Quinn said. "You get a real good look and remember I'm the one who pulled you out of that fire."

"After you shot out my tires," he cried.

"After you tried to kill me! Now shut up and listen," Quinn countered. "If you don't die here today, you'll be seeing my face again in court, and you better pray to God that they put you in prison for life, because if I ever see you loose on the streets again I will shoot you without hesitation. And when I do, I won't hit your hat again. That bullet will land right between your eyes."

Anton coughed and turned his head toward the nearby cops.

"You heard her threaten me," he cried, as though there was any chance he would appear innocent in all of this.

Nick kicked the bottom of Anton's other shoe.

"I didn't hear a thing."

Anton frantically looked at the cops around him, but they were looking up the road.

"The ambulance is here," one of them said, pointing over Nick's shoulder.

Nick put his arm around Quinn and waited on the scene until Baba was gone.

"That was quite the promise you just made him," he said, tilting her chin up so he could look at her. "If you want him dead, why pull him from the truck when you could have left him to die?"

Quinn closed her eyes, thinking a moment before answering. "Part of me wants him dead—but that's mostly the angry, scared part of me. The rest of me wants him to answer for his crimes, for what he's done to so many women over the years—not just to me."

Nick pulled her close, knowing with more certainty than ever that this was the woman of his dreams.

A couple of cops were stringing crime-scene tape around the truck when Quinn started to come down from the adrenaline rush.

"How long do we have to be here?" she asked.

"Until we've given our statements for sure, unless they let us come down to the precinct tomorrow to do it."

"Then I need to sit down."

Her face was white beneath the dirt as he picked her up in his arms and carried her over to one of the patrol cars. The engine was still running, the air-conditioning blasting cool air as he put her in the back seat.

"Wait in here where it's cooler, baby. I'm going to go see what I can do to speed this up."

She was already curling up on the back seat as he closed the door. He glanced in the window to make sure she was okay, then jogged over to one of the cops.

"Hey, Quinn was feeling faint. I just put her in the back seat of your patrol car."

The cop grinned.

"I'd feel faint, too, if I'd been on a Harley for ten miles in this heat chasing down the man who tried to kill me. Baba said she shot out his back tires."

Nick shook his head. "She's never been one to back away from trouble. I guess he finally pissed her off enough to take action."

"It's all that red hair," the cop said, then clapped Nick on the shoulder. "I see you two have a thing going…so, congratulations. She seems like a great lady, but I feel obligated to warn you—don't make her mad."

Nick grinned.

"Duly noted."

Star was doing her daily best to reestablish a normal life back in her hometown of Nashville, but it still felt strange. Part of the time it almost felt like the last seven years was a nightmare that didn't really happen, and then she'd catch a glimpse of Sammy, and it would all come flooding back.

Right now, she was alone in her parents' house except for Sammy, and it felt good to be in control of the space, even if it was temporary.

Her mother had gone to the supermarket, and she had just put a pan of sugar cookies in the oven.

Sammy was standing at the kitchen door, looking

out into the backyard, where his grandpa John was on the riding lawn mower cutting grass. He banged on the glass, clearly wanting a ride.

Starla turned around.

"Sammy. No hitting the door, please."

He whacked it again, yelling, "I ride, I ride."

"Sammy! What did I just say?" she said, this time in a sterner voice.

He stopped, patted the Plexiglas in an apologetic way and then toddled over to the counter and hugged her leg.

"Mama not mad at me," he said.

She dropped to her knees.

"No. I'm not mad, sweetheart. But you can't hit things like that. They might break, okay?"

"'Kay," he said and pointed at the oven. "Cookies for me."

She scooped him up in her arms with a laugh.

"Cookies for everyone but not until they are through baking."

He patted his hands on her cheeks and smiled.

An overwhelming rush of love washed through her as she cuddled him close.

"I sure do love you," she said.

"Love you!" he said and patted her cheeks again.

She was still smiling when the phone began to ring. She set him down and pointed at his toys beneath the window.

"Go play," she said and then ran for the phone.

"Hello?"

"Hey, sis, it's Justin."

She turned toward the window to watch Sammy as she talked.

"It's so good to hear your voice," she said.

"I have some really good news for you," he said.

She grinned. "I could always use good news. Spill it."

"Anton Baba is in a hospital, officially under arrest, and if he doesn't die from his wounds he'll soon be behind bars."

"Oh, my God!" Star gasped. "How did they find him? Why is he in the hospital?"

"Remember that woman, Quinn O'Meara, who found Sammy out in the desert and brought him into Vegas?"

"Yes. She saved his life. She was in the hospital. Is she all right?"

"All right enough to be the one who took him down. It's a long story, and I don't have much time, but I wanted to let you know that you're safe. His empire is imploding. That Stewart guy who first kidnapped you and sold you to Baba is dead, and they're laying that at Baba's feet, too. You are free from everything now but bad memories. I just wish I could get rid of those for you, too."

Star started to cry.

"Will I have to still testify in court?"

"I don't know, but I wouldn't count on it. I'm betting Baba will try to make some deal with the Feds and go straight to prison."

"But won't that mean he gets out early?"

"Besides everything they already have on him, they now have him for Stewart's murder and two attempted murder charges for trying to kill Quinn O'Meara. He will never see freedom again, I promise you that."

Tears were rolling now.

"Thank you, Justin. Thank you from the bottom of my heart for everything."

"Hey, kid, no tears. I love you. What else would I do? Listen, I gotta go. Tell Mom and Dad I said hi. I'll call them this weekend."

"I will," she said and hung up.

Sammy saw her tears from across the room and came running, patting her leg to be lifted up. She picked him up and kissed his little round cheek.

"Mama is okay," she said. "Happy tears. These are happy tears."

The timer went off at the stove.

"And cookies are done!" she cried.

"Cookies done!" Sammy shrieked and wiggled out of her lap.

"Nope, too hot to eat now," she said. "Go play. We'll eat cookies later."

Sammy still followed her to the stove, watched her putting the cookies on a rack to cool, and then when he felt the heat from the oven, he backed away with a frown and went back to play.

A short while later her dad came in through the kitchen door.

"Wow, something sure smells good in here," he said, as he gave her a hug.

"Cookies, Papa!" Sammy shrieked.

John scooped him up, laughing.

"How many has he already had?"

"None yet."

"Well, heck fire, boy! Let me wash my hands and we'll both have a cookie, okay?"

"Heck fire! Wash my hands!" Sammy yelled.

John grimaced.

"Sorry about that."

Star just shook her head.

"Go. Wash. Eat. I have news."

John poked Sammy in the belly just to make him laugh, and then both of them headed to the bathroom to clean up.

Star took a deep breath and felt a huge wave of relief sweep through her as she counted out her blessings.

The staples were out of her back.

Her wounds were healing.

She and Sammy were safe.

They were home.

She couldn't wish for anything more. Then she heard Sammy's chatter and her father's laugh.

She wiped her face one last time and lifted her chin.

"Cookie time," she said. Man, did she have a tale to tell.

Twenty

Nick and Quinn were still at the scene of the crash later that afternoon when the Feds showed up.

Agent Gleason and his partner, Agent Powers, showed up unannounced and headed straight for Quinn.

She was leaning against a patrol car with her arms crossed beneath her breasts, wearing a patrolman's hat to shade her from the sun.

Nick was back on the county road helping measure skid marks when he saw the Feds drive up.

"Sorry, guys. Those are Feds. I need to make sure Quinn doesn't lose it on them, too. She's reached her limit of everything today."

"Yeah, sure thing. Thanks for the help, Saldano."

He took off toward Quinn at a lope, reaching her just moments after the agents' arrival. No one was talking, and he didn't know exactly what was happening, but they were all staring at each other, as if waiting for a question to be answered. He walked up behind her, slid an arm around her waist and nodded at the men.

"Afternoon. Are you lost, or just sightseeing?"

"We heard about what happened and came to make sure Miss O'Meara was okay."

Quinn looked up at Nick.

"What he just said is...they came to see if their witness was still breathing, no damn thanks to them."

Nick raised his eyebrows.

"As you can see, she's fine. In fact, we have her to thank for running Baba down. I'm sure you've heard that, too."

Gleason nodded.

"A very brave thing to do," he said.

"I got tired of sleeping with one eye open," Quinn snapped. "So, is he still alive, or did we all get lucky?"

"He was coming out of surgery last I heard."

"Too bad," she said.

"And yet I heard you are the one who also pulled him out of the fire," Powers added.

"Yes, I did do that," she said.

"Out of curiosity, what prompted you to do that?"

Quinn shrugged. She didn't owe this man any explanation. She'd basically done his job for him anyway.

Gleason sighed. She had the right to be angry. A lot of bad stuff had happened to her for trying to do a good deed.

"Have you officially served your arrest warrant on him?" Nick asked.

"We're on the way to do that. We'll have to wait until he comes to enough to hear us out, but by the time he wakes up in his room, he will find himself handcuffed to the bed and one of our men on his door until he can be released into our custody."

"That's good," Nick said.

"When can we go home?" Quinn asked.

"Probably right now if you're ready. We can give you a ride into Vegas," Gleason said.

"We have a ride," Quinn said.

The agents eyed the Harley, then shrugged.

"If this goes to court, we'll let you know," Gleason said.

Quinn turned her back on them, tossed the patrolman's hat back inside his car and headed for her bike.

"Well, gentlemen, it's been nice seeing you again, but I don't want to miss my ride," Nick said, and he left them standing in the sun staring at the remnants of a burned-out truck.

Quinn was already at the Harley, checking it out before starting it back up.

"Can I drive?" Nick asked.

For the first time in hours, she smiled.

"Do you know how?"

"Yes, ma'am."

"Then I would appreciate the ride home," she said and picked up the helmet. "I don't think this will fit you. I have some goggles, though."

"You wear the helmet. I'll take the goggles," Nick said.

She dug them out of a compartment on the back of the bike and handed them to him. He adjusted them a couple of times before they felt right, and then threw one leg over the Harley and toed up the kickstand.

Quinn pulled the helmet onto her head and got on behind him, settling into the seat and wrapping her arms around his waist.

"Take me home, Nick."

"You got it, baby. Just hang on."

The Harley roared to life as Nick put it into gear and accelerated, zipping through the desert and then back onto the county road toward the main highway.

The heat waves were endless, dancing just above the pavement. A buzzard circled high above them in the sky, and the traffic and the roar of the engine was constant. Another biker passed them, giving them a thumbs-up. If only he knew.

The farther they rode, the more relaxed Quinn became until the tight grip she'd had on Nick eased. They rode into Vegas without stopping and headed straight for his house. Unknowingly, both of them were thinking about the chaos they'd left behind and all of the unpacking yet to do, but when they turned the corner on his street and Nick saw all the cars at his place, he smiled.

They rode up the driveway, weaving between the cars and all the way into the garage before he killed the engine.

Quinn took off her helmet.

"What's going on?" she asked.

"I'm guessing one of the neighbors called my family. My car has a new back tire, and I can bet Aunt Juana is in the kitchen cooking."

Quinn groaned.

"I look like a sewer rat, but I suddenly do not care. Lord, but I am so hungry."

At that moment, Donny, the teen from the neighborhood, came running into the garage.

"Hey, Nick. Mom and Dad are in the kitchen with your parents. Dad got you a new tire. He said I was worth about that much to him. Are you guys okay? Did you catch the dude who shot at you?"

"Yeah, we sure did, D-Man. He's under arrest in a hospital and then headed to jail later," Nick said. "Let's go into the house. It seems Quinn and I have some people to thank."

Donny followed them inside and into the kitchen. The noise level was already loud, but when they saw Nick and Quinn, it erupted.

"What happened! Are you two okay?" Tonio asked.

"Is any of that yours?" Juana asked, pointing to the blood splatters on Quinn.

"No, ma'am. Nick shot Baba twice before he got away," Quinn said.

Juana frowned.

"Nick's not the one covered in blood, so how did all that get on you?"

Quinn sighed.

"It's a long story and I'm filthy, but could I maybe have a tortilla and some guacamole before I go shower? I'm starving."

"Poor baby," Juana cried and headed for the table.

Lara slipped through the crowd and put her arms around Quinn's neck, hugging her as she whispered in her ear.

"I am so glad you're okay. Is there anything I can do to help you?"

Quinn's eyes welled. "Just don't let them eat all the good stuff before I get back."

Lara grinned. "I'll do what I can, but you know Santino. He is shameless."

Quinn held on to the laughter to keep from crying. She'd always been better with anger than sympathy. And then Juana came back with a soft, homemade tortilla filled with spicy carne asada and topped off with sour cream and guacamole.

"Here you are, daughter. You go make yourself feel better, and we'll be here when you get back."

"Thank you," Quinn said and took a quick bite to keep from crying as she hurried out of the room. She had never been anyone's daughter before.

Nick tried to pay Donny's parents for the tire, but they immediately refused and thanked Nick for making sure their son stayed safe during the shooting. After more hugs and well wishes, they left the family on their own to catch up.

As soon as the neighbors were gone, the family started in on Nick.

"What really happened out there, Nick? What happened to Quinn?"

"If I told you she rode Anton Baba down out in the desert, shot out both of his back tires and then pulled him out of the burning wreck, would you believe me?"

There was a collective gasp and then silence until Santino spoke up.

"Are you serious?"

He nodded.

Juana pressed a hand to her lips to keep from crying, then made the sign of the cross.

"She is blessed by God," Tonio said.

Nick wasn't going to argue with that.

"Hey, guys, I'm going to change shirts and wash up a little myself. I'll be right back."

"No worries," Juana said. "I'm still making queso."

Nick gave her a hug and hurried down the hall to his bedroom. Quinn's door was closed. He honored her need for privacy and went into his room to change.

Quinn stood looking out her bedroom windows as she ate, too dirty to sit down on anything in the room. Once she'd polished off the food, she stripped where she stood and headed for the bathroom.

She turned on the water in the shower and then checked the healing wound on her shoulder. It looked fine. Nothing had come open. Nothing was bleeding.

She grabbed a clean washcloth, checked to make sure there was shampoo and conditioner inside the shower and then stepped inside.

The water was hot, almost too hot, but she didn't care; she wanted every trace of Anton Baba scrubbed from her skin. She was angry enough about being shot at, but when those two federal agents showed up to make sure their witness was okay, she lost it. They weren't worried about her. They were just worried about their case. She was sick and tired of always feeling used, but she no longer felt like a victim.

Pointing a gun at the man who's trying to kill you is an empowering moment. Pulling the trigger a second before him was even better. Knowing she'd scared the crap out of him was priceless. By reacting instead of hiding, she'd taken herself off the victim list and liked how that felt. She felt powerful. She'd stood up for herself in a way that she'd never done before.

The water was hitting her in the chest now, just below her chin. This was the moment where her stomach always knotted and her panic exacerbated, only that wasn't happening this time. Everything suddenly felt different, and she remembered hearing once that as long as you continue to do the same things, you will always have the same results. It's only when you change, the world will change around you.

She lifted her hand up to face the showerhead and felt the jets pulsing against her palm.

"It's time to do something different," she said and took a deep breath and stepped beneath the spray.

The only thing that happened was she got wet. There was no panic, no heart-stopping feeling of drowning. She squirted a handful of shampoo in her palm and started washing her hair, thinking that she wished she'd had a shot at Pappy Whitlaw when he'd tried to hurt her instead of running away. That's when this fear had all begun. He'd made her feel so helpless that all she'd known to do was hide.

She rinsed, conditioned and rinsed again, then grabbed a bar of soap and scrubbed until her skin tingled. After enjoying the warmth of the water a few moments more, she got out of the shower and wrapped a towel around her hair.

Now that she was finished, she couldn't move fast

enough to get back into the kitchen. She dried herself, then towel-dried her hair and headed for the closet.

Again, her choice of clothing was minimal. One of these days she'd have to rectify that, but for now she just chose what was clean.

When she left her room, she had on jeans and a long, loose T-shirt. Her hair was damp and hanging loose around her face as she hurried barefoot down the hall.

The sound of Nick's voice and his laughter made her heart skip a beat as she moved toward the sound of happy voices.

She was getting the hang of having family.

Epilogue

Paco Cruz heard about Anton Baba's arrest as he was getting a haircut down in the barrio and his heart nearly stopped.

He will blame me. He will think I set him up.

The longer he thought about it, the more panicked he became. His brother, Jesus, had been trying to get him to go to Denver for months now. The marijuana business was legal there, and if Paco knew anything, he knew about weed. By the time the barber was through with his cut, he'd made up his mind. He was sick of cleaning other people's toilets and emptying their trash. Who would have ever guessed something he'd been put in jail for was now a legal business?

He paid for his haircut and headed out the door. It was time to get away from this place and all the people in it. Nothing good had ever come to him here and he needed to get lost. Maybe he would start his life over. It was never too late until you took your last breath.

* * *

Anton Baba woke up handcuffed to a hospital bed, one guard inside his room and one standing outside the door. Neither one would talk to him. He asked to contact his lawyer. Two Feds named Gleason and Powers came instead, officially arrested him for the murder of Dale Stewart, the attempted murder of Starla Davis and Quinn O'Meara, and a litany of other infractions he knew they could prove.

"Do you understand the charges as we have read them?" Gleason asked.

"Yes. I want my lawyer."

"I'll bet you do," Gleason said and then turned to the guard in the room. "He is allowed to make one call. Then I want the phone taken out of this room."

"Yes, sir," the guard said.

"But what if he needs to call me back?" Anton said.

"You better say all you need to say the first time, because technically, you're already in jail," Gleason said.

Anton's gut turned. Everything he'd ever feared was coming true. He'd like to blame Star or Quinn or even some snitch, but he was honest enough to know he had started all of this himself. He just hadn't expected anyone to fight back.

Three days later Quinn woke up alone in the bed, then rolled over to find Nick sitting in a chair on the other side of the room watching her sleep. He was not only already dressed, but he'd also showered and shaved.

"What's happening? Are we supposed to be somewhere? Did I make us late?" she asked as she threw back the covers and started to get out of bed.

"Everything is fine," Nick said. "I just like watching you sleep."

She made a face at him.

"That's a little creepy. Was my mouth open?"

"Yes, and you were drooling," he said.

"You lie," she said calmly, then laughed and threw a pillow at him.

Nick got up and walked over to the bed to sit beside her.

"I need to tell you something," he said.

She got a knot in her stomach. The first thing that went through her head was *I knew this was too good to be true.*

He took her hand, then lifted it to his lips and kissed it.

"This better not be my walking papers," she said.

"On the contrary. It's an invitation."

"Oh, well, then," she said. "Where am I going?"

"To spend the rest of your life with me," he said and slipped a ring onto the third finger of her left hand.

Quinn stared blankly at the ring and then at Nick.

"You just proposed to me, didn't you?"

He nodded.

"Then I say yes," she said and began to cry.

Nick put his arms around her and held her close.

"You're supposed to be happy," he said.

"I am happy. But I'm also a girl. I have imagined this moment for as long as I can remember and never knew it would be this perfect."

"This seals the deal," he said and leaned in for a kiss.

"You've chosen poorly," she said primly.

He grinned.

"How's that possible?"

"I have no dowry. No money. No work skills. At the same time, I do not have a police record, so there's that."

Nick laughed out loud.

"You are so full of shit. Dowry? Police records? Why do I think you are messing with me? What are you up to?"

She grinned.

"I'm just playing fair. No secrets between us."

"Ha, then that's what's wrong. This isn't a game, and I'm not playing."

She crawled into his lap and put her arms around his neck.

"You pass," she said.

"Pass what?"

"The confirmation I needed to know that you are indeed in love with me, and are marrying me for my fine body, good teeth and my skills in bed."

Nick rolled with her in his arms until she was lying beneath him, grinning.

"Crazy redhead," he whispered. "I do so love you—and for much more than your teeth."

"Pretty dark-eyed man, I do so love you, too. The ring is stunning. I am so blessed. Thank you for having me."

"Oh, it's going to be my pleasure, for sure," he said. "Do you want to get dressed, and we'll go out for breakfast and talk about planning a wedding?"

"No. I want to get undressed, no talking, and make mad crazy love to you."

Nick smiled.

"Yes, Your Majesty. Your wish is my command."

Nashville—one week later.

It was midafternoon, and the sky was turning darker by the minute. Star had Sammy in her arms and was just waiting for her dad to say the word that they were going to the storm cellar when the home phone rang.

Connie jumped up from her chair and ran to answer, leaving John watching the weather report and the clouds.

"Hello?" she said.

"Hi, Mom, it's me, Justin."

"Hello, son. You caught us at a bad time. We're on the verge of going to the storm cellar."

"Oh, wow...tornado warning?"

"Yes, in the area."

"Then I'll keep this short and sweet. Tell sis that there's not going to be a trial. She won't have to come back here and testify. Baba's lawyer has done a deal with the Feds. I don't know what all he gave up to them, but the bottom line is he's in for life. No possibility of parole."

"Oh, thank goodness!" Connie said. "That's wonderful news. I'll tell her."

"Be careful in that storm," Justin said.

"We will. Love to all."

"Thanks," Justin said, and then he was gone.

Connie came running back into the room smiling.

"Starla, that was Justin. There won't be a trial, and Baba is already in prison. He made a deal with the Feds, but he'll never get out. He's in for life with no possibility of parole."

Starla looked down at the sleeping baby in her arms and started crying.

"I can't believe it's finally over," she whispered, holding Sammy close.

"I'm so glad for you," Connie said.

John suddenly yelled out from the other room.

"Danger over. Storm weakened before it got here. All we'll get is some much-needed rain."

Connie looked at her daughter and smiled.

"See, it is a sign, honey. Your life is calming. The danger to you and Sammy is over, just like this storm."

"Then I'm going to put him back to bed," Star whispered, and tiptoed out of the room and down the hall to his bedroom.

She elbowed the door inward and carried Sammy to his crib and laid him down, then pulled his blanket up and over his shoulders.

She stayed for a moment, watching to make sure he stayed asleep, and grinned when he popped his thumb in his mouth and started sucking.

She thought about all she'd gone through to keep him in her life—and how close she'd come to losing him.

Thank you, God.

Then she turned and walked out of the room.

* * * * *